The House At Flynn's Crossing

Elisabeth Rose

16pt

Read How You Want
LARGE PRINT BOOKS, BRAILLE & DAISY

Copyright Page from the Original Book

Title: The House At Flynn's Crossing

Copyright © 2018 by Elisabeth Rose

www.escapepublishing.com.au

TABLE OF CONTENTS

The House at Flynn's Crossing
Elisabeth Rose

She's been through hell, so risking her heart should be easy...

Anxious to rid herself and her twins of the dark memories from their past, twenty–three–year old Antonia moves to the small rural town of Flynn's Crossing. Antonia is frightened but determined to be independent for the first time in her life, so she rents Mango House and settles in to the community to begin the process of healing.

Town councillor and local real estate agent Flynn has secrets. Guilt–ridden over a tragic childhood event, he fled the city and devotes his life to assisting others. He has big plans for Flynn's Crossing. Without change, the town will shrivel and die. But the townspeople are resistant to his ideas, and his discussions with a luxury resort developer.

When Flynn first meets Antonia, he doesn't know her sensationalised past, and Antonia feels normal for the first time. Slowly, as they get to know each other, to trust each other, Antonia begins to consider the possibility of something more. But when tensions over the resort development reach breaking point, she discovers that Flynn hasn't been entirely honest, and her new beginning is at risk of ending. When Flynn has to choose between the town he's devoted his life to and the woman he barely knows, can she trust that the man who healed her heart will treat it with care?

About the author

Multi-published in romance and romantic suspense, writer **ELISABETH ROSE** lives very happily in Canberra with her musician husband. Travel is a big part of their lives now the family has left home. Elisabeth's original training was in clarinet performance, but she was also a tai chi instructor for twenty-five years. An avid reader, her preference is for a happy ending regardless of genre and is most annoyed if a main character dies or leaves—unless, of course, it's the villain.

If you'd like to know more about me, my books, or to connect with me online, you can visit my webpage elisabethrose.com.au or like my Facebook page www.facebook.com/Elisabethroseauthor.

Acknowledgements

I drew quite a bit on my own accumulated knowledge for this story, but as I often do, called on my daughter Carla for assistance, this time in the legal area concerning trials. She steered me towards a lawyer friend, Matthew Bogunovich, who generously provided lots of information to help with the process and time frame of a conviction.

Thank you to the RWA members for their enthusiastic sharing of information. Someone can always supply the answers to random questions.

As always, thank you to the terrific team at Escape and the wonderful Kate who keeps having faith in my writing.

To Colin, Carla, Nick and Paige

Chapter 1

Movement caught Simon's eye and he turned, straightened and rubbed his lower back, squinting into the bright sun already stinging his skin this early in the day. A woman walked slowly, almost hesitantly along the grassy track from the houses. Something about the way she held herself, the slim body, the long dark hair, tickled his memory.

Lauren, across the other side of the large plot, was still digging holes ready for the new batch of lettuces waiting in trays beside the garden beds. Her wide-brimmed straw hat shaded her face but he knew she would be humming softly to herself, her lips curved in that natural smile, loving every minute spent grubbing about in the rich dark soil, making plants grow, tending and caring for them.

He started along the row to meet the visitor. Lauren hadn't seen her, too far away, back turned.

After the silverbeet planting was done, he'd have to chip the weeds out between the strawberries. The stormy rain they'd had this week made it easy to plant seedlings but it sure made everything grow, including weeds. Thunderstorms were forecast all week, and if they got hail the new crops would suffer. Fingers crossed. Farming was a perpetual fingers-crossed activity.

The woman came closer and the nervous way she trod through the thick, wet, grass clumps made him think of a deer, timid and fearful. Frightened of him? Why on earth would she be?

'G'day.' He smiled. The sun was in his eyes and he raised his hand to block the glare. She came into focus. Something twisted in his gut. He knew her...

'Simon?'

The world reeled as a rush of memories, guilt, remorse, sorrow and most of all complete and overwhelming amazement sucked the air from his lungs.

'Antonia! I thought you were dead ... we all did ... we thought...' He couldn't go on.

'I'm not dead.' The same voice, the same clear skin and deep brown eyes but now shadowed with a depth of experience she hadn't had before.

'Antonia...' He shook his head, uncomprehending. How could this be? 'What happened to you?'

'It's a long story.'

'I can't believe it.' He reached out a tentative hand then saw his fingers were caked with earth and she was clean and fresh in a pale blue and white summer dress. He grimaced. 'Sorry. Filthy.'

She smiled and his heart rolled over at the memory. 'Mum couldn't stop touching me when I first came back. Checking I was real.'

'When did you? When was that?' So many other questions fighting to be asked. He shook his head, still half disbelieving his own eyes and ears. He could understand Robin's reaction after years of believing her daughter abducted and murdered.

'Last June. I'm surprised you didn't read about it or see it on TV.'

Eight months ago. He couldn't speak, could only shake his head and stare, taking her in from the glossy crown of her head to her feet in purple leather sandals. She was stunning. She'd been seventeen, they both were, when he'd seen her last—just under six years missing. Then, she was a pretty girl; now she was a beautiful woman.

'We should go in. Talk.' He gestured at the cluster of cottages she'd walked past.

'Hello.' Lauren stood by his side and he hadn't even noticed her arrive. 'I'm Lauren.'

'Hi, I'm Antonia.'

'I won't shake hands, I'm all dirty,' Lauren said. 'Planting lettuces.'

'We're old friends,' Simon said with an attempt at normal. 'We went to school together.'

'Oh, right.' The way she said it and the way her clear blue eyes studied Antonia implied there should be more said, an explanation for her sudden appearance. Antonia said nothing.

'We were just going inside for a drink, catch up,' he said. 'Coming in?'

Lauren's gaze swept to him then passed on to the garden, leaving a slight chill in its wake. 'No, I'd better get these seedlings in. I reckon it'll rain again this afternoon.' But she didn't move.

'The garden looks good. You must have great soil here.' Antonia's soft voice broke the silence.

'Yes.' Lauren flicked her a smile. 'Do you grow vegetables?'

'I used to. I did. We ... where I lived we were almost self-sufficient.' She seemed to withdraw into herself, face closed, eyes gone blank, suddenly years older.

'Where was that?' Lauren either didn't notice or didn't choose to notice Antonia's reaction. Unusual for her.

'South of Sydney.'

'Come on.' Simon started walking with this new information churning in his head. South of Sydney? What was she doing there, so close to home and not contacting anyone? Her parents were devastated, her family broke up not long after because of it. All she had to do was pick up the phone and call someone. Instead she left them in limbo. Why would she do that to the people who loved her?

Behind him, Antonia said, 'Nice to meet you, Lauren.'

'Likewise.' But Lauren didn't sound at all pleased about it. Why the hell not? She was usually friendly and welcoming to everyone and she didn't know Antonia at all. Maybe she was pissed off because he'd walked out on the planting. He'd finish it later.

Antonia's quick footsteps brushed the grass in his wake and he slowed to let her catch up. She was different to the girlfriend he'd had at school. That Antonia was bubbly, opinionated, ready to try almost anything, oozing confidence. He'd been besotted, shy and ready to take her lead, amazed she was interested in him at all.

This older, twenty-three-year-old Antonia was quiet, reserved and had a profound air about her more usual in someone much, much older. Where had she been? What had happened to her?

He led her to his cottage, the one at the end of the horseshoe-shaped row closest to the encroaching forest of multi-hued green—trees, creepers, climbing vines, ferns, all flourishing in a tangle of nature at its riotous best. Potted herbs clustered about the door, bright red geraniums climbed the wall.

He loved his little A-framed home built of timber, sweat and love. Here, for the first time in his life he felt really and truly comfortable, physically and spiritually.

He pulled open the screen door and held it for her. 'Go in.'

Antonia stepped silently inside while he yanked off his muddy boots and left them on the step. The laundry and bathroom were in an annexe right next to the entrance and he went in to scrub the mud from his hands and arms and splash water on his face.

When he joined her she was looking at the photos on the wall in the small living area. She lingered in front of his favourite—a close-up of a magnificent tree fern clinging to an ancient eucalypt. Next to it was his shot of an orchid growing delicate and fragile in a jumble of tree litter. He'd tramped the bush for days searching for that flower because Flynn had seen one in the area but wasn't exactly sure where.

'These are beautiful.'

'Thanks.'

'Did you take them?' She looked over her shoulder in surprise.

'Yes. Tea or cool drink?'

'Cool drink, please.

'Fresh pineapple and mango juice okay?'

'Yes, thanks. How come you didn't read about me?' she said again. 'It was a pretty big story.'

Sitting opposite her, holding his own glass, he was barely able to look away. She didn't seem perturbed by his scrutiny.

'I don't read the papers much and I don't have TV. I can't believe it's you,' he said. 'What happened to you? You didn't run away, did you?'

'No. You knew that ... you and Bryony.' He hadn't given Bryony a thought since they left school. Antonia's best friend and the third member of the trio—third member of the pact. She ran her tongue over lips. 'I was abducted by a man who kept me locked up in a house near Coalcliff.'

'Coalcliff?' was all Simon could articulate through the unimaginable horror of what she'd said so baldly.

'It's south of Sydney, near Bulli. He had other women there too. And children.'

He swallowed, uncomprehending. 'But how? Where did he take you from?' She spoke so calmly. How could she?

'Outside the abortion clinic. He hung around waiting for girls on their own, like me. He had a woman with him—Hannah. He talked to me and was kind and offered to help and give me a place to stay while I decided what I really wanted to do. Until I said I wanted to go home, then he wasn't so nice.'

'My God!' He couldn't ask the next question. The answer would be too horrible. 'I should have gone with you. I should have ... I was such a bloody wimp.'

'Simon, we'd decided, remember? You would have been in too much trouble if our parents found out.'

'We were so stupid. The three of us. And Bryony and me ... when the police asked us questions. We never said ... it was unbelievably stupid. Whatever they'd done or said to us wouldn't have been as bad as what happened to you ... I'm so, so sorry.'

'Simon, I haven't come to see you because I blame you for what happened. I never thought that, ever...' She took a mouthful of juice, and to his surprise her hand was shaking as she held the glass. A worm of suspicion began squirming deep in his gut.

'Were you abducted before or after you went in to the clinic?' he asked slowly.

She looked him in the eye. 'Before. He wanted our babies so he could imagine he had a family.' Her lip curled in her first show of disgust for the monster who'd stolen her. 'He was sterile. He had ... sexual problems.'

'Was he violent?' he whispered.

She nodded. 'But not with the children. I think I would have found a way to kill him if he'd harmed them.'

He swallowed. She continued to stare into his eyes, waiting for him to acknowledge what she'd told him.

'Am I a father?' His voice was hoarse.

Another nod. 'Twins.'

'Twins?'

She sat frozen in place while he digested the news and it dawned on him with a chill that she was petrified. She'd lived with a man who used violence to express himself and she didn't know how he would react.

She'd hit him with a triple whammy and he could hardly speak, but anger wasn't anywhere in the whirlpool of emotions he was feeling. He slumped back into the cushions on the cane chair. 'Twins? That's ... amazing.'

The tension leaked out of her body. 'Sarah and Jacob. They're five.'

'I'm the father of twins! What are they like? Have you got a picture? Where are they?' A horrible thought struck him. 'They're okay, aren't they? The birth was okay?'

'It wasn't much fun, but yes, they're beautiful.' She pulled an iPad from her bag and showed him a photo. Two small, dark-haired children gazed solemnly at him. Jacob was the image of himself at the same age.

'I looked like that when I was five.' A crazy laugh bubbled up from nowhere. 'My God, I can't believe it. Where are they now?'

'Staying with Mum in Sydney. I came here on my own.'

'They're beautiful. Perfect. But...' He looked up quickly. 'I thought you didn't want to have the baby back then, that you'd made up your mind. How come you went with him?'

'I've wondered that too, many times.' A tiny smile. 'I wish I'd done everything differently.' She took a deep breath and exhaled slowly. 'It was a hard thing to do, walk into the clinic. Such a big step when I actually got there. He knew that and took advantage. And Hannah was there. She was ... reassuring.'

Simon nodded. 'I should have gone with you.'

'Don't,' she said softly. 'If you had I wouldn't have my children. Our children.'

Looking at her now, he saw what was so different. She was a mother and being a mother trumped any hardship, deprivation and abuse she suffered after the children were born.

She took another mouthful of juice. 'This is lovely.'

'We have our own fruit here. How did you get away from that crazy guy?'

'Dad and Jax, remember her from school? She saw me quite by chance when I was with him at Central Station.

He used to take me or Hannah along to try to abduct a new girl. We'd hang out with the anti-abortion protesters. Jax told Dad and the police. He never gave up looking for me. They rescued us, all of us.'

'Wow. Unbelievable.' Her father Connor was a big, quiet man but with expectations of his daughter she rebelled against. Simon had kept out of his way.

'Dad didn't think I should just front up and dump this on you but ... I wasn't sure how else to tell you. Jax said I should do what I felt was right. They're getting married,' she added. 'She's good for Dad.'

'What are you doing? I mean where are you living?'

'Hannah and her kids and I share a place but I'd like to move out of the city. She wants to stay.'

Her unspoken words hung in the air. Was that why she'd come here? She wanted to move in with him?

'Where would you go?' The reticence in his voice shamed him even as he spoke.

'Simon, I haven't come here to ask you to take us in and I don't want money from you.' He began to protest but she shook her head and continued in her quiet, slightly hesitant voice, so unlike the bold girl he remembered. 'I thought you should know about your children, and if you wanted to I thought you could meet them. I'd like them to know their father—their real father.'

'God yes! Absolutely I want to meet them.' He couldn't let those little innocents think that insane perverted monster was their father. 'I'd love to. And I want to help financially.' Not that he could do much dollar-wise but there was no way she should be coping with this by herself.

'Thanks, Simon. Mum and Dad have been generous, helping me and the kids but I want...' She looked at the empty glass in her hand and put it on the table. 'Do you think I could stay in the town for a bit? Rent somewhere? I thought I could find a place, maybe get a job.' Again the doubtful tone, the fear of being smacked down.

'What sort of work?' He'd have to rethink the Antonia he knew before.

This girl was tentative, unsure of herself, unsure of her place in the world and the reaction she would get when she voiced an opinion. That bastard!

'Maybe in a cafe. Cooking. I like that and I'm good at it. Or waitressing ... anything.'

'Great. There are a couple of cafes, a restaurant and the pub. We supply them with fruit and vegetables. I'm sure I can organise something. And I'll introduce you to Flynn. He's the man to see in town. He's the real estate agent and he owns the pub. I'll make sure he finds you something really good.'

'Thanks Simon.' She stood up. 'I'm really happy you want to see the twins.'

'Tonia, of course I would. Did you think I wouldn't?'

She smoothed the fabric of her dress over her knees. 'I wasn't sure. I hoped ... but...' Her eyes met his. 'Dad said be prepared for you to say no, that you might have a family, a wife...'

'I don't.'

'What about Lauren?'

He frowned. 'What about her?'

'Isn't she your girlfriend?'

'No, she's just a friend.'

Antonia studied him for a moment with one of the inscrutable female expressions he could never figure out. Lauren did it too, sometimes. Antonia's had a hint of amusement. She picked up her handbag.

'Do me a favour, Simon? Please don't tell anyone about my past, what happened to me. I want to start fresh. A new life. I don't want to be pitied or discussed.'

'What about the kids? I'm not ashamed of having them.' He smiled. 'I'm proud. Twins. That's fantastic!'

A genuine smile lit her face and the teenage Antonia he'd loved so much made a reappearance. 'I guess we can tell the truth about them. You thought I'd had an abortion. We split up and I was living somewhere else with my parents. Kind of blame our parents.'

He laughed because that was so Antonia at seventeen.

'Be vague. Okay, I can do that.'

She said, 'When can I meet this Flynn person? Is the town named after him?'

Chapter 2

Antonia followed Simon's battered ute back into the small town of Flynn's Crossing, quivering with relief. He'd taken the news amazingly well, although in some deep-down part of her mind she knew he would despite Dad's warning. Dad meant well but he didn't know Simon the way she did; he barely knew Simon at all, that had been the problem. Part of the problem, she corrected herself. Dad wasn't to blame for her appalling decisions and he said several times he and Mum would have stood by her and supported her through whatever choice she made about her pregnancy. If she'd given them a chance by telling them.

But that was then. This was now and she meant what she'd told Simon. Fresh start. New place, new friends, new happy memories. Sarah and Jacob would go to the white weatherboard primary school and gradually forget they'd spent the first five years of their lives as captives. Already they were blossoming in the knowledge they wouldn't be shouted at or told to be quiet, and that their mother wouldn't be bashed by the man who told them he was their father. They had grandparents and an uncle who loved them unreservedly. Now they would have their real father.

New life, new thoughts. She clamped her hands on the steering wheel and focused on the road. Driving was still a novelty. Dad had bought her this second-hand red Honda and she loved it and what it represented. Her freedom. She'd gained her licence shortly before her abduction but ... No. That part of her life was over.

Who was this Flynn? He sounded like one of those wealthy landowners in a soapie who thought they owned everyone and everything in the district. Maybe he did, though Simon laughed at her question and said the town was named after some early settler. She didn't care so long as he had a house she could rent at a reasonable rate, and if he owned the pub maybe he could give her a job in the kitchen as well. He and Simon seemed to be mates, judging by the conversation they'd had when Simon phoned him.

She chuckled softly. Simon was still as clueless about girls as ever. Lauren was clearly in love with him but he was oblivious. Poor girl. She seemed nice, and who could blame her for a bit of jealousy when some old girlfriend turns up out of the blue and goes off with her man?

Lauren needn't worry, that wasn't going to happen. She and Simon had run their course six years ago and seeing him now didn't reignite any emotion beyond relief and gratitude that he was prepared to love his children. That was enough for her. She couldn't face any sort of relationship with a man. Now she wanted to be herself, find out who she was and what she could do, explore life with Sarah and Jacob and teach them they could do or be anything, work on enjoying the freedom and new experiences. Be happy again. The last thing she needed was a man messing with her life.

Her fingers ached and she realised she'd begun gripping the steering wheel in a stranglehold. She breathed in slowly and relaxed her hands, shaking first one then the other to remove the tension. *She* was in control of her life now.

Simon slowed at the town sign and Antonia did likewise as they drove down the main street. She liked the small country town feel of the place. Apart from the two-storey pub, the buildings were neat, small, wooden-framed with shaded verandahs, all nestled snugly into the folds and curves of the hilly terrain and surrounded by lush gardens. When she arrived earlier, she'd asked for directions at the Bluebird Cafe and the red-haired woman had been very friendly and helpful, directing her to the Mountain View Motel where she booked a room for the night, giving her a run-down of Simon's gardening business and introducing herself as Bettina.

'It's a cooperative,' she'd said, leaning on the counter, ready to deliver a thorough explanation of what that entailed. A group of six people running a market garden-style operation and supplying the local area with fresh organically grown fruit and vegetables and honey. Very successful, too, though they weren't concerned with making money. They liked the lifestyle. Simon wasn't one of the founders but he'd been there for about four years. The original people were Aidan and Georgia with their friend Rufus. The others had come in later, Lauren being the most recent, as the business expanded. She couldn't remember who the sixth one was but Bettina thought Lauren and Simon would be a good match.

All the information came with barely any prompting on Antonia's part and she knew Bettina, itching to discover exactly who she was and why she was looking for Simon, would expect an explanation of her own in return. She didn't get it. She'd find out soon enough.

Simon parked outside the pub and she swung the Honda in beside him and got out.

A man stood on the wide wooden verandah watching, hands on hips, as she and Simon came up the steps towards him: white shirt tucked into worn blue jeans, slightly tousled sun bleached hair, well-built, strong but not musclebound, an aura of confidence.

Good looking and knew it. A man sure of his place and his worth, the owner of the town. Just seeing him made her breathing shallow, made her tense.

'G'day, mate,' he said. White teeth flashed in the tanned face.

'G'day, Flynn.' Their palms smacked together in a handshake. A pair of piercing blue eyes met hers. 'Antonia. Welcome to Flynn's Crossing.'

'Hello.' Her hand disappeared into his and she couldn't prevent the instinctive flinch as he gripped her fingers.

'Sorry.' He let go instantly, his face collapsed in remorse. 'Don't know my own strength.'

She managed a tiny smile. 'It's okay, Mr Flynn.'

'Just Flynn.' His smile was reassuringly warm, the voice and expression softer when he said, 'Simon tells me you're looking for a place to rent. A house.'

'Yes. Two bedrooms would do. It's just me and my children.' She waited for the inevitable query about a husband or partner but Simon jumped in.

'You need three or four bedrooms,' he said. 'Two isn't enough. What about visitors?'

'Come inside.' Flynn led them through the empty bar area to a courtyard with tables and chairs. Potted flowering plants set about on the brick paving and a trellis covered with bright purple flowers made it a cool, welcoming space. 'Can I get you a drink?'

'No thanks.'

'How many children?' he asked when they'd chosen a table in the shade.

'I have five-year-old twins.'

'They must be a handful.' Again that sparkling smile, but it had an assessing edge. He must be doing quick mental arithmetic, figuring she'd been a teenage mother, but he oozed charm. A man confident in his looks and ability to get his own way. Her skin prickled uncomfortably. He made her edgy, unsettled, the way he looked at her. They should leave.

'No ... they ... they're very good. They're very quiet. No trouble.' She glanced at Simon for help, forcing herself to stay seated when she wanted to run for the car.

'Is there anything suitable in the area?' he asked.

'As a matter of fact, there is a house.' The blue searchlights turned their beam on her. 'Perfect for you—but the owner really wants to sell it rather than rent.'

'Oh.' Antonia nodded. 'Okay, well, thank you.' She looked at Simon. 'We should go and not waste Flynn's time.'

It had been a long shot. Flynn's Crossing was small, a bit out of the way to attract many tourists and retirees even though it was a throughway to the mountains. Apart from the hikers and travellers, people came and stayed put or had been here for generations. The whole venture was fraught with maybes and ifs. She pushed her chair back.

'When would you be wanting to move up here?'

She may as well not have spoken.

'As soon as possible. But if there's nothing available ... I can look elsewhere.'

'You must know of something,' said Simon. 'Come on, Flynn. You know everything.'

She waited, hands on the arms of the metal chair, ready to rise and escape.

'There's a place out on the river road ... but...'

'You mean Higgin's old place? That's a dump. She can't go there!'

'How bad is it?' she asked.

'No. You can't live there,' Simon said sharply. 'It's too isolated for a start.'

Antonia nodded and bit her lip. He reached out and squeezed her hand gently. 'Sorry,' he murmured.

A wrinkle appeared in Flynn's brow. He missed nothing. 'You're right. It's in terrible condition and too far out of town.'

'How much does the owner want for that other house?' she asked.

He rubbed his lips together. 'Three-twenty but may negotiate.' He obviously thought she wasn't buyer material. No profit for him here.

'Can I see it?'

'Sure.'

'But Tonia...' Simon began.

'Let me look at it, Simon.'

He smiled. 'Sure, why not?'

She risked a quick glance at Flynn. 'Maybe the owner will rent it to me if you ask him.'

He tilted his head. Considering. 'Maybe.' Which meant 'unlikely'.

'Which place is it?' asked Simon.

'On Randall Road. Old Mrs Tracey died last year and the heir wants to sell up. It's been empty for months.'

'The white house down the end with the mango tree at the front?'

'That's the one. Shall we go?' Flynn clearly didn't like to sit about wasting time.

Neither did she in this case. A mango tree. How wonderfully exotic. The house sounded perfect already. If they would rent to her and she could get a job, Mum and Dad would help her with a deposit, buying wasn't out of the question ... So many ifs. Too many. The little bubble of euphoria popped.

'You can come with me in my car,' said Flynn. He led them back out to the front of the pub where the increasing heat made shimmery waves over the road.

'I'll take the ute, thanks mate. I have to drop into Kev's and pick up the generator.'

'Right. We'll meet you there.'

Get in a car with a strange man? Every fibre screamed no. Antonia hesitated. 'I'll follow in my car.'

Flynn didn't care. 'Okay, if you prefer. Mine's the BMW.' He pointed to a black car parked in the shade. 'We go back the way you came in.' He strode away, car keys jingling in his hand. An electronic chirrup sounded and the BMW flashed its lights.

'I won't be long,' said Simon. 'Don't worry. Flynn's a good bloke. He won't rip you off. Trust him. Trust me.'

'He's very ... confident.' She wanted to add smarmy and slick but he was Simon's friend and she had to trust his judgement. Had to trust someone.

'Yeah, I guess. Anyway you'd better go. He's waiting.'

'Okay.'

'See you soon. Don't worry. I'm so pleased you came.' He dropped a soft kiss on her cheek, which surprised her, but he was gone before she could react.

Flynn drove faster than she was comfortable with along the quiet roads but she had to keep pace or lose him. She didn't want to annoy him by keeping him waiting. He took a left turn just before the primary school, followed around the block and turned again down a street with a lopsided white signpost saying Randall Road. It was a cul-de-sac with three houses down each side and two at the bottom. Towering gum trees formed a backdrop along the right-hand side. Flynn drove to the end and pulled into an overgrown driveway on the right, leading to a low white weatherboard cottage with green trim and a long verandah. A large tree with big dark green leaves spread its branches regally over the front yard. The mango tree, with plump fruit hanging like green treasures. Antonia laughed with delight. She got out of the car still smiling, gazing up at the magnificent tree, its thick leaves casting dappled shadows on the lush green of the yard. A swing for the twins would be brilliant on that lower branch.

Flynn came and stood beside her, grinning. 'It's a monster.'

'It's beautiful. Look at all that fruit.'

'Take some when you go,' he said.

'But I couldn't do that. It's not mine.'

'The neighbours will be collecting it and if it's left, it'll just rot.'

'Oh. Well, if you think so. Thank you.'

'No worries.'

'It's a magnificent tree.'

'It needs a trim.'

'No!'

He looked at her, eyebrows raised.

'I think it should be left the way it is ... free ... to grow.' She stopped abruptly, breathing hard. 'I'm sorry. I...'

'That's okay. Jean Tracey felt the same way about it.'

'Did she?' She stole a glance and discovered he was watching her with a tiny smile playing on his lips. He nodded.

'That's why it's such a monster. She was ninety-one when she died and she reckoned her father planted it when he was ten. Never cut so much as a twig off it, although the odd branch has come down in a storm.'

She couldn't stop her own smile mirroring his. 'It must be nearly two hundred.'

'Come and have a look inside,' he said after a moment.

The garden had been organised and cared for once, but during the months of neglect had begun a life of its own in the warm moist conditions.

'This needs work,' she murmured looking about, assessing and calculating what she would do first. Clear the weeds from the path and the rose beds. Prune and trim, take out some of the overblown flowers. Not too bad. Jean Tracey had been a gardener.

Flynn said, 'Hey. Inside. Remember?' He stood on the top step with the green painted front door already open. The paint was flaking and cracked. The same deterioration showed on the verandah railings where the paint had disappeared completely. Where the guttering had leaked onto the verandah, some of the wood was rotten.

Antonia rushed forward. 'I'm so sorry, I was daydreaming. I know you must be busy.'

'No worries.' He stepped aside to allow her entry but she hesitated on the verandah as a rush of memory froze her in place. Alone in a house with a strange man. At his mercy. He had no mercy, the other. Her breathing accelerated, skin clammy despite the heat of the day.

'Antonia, are you all right?' The concern in his voice was genuine. She focused on his face. Not the same man. They weren't all the same. Trust him, Simon said. Simon would be here soon. Any minute. Should she wait for him?

She exhaled slowly and took another deep slow breath. She could do this. She must if she had any chance of making a new life. 'Yes, I'm ... I'm okay.'

She caught a reassuring whiff of a woody fresh scent as she passed him to enter the dim, cool interior.

As houses go, it was a basic, old-fashioned floor plan with wooden floors, white painted walls going cream with age and the occasional water stain, a big living room, three decent-sized bedrooms with large windows, a bathroom with a showerhead over the bath but also a newer-looking shower cubicle, separate toilet and a kitchen big enough for the red formica-topped table and four chairs still in residence. Mrs Tracey's relatives had cleared personal items but left some of the larger pieces of furniture. A reasonably new fridge stood with its door open. Partly furnished was good.

The stuffy closed-up smell would dissipate in no time and she wasn't afraid of scrubbing and dusting. As long as the roof didn't leak, she could live here.

'There's only one bathroom but she had the hot water system switched over to solar twenty years ago. It's on the town water, electricity and sewerage. The water's still connected but you'd have to arrange for the power.'

A verandah ran the length of the house at the rear and along both sides to join the one at the front. The back garden was half-vegetable plot, again neglected but flourishing. A green garden shed looked quite new. The back fence struggled against the encroaching bush, but neighbours on both sides meant the house wasn't isolated. Music floated over from next door. An orchestra playing Mozart. They wouldn't mind her practising flute.

'It's rather run-down but the owner won't spend any money on it. She wants to sell as is.'

'Would she rent until someone wants to buy? I mean, it's empty. She could make something out of it in the meantime.'

He rubbed his chin. 'I agree. I'll call and see what she says. Excuse me.' He pulled his phone from his pocket and headed out into the back garden.

Antonia wandered about the empty rooms. 'Poor neglected house,' she murmured. 'Mrs Tracey loved you and so do I.'

In the living room, an old sofa covered in floral-patterned fabric had been left behind, as had a wooden bookcase and an old-fashioned wooden dresser. Mrs Tracey would have had her best china in the glass-fronted cabinet and her photos on the top, with perhaps a vase of roses from the garden. 'What books did you have? What did you like to read?' she asked softly.

Already she knew which of the bedrooms she would choose and which would be the twins' room. Eventually they could have a room each, but for now they'd prefer to share. And they'd have a spare room, as Simon said, for visitors. 'Please, please, please, let me live here,' she whispered.

A car engine sounded outside. Simon. She went to meet him.

'Like it?' he asked.

'I love it. It's perfect. Flynn was right.'

Simon grinned. 'That's great. Where is he?'

'Phoning the owner to see if she'll rent to me. If she won't, I think Mum and Dad might be able to help me buy it but I don't want to ask them.'

'Really? You want to stay here permanently?' His delight was genuine.

'I think so. Yes.' She looked around at the doors leading to empty rooms, the silent passageway leading to the rest of the house. 'It feels like home. As if it's been waiting for me.' She ducked her head. 'That's silly.'

Simon touched her under the chin. 'No, no it's not. I feel the same way about my place.'

'Thanks, Simon,' she said softly.

The screen door banged, feet clumped on the wooden floor. 'Ah, there you are,' said Flynn. His gaze flitted from Antonia to Simon. She took a step back, cheeks warming uncomfortably.

'What did she say?'

'She wanted three hundred a week but I beat her down because there's no way she'd get anything like that for this place in the state it's in and the current market. How does two-twenty per week sound?'

'Two hundred and twenty dollars? I...' She looked at Simon. 'Does that sound okay?'

'Absolutely. It's a great price.'

It sounded astronomical to her. Would Dad pay that? Panic gripped her for an instant. Her dream began to crumble.

'I need a job,' she blurted.

'Talk to Raoul at the Belle Cuisine,' said Flynn. 'He might have something. That's if you don't mind restaurant work. Otherwise there's cleaning.' He sounded doubtful. 'What can you do?'

'Anything. I'll do anything.'

'Okay. Let me make some calls and let you know.'

'You don't need to. I can ask around. You've done enough for me already, finding this house.'

'It's no problem.'

'Flynn likes to know what's going on,' said Simon. 'He likes to be in control.'

Antonia nodded. 'But I want to be in control of my life.' She sucked in air quickly. 'Sorry, that was rude. You've been ... are ... very kind.'

Again the blue eyes examined her. 'You'll need to come and sign the lease agreement and pay a bond. She wants a month in advance, which is standard.' He named the total amount. Another astronomical figure. Antonia nodded and shook his proffered hand. This time his grip was firm but gentle.

'Done,' he said. 'Come in tomorrow afternoon and we'll complete the deal. Don't forget the mangoes.'

Antonia drove to the motel on automatic. She'd done it. She'd found

Simon, told him about the twins and found a home all in one day. This afternoon she'd ask around for work and this evening she'd drive out to have dinner with Simon at his invitation. Tomorrow she'd meet Flynn and sign those papers, but now she needed to scrape up that money. And she had a shopping bag half-full of fresh mangoes to take home to Sydney.

She lay on the bed and phoned her father. After that she'd find some lunch and a job.

***

In a state bordering on emotional shock, Flynn drove back to the pub to have a counter lunch in the bar, washed down by a cold beer. Donna pulled the beer, took his order of chicken Caesar salad then began unloading a tray of clean glasses and stacking them under the bar.

The chill of the beer steadied his overheated hormones. What the hell was the matter with him? Something had happened that morning when Antonia got out of the car and walked towards him. Something slammed into his heart and stopped it for a few beats, something jammed his lungs and when his vital functions started working again, the world had changed colour. His whole world had changed because Antonia was in it where she hadn't been before. Until that car door opened and she appeared like a goddess, unbeknownst to him he'd been operating in a twilight state. She'd dazzled him and electrified him into a new awareness.

Unfortunately, he hadn't done the same to her. He had the horrible impression he repelled her at first sight. But she'd gradually relaxed and whatever had bothered her had faded. Maybe he looked like her ex. He downed a third of the beer in one swallow.

'How are things?' he asked Donna. 'How are the kids?'

'I'll be glad when school starts,' she said with a groan. 'All they do is sit around with their electronic doodads and complain about living in the sticks.'

'I suppose it is quiet for kids.'

'They loved it when they were little but now they can't wait to grow up and get out of here.'

Flynn nodded. 'And yet people like Simon and the cooperative choose to come here for the same reasons the teenagers want to leave.'

'That mob aren't afraid of work,' she said. 'I'll say that for them.'

'A friend of Simon's turned up today. She's moving into Jean's old place with her kids. We shook on it just now.' And his palm still tingled from the contact.

Donna finished stacking and leaned on the bar. 'That's good. How old are the kids?'

'Five-year-old twins. She's not much over twenty-two or so herself, I reckon.'

'Single mum?'

'Yep.'

A bell rang. 'That's your salad.'

Antonia. He wanted to linger, talk to her and find out why she was so skittish, almost frightened of him one minute, quite forceful the next, but apologetic after stating her mind. What was that about? If he had to guess he'd say she'd been in an abusive relationship and was trying to start afresh. Had someone deliberately harmed her? The thought made his teeth grind.

What was her relationship with Simon? They were comfortable and affectionate together; that was plain. Simon almost fell over himself to help her. Old friends, old lovers? He didn't know much about Simon beyond the superficial—hardworking, honest and extremely amiable, loved the life he'd chosen here at Flynn's Crossing, liked photography, as did Flynn. He'd grown up in Sydney and his family situation hadn't been particularly happy. That was about it apart from an overall impression of naivety and perhaps cluelessness about life in general.

But Antonia. She was a mystery. An enigma with dark haunted eyes and glossy deep brown hair. Serious and quiet, slim and fragile. He'd hurt her hand crushing it in his big clumsy paw. Mortifying. He made sure not to do it again. But that smile had dazzled him, coming from nowhere, laughing with him underneath the mango tree, snatching the thoughts—those he'd just begun to make coherent—from his head for a few moments of oblivion. He'd had a glimpse of a different carefree, sensitive and lovely young woman.

Donna slid his salad in front of him. 'Another beer?'

'No, thanks. This friend of Simon's needs a job. Have we got anything?'

'Not really.'

'That's what I thought.'

'I think Cath wants someone for a couple of shifts at the Paragon. Can she cook?'

'She said she'd do anything.'

Donna shrugged. 'Worth her asking.' She moved away to serve a couple of newcomers.

Flynn finished his lunch and strolled down the street to his office. Brandon should be there at the moment. Business was a bit quiet given the jittery state of the economy. Clients like that stupid, greedy Tracey woman had no clue about country real estate and the ups and downs of demand and prices. All she saw was free money courtesy of her great-aunt who'd been a sweet, generous and beloved member of the community all her life. He'd taken great satisfaction in beating her down to a more than reasonable rental, giving her the argument that the house wouldn't sell quickly, this money was better than nothing and the tenant would clean up the garden, which desperately needed doing if she was to have any chance of attracting a buyer.

He didn't mention Antonia's interest in the property beyond renting. Where would she get the money? She didn't have a job or career skills and probably barely finished high school. He couldn't in all conscience go forward with a sale if the buyer was a financial risk. Simon might have a few answers if it came to that.

Brandon looked up from a folder of papers. 'G'day, boss.'

'Afternoon. I've got a tenant for the Tracey place.'

'A tenant? I thought they wanted a buyer.'

'I talked her into renting it out. Could turn into a sale though. Antonia's coming in tomorrow afternoon to sign the papers. Can you get that organised, please?'

'Okay. What's her last name?'

'I don't know. Hang on.' Idiot. He'd been so dazzled he hadn't even asked for that or a contact number. He rang Simon.

G'day, mate. Listen, we're getting the paperwork ready for Antonia. What's her last name? And do you a have a contact number for her?'

'Farris,' he repeated to Brandon and scribbled the number Simon gave him on a piece of paper. Was that a married name or her family's? She wouldn't keep the name of her abuser, surely?

'Come for dinner tonight,' said Simon. 'Antonia's coming to meet everyone.'

'Okay. Thanks.'

'See you at seven.'

Flynn copied her number into his phone and slipped it into his pocket.

'She'll be in tomorrow afternoon. See you later, Brandon.'

Back on the street, his strolling feet took him in the direction of the Paragon and Cath.

Chapter 3

'I'll transfer the money into your account as soon as I hang up,' her father said. 'Are you sure it's what you want, sweetheart?'

'Yes, positive. There's something about the house and the garden—it's just the feel of it. And it backs onto the bush. It's beautiful. I can't explain exactly.'

'You don't have to, I understand.' And he did, she knew. He was a landscape gardener, he had an intuitive sense of what worked and what didn't, what fitted and what fought against the environment.

'Thanks, Dad.'

'Have you called your mother?'

Antonia closed her eyes and exhaled. 'She won't like it. She didn't want me to come at all.'

'I know but she's worried, that's all.'

'Dad, can you call her?' She sat up and swung her legs over the side of the bed.

'It will just make her more upset if you don't tell her yourself.'

'I suppose…'

'Start off by telling her about Simon and how keen he is to meet the twins—which is great, by the way. Then you can say you've decided they should all get to know each other so you want to stay up there for a while.'

'It sounds reasonable, doesn't it?' She hadn't plucked up the courage to mention the idea of buying the mango tree house.

'Yes, it does. Frank will back you up.'

'I like him.'

'Me too.'

'Mum wanted them all to traipse up here to see Simon together but Frank said no, I should go on my own.'

That scene was imprinted on her memory. It had taken all her courage to broach the subject knowing the reaction she'd get, but in his quiet, eminently rational way, stepfather Frank had listened to the hysterical objections from her mother and calmly pointed out all the reasons it was a good idea for Antonia to see Simon alone.

'We don't want the twins to be there if it all goes pear-shaped,' he said. 'It's a small country town and everyone would know all about Antonia and the children within five minutes. Or think they did, which is worse. We don't want that to happen, do we?'

'I'm her mother,' she insisted, face pale, hands clenched. 'I need to be there with her. I want to go with her. She hasn't recovered yet.'

'Mum, I want to do this for myself. I can't ... do ... be ... anything if you smother me. I know you're trying to protect me but...' She spread her hands. 'What else can happen to me, worse than what did?'

It was a cruel remark because it was guilt driving her mother's fear, she knew that. Guilt at not knowing her teenage daughter was pregnant, not knowing she planned an abortion, and guilt at believing her dead when Dad never gave up hope. But she had to fight for her independence or she'd continue to be a victim. She wasn't a victim, not now.

Frank smiled. 'She's right, Rob. Nothing will happen. She'll be fine.'

'But she's an innocent, the world has changed in that time. And what if

Simon is cruel and nasty and won't have anything to do with her? Who would she turn to then?'

'If that happens, which I doubt, I'll come straight back to Sydney.' Her mother had no idea what depths of cruelty and nastiness Antonia had endured. Simon wouldn't have the capacity to think of them, let alone employ them.

'But the roads are so dangerous and you're not used to driving. I can't lose you again,' she wailed. Frank put his arms around her as she sobbed.

'Don't worry,' he mouthed at Antonia.

'Mum, I have to learn to be an adult. I want to do this alone. I need to.'

So her mother grudgingly agreed to stay at home and mind the twins with the proviso Antonia call each morning and night and in between if she wanted to. She suspected Frank had confiscated her mum's phone because she'd had no panicky calls since she left the day before yesterday. She would have driven to Flynn's Crossing in one long day but all the parents united in making her promise to limit her daily driving time to five or six hours, for which she was grateful when, stiff and exhausted, she arrived at her first stop near Kempsey.

Connor said, 'How long do you think you'll stay?'

'Flynn said I can rent until someone wants to buy the house ... but that might take ages. I don't know, at least one term so the twins can start kindy. It'll be ideal because it's a small school and they'll be able to walk there. I should enrol them. How do I do that?'

'Just go in when it opens and sign them up.'

'Okay. Dad ... thanks for helping me do this, I know you don't want me to move so far away either ... and it's so much money.'

'What I want is you to be happy,' he said. 'That's all any of us want. You missed five years and you need to recover them in a way that suits you. The money is nothing compared to what happened and I'm just glad Jax and I are in a situation where we can provide for you. So are your mother and Frank. We love you. Never forget that.'

'No, I won't. Love you.'

Antonia tossed the phone on the bed with tears gathering. Super Dad. If only she'd known when she was a teenager. She dashed the moisture away and went to the bathroom. Before she called her mother, she'd have lunch and do some job hunting. That conversation was not something she wanted to face on an empty stomach, and if she could land some work her case would be all the stronger.

The motel was just on the outskirts of the town. From what she could tell, it catered mainly to hikers who came to spend a few days or more trekking through the spectacular mountainous national parkland that bordered Flynn's Crossing. The reception area had a carousel loaded with maps and information about the best views and scenic spots. Some of the trails looked accessible by five-year-olds and there was a waterfall with a picnic area, which was a very short distance by foot from the access road. Judging by the photos Simon had taken, it was a beautiful area.

Rather than walk back to the main street, she took the car. The temperature had risen dramatically since she'd been at the house and the humidity climbed with it, cloying and sticky. It felt like a storm coming. But it was midsummer and everywhere was hot. She didn't care, she was free. A fact that was very slowly sinking in.

A few elderly men lounged in chairs on the verandah of the pub, their beers on a small table between them. She'd need to stop in to buy wine to take to Simon's for dinner. Assuming they drank wine. She should take something else as well in case. What? They had their own juice, they probably wouldn't drink soft drink ... beer? Cider? The person in the bottle shop would know. She'd never had to make this type of decision.

She drove slowly along until she spied the Bluebird Cafe where she'd asked for directions earlier. A couple of hikers in shorts sat at an outdoor table on the footpath eating toasted sandwiches, their backpacks leaning against the wall. Inside the air con was pumping chilled air over a couple of bikers eating burgers. Most tables stood empty. Red-haired Bettina greeted her like an old friend.

'Hello, darl. Did you find Simon?'

'Yes, thank you. I'd like to have lunch, please.'

'Take that table by the window and I'll be with you in a minute. Would you like a drink?'

'Just water, thanks.'

'Help yourself, darl.' She pointed to a pile of glasses and water jugs on a table at the end of the counter.

'Thank you.'

Sipping the cold water, Antonia studied the menu. Basic cafe fare of toasted and open sandwiches, burgers, pies, curry and rice, schnitzel or fish and chips, steak sandwich and soup of the day.

'Made up your mind yet, or do you need a few more minutes?' Bettina stood beside her, pen poised over her notepad.

She would have like a salad but it wasn't an option at the Bluebird. She couldn't walk out now. 'A cheese and tomato sandwich please, toasted.'

'Anything else?'

'Not at the moment. Thank you.'

'Staying in town long?'

'No, but I'll be back.'

Bettina nodded. 'Of course, you'll be moving your children in to Jean's place.'

'Oh. You know already?'

Bettina smiled showing a row of teeth jostling for a front row position. 'Word gets around.' She moved away.

Word got around all right and the only person who had a word to spread so fast was Flynn. She pressed her lips together. Flynn. She'd have to be very careful what she said around him. Mr Flynn's Crossing wheeler-dealer.

Five minutes later her sandwich appeared. Very ordinary. White bread, plastic packaged cheese. Only the tomato was rich and tasty and that would be because it was locally grown by Simon and his friends.

'I hear you're after work,' said Bettina as she cleared the next table.

Antonia hid the jolt of surprise by pretending the tomato had burnt her tongue. She swallowed, collecting her thoughts.

'Yes. You don't have anything here, I suppose?'

'Sorry, darl. It's only me, and Shazza out the back doing the cooking.'

Antonia nodded. 'Oh well, if you ever need a break or something...'

'Try the Paragon. Across the road and along about a hundred metres. I think Cath might be in need of help. She's had a bit of trouble with the girl she had.' She leaned closer. 'Fingers in the till.'

'Really? My goodness. Was she a local girl?'

'From Kurrajong—that's the next town but no one's surprised, given the family she comes from. Cardews. Drunks and thieves, the lot of them. Cath tried to do the girl a good turn and look what she gets by way of thanks.' She wandered off with her load of dirty dishes and gossip.

Cath at the Paragon. Antonia swallowed the remains of her sandwich and stood up. She took her plate and glass to the counter and paid Bettina.

'Thanks, darl. See you again, no doubt.'

'Probably.' Or not.

Cath at the Paragon was a small wiry blonde with a big smile and a red-checked apron over blue denim shorts and a red sleeveless shirt.

'You must be Antonia,' she said when she spied Antonia hovering just inside the door. The place was full of chattering customers eating food that shamed Bettina's toasted sandwich effort.

'Yes, I am.' This time she was prepared. If Bettina knew about her, just about everyone else would too.

'Thought so. Flynn said you'd be in.'

Flynn again. If she didn't know better, she'd suspect he was a spy for her mother.

'I heard you may have a job vacancy.'

'Can you waitress?'

'Yes.' She held Cath's eye firmly. She'd served pizzas the summer before she was ... That counted.

'When can you start?'

'Um ... when suits you?'

'Now?' Cath laughed and gestured at the crowd. 'I'm flat chat.'

Antonia sucked in a deep breath. 'Okay. Tell me what to do.'

If Cath was surprised she swallowed it quickly. 'Leave your bag out the back and grab an apron. I'll show you.'

***

At four-thirty Cath closed the door and locked it behind the stragglers. Antonia cleared the last table and took the tray to the kitchen where Len was wiping down the cooktop.

'Last lot,' she said.

'In the dishwasher, thanks, love.'

Cath came in with a handful of cash. 'Here you go, Antonia. Your pay. Three hours.'

Antonia straightened and took the notes. Three hours? The time had raced by. She stared at the money in her hand. Her very first pay in her new home. The symbol of her new life. Her throat clogged suddenly.

'Sorry,' said Cath. 'It's not much but...'

Antonia swallowed and sniffed. 'No, no ... it's plenty. I'm just ... really happy ... to have a job.'

'So you'll be back tomorrow?' asked Len. 'We haven't frightened you off?'

'Oh!' She pressed a hand to her mouth. They were expecting her full-time. 'I'm so sorry—I can come in the morning but I have to sign the lease in the afternoon and leave the day after to organise...' She stopped in a muddle of confusion and dismay. Had she blown her new job already? Hadn't Flynn explained she hadn't moved yet?

Cath patted her on the shoulder. 'It's fine. Dad, don't bully her. She has to move herself into Jean's old house and get her kids settled. She can't work here and do that at the same time.'

'Sorry, love.' Les grinned. 'I came over all excited; it was so nice to have a pretty face around instead of that shocker Cath hired. Bloody nightmare she was, with her tattoos and nose rings and what have you.'

'Don't start,' Cath said. She turned to Antonia. 'When do you think you'll be ready? I could sure use you as soon as possible. You saw how busy we are and it'll be like this till the weather cools. You did well today. Thanks for jumping right in.'

'I need to go back to Sydney and pack up. I don't have any furniture or anything so I'll have to buy beds and chairs. Kitchen stuff...' The task seemed overwhelming all of a sudden. On her own. She'd insisted she could do it by herself but could she? Her mother would have a fit if she saw the mango tree house before she'd had a chance to do some work on it.

'If you don't mind second-hand, we can ask around for some things to get you started,' said Len. 'Make a list of what you need and we'll see what we can rustle up.'

'You don't need to do that.'

'It's how it works in the country,' he said. 'We're real stickybeaks and know all about each other's business, but we help each other out too.'

'You'll get used to it,' said Cath with her big bright smile. 'Not having any privacy.'

Antonia managed a weak smile. 'Thanks,' she said. 'I don't mind second-hand.'

Out on the street now baking in the late afternoon sun, earned money in her purse, a house and a job, Antonia had a surge of optimism. Cath and Len were friendly and welcoming, knew her circumstances and arranged her shifts accordingly. The Paragon opened for breakfast and lunch five days per week and closed Sunday and Monday but Cath knew Saturday would be difficult for a single mother with school-age children, at least at first until they made friends.

'See how we go,' she said. 'You might be able to get a sitter for them.'

Antonia mumbled her agreement, knowing that wouldn't happen for a long time. Sarah and Jacob were wary of strangers, especially adult males, but they were gradually learning that most people weren't like the monster they'd spent the first years of their lives with—the only man they'd known until their grandfather burst into their lives.

They knew their captor wasn't their father, she'd told them right from the start that whatever he said, and although he insisted they call him 'father', he wasn't. It was a secret they must never tell. 'One day,' she'd whisper to them. 'You'll meet your real father. His name is Simon.'

She smiled. And Simon had turned out to be as thrilled to be a father as the twins would be to finally meet him. She crossed the road and began walking to her car still parked outside Bettina's cafe.

What she really wanted to do was cook. When she knew Cath and Len better, she'd ask … Len could teach her a lot. He used to work in Brisbane as a chef, he told her. He'd trained with the best but tossed it in to come back where he'd grown up. 'I love it here,' he said. 'And I talked Cath into coming after her marriage collapsed. The less said about that loser the better. Wasted the best years of her life on him,' he muttered.

'Afternoon.'

The voice pulled her up short. Flynn. Again. Where had he sprung from? She'd been walking without noticing where she was. She glanced around and saw real estate photos stuck in the window of a nearby shopfront. His agency.

'Hello.'

He smiled that lazy, charming smile which didn't fool her one bit. At the same time as being Mr Casual he was assessing her, wondering if he could sell her the mango tree house, how much commission he could screw out of the sale.

'How'd it go with Cath?'

'Fine, thanks.' The euphoria of her little success fizzled. He put her on edge, wary and suspicious.

He nodded. 'Good.'

'I can't do weekends. I'll need to find something else when the Paragon is closed.'

'Okay.'

She frowned. 'Okay? What does that mean?'

'I'll ask around.'

'I can do that myself, thank you.'

'I know everyone in town and who's more likely to have work.' He kept his gaze firmly on her face. The skin around his eyes had crinkles from being outdoors. Like her dad. 'I thought I could be helpful.'

She licked her lips and moved into the shade of the overhanging shopfront. 'Cath said I'd get used to everybody...'

'Helping out?'

'Knowing everyone's business.'

'Well, I suppose for a city girl that's hard to get your head around, but if you're going to live here that's part of the deal.' The smile stayed in place but the tone had sharpened.

'I'm sorry.' She grimaced and rubbed her fingers lightly on her forehead. They came away sticky with sweat. 'I'm so sorry. Thank you. You are being helpful. And everyone has been friendly and kind.' She sneaked a quick, anxious look at his face. 'I do want to live here. I ... I like it.'

The assessing look had gone replaced by one that surprised her—remorse.

'No. I'm sorry, Antonia. That was rude and unfair. You have every right to live wherever you like. Believe me, I'm not trying to pry into your affairs,' he said. 'Just getting to know you.'

An apology from Flynn. That was unexpected and difficult to deal with. He was confusing, very confusing. Why on earth would he want to get to know her? There was nothing to know.

'Thanks,' she muttered, looking at her feet and wishing he'd go away. Her car was a hundred metres along outside the Bluebird Cafe. He'd probably want to walk with her, asking questions she couldn't answer, making her uncomfortable.

'Would you like a lift to Simon's for dinner this evening? He invited me too.'

Her chin lifted abruptly. 'Simon did?' Why would he do that? Why include Flynn more than necessary?

'Yes. We're friends.'

'Oh.' She swallowed. She'd forgotten about friendships, that easy camaraderie she'd had with her schoolmates—boys and girls. She'd have to relearn. Especially about men.

'I thought seeing as we're both going to the same place from the same place we could travel together. And there's a lot of wildlife on the road at night. Dangerous if you're not used to it. Storm coming too.'

Put that way it was supremely logical, but Flynn always managed to sound logical. She couldn't keep up.

'You might want to stay later,' she said weakly.

'I'll be happy to leave whenever you want to.'

Standing in the street arguing over something so petty as a lift suddenly struck her as ridiculous. He wasn't going to abduct her. Simon said to trust him and trust Flynn. She had to start somewhere or her mother would be proved right—that she wasn't ready or capable to go it on her own. If she was to live in Flynn's Crossing she had to make friends.

'All right. Thank you,' she said loudly and clearly. Too loudly.

Flynn grinned. 'Right. I'll pick you up at a quarter to seven.' He turned to go.

'Flynn, what should I take? Do they drink wine?'

He stopped. 'Sure do. I was going to take a red.'

'Should I take a white wine then?'

'Good idea.'

'Thank you. I'll see you later.'

She walked to her car, keeping in the shade of the shopfronts because the afternoon sun was scorching. She needed a hat. A teenage girl said 'hello' as she went by, a woman coming out of the chemist shop said, 'Hot one today,' two little boys slurping ice-creams nearly crashed into her as they barrelled out of the supermarket with their mother yelling, 'Be careful,' from inside then rolling her eyes at Antonia with a resigned grin.

All normal, friendly people. No perverted, lunatic criminals. Although—with a little spurt of laughter she remembered Bettina's comment—there were the ... what was their name? The drunken, criminal Cardews from the next town.

***

The storm didn't eventuate though rain looked imminent when Flynn drove to the motel. Antonia was waiting under a poinciana out the front. She clutched a bottle-shaped brown paper bag in her hand, waiflike and lonely, slim in her pink dress with her long brown hair hanging loose. Was she lonely? She had two children who must have a father somewhere. Some loser who'd made her pregnant and left. Raped her? Possible. It would explain the jumpy wariness, the lack of confidence and the anxiety when she thought she'd offended him.

But her twins were five. Maybe she'd been in an abusive relationship and only just escaped. That would make more sense. And she'd sought out an old schoolfriend, Simon, knowing he lived in a little corner of paradise. Simon was safe. He wouldn't harm anyone or anything and he was very pleased to have her here. Anyone with half an eye could see that. Why was that thought so shamefully displeasing?

Flynn stopped the BMW beside her and jumped out to open her door.

'You look lovely.' He would have said something similar regardless of the woman or her appearance, but belying the glibness of the compliment, he really meant the words. She was lovely with an innocence all her own, childlike with an air of having experienced suffering. As a teenage mother; that was understandable, but he sensed more.

A deep flush stained her cheeks. 'Thanks,' she murmured, dropping her gaze to the bottle in her hand. She held it out. 'Will this be all right? The man at the shop said it would.'

He gave the label a quick look, hoping Jordan hadn't taken advantage of her naivety and sold her the most expensive wine in the place. He hadn't.

'That's perfect. Good choice.'

The little smile appeared, pleasing him far more than he expected. 'He chose, not me.'

'Right.' He laughed. 'But you can pretend you chose.'

The smile widened, lighting her eyes. 'I couldn't fool Simon. He knows I know nothing about wine.'

He ushered her into the car. When they were underway, he said, 'When did you and Simon meet?'

'We went to the same high school.'

'Boyfriend?'

'For a while, but we broke up.'

'But stayed friends.'

'Of course.'

She didn't elaborate as to why that would be the case. He wasn't friends with any of his exes. The farther away they were the better. Except Lou, but she didn't really count as an ex. She lived in the apartment next door when he'd lived in Brisbane, and she was still there. They dated once and acknowledged there was nothing more there than a genuine friendship. Pure and simple.

'Are you friends with all your old boyfriends?'

She nodded but her cheeks had turned pink again.

'The twins' father?'

Another nod. 'Do you have a ... a...'

'Girlfriend?' he supplied.

'Yes, but girlfriend doesn't seem like the right word.'

'Why not?'

'You're too ... it's a bit ... high school.'

He laughed. 'What you're trying to say is I'm too old to have a girlfriend?'

'No! Of course you're not, but the word ... isn't right.'

'Well, I don't know what word is right but the answer is no, I don't have a significant other. Female or male.' He slid her a quick sideways look and found her watching him. 'And I'm thirty-three. Is that too old?'

He concentrated on the driving again. The rain had begun in a steady grey drizzle, obscuring vision. This stretch was winding and hilly with thick vegetation coming close to the roadside. Kangaroos and other wildlife were likely to appear at any moment and the last thing he wanted was to hit something.

'Ten years older than I am,' she murmured.

'Ancient.'

As he'd hoped, that brought the laugh that delighted him at the Tracey house when they discussed the mango tree.

As if reading his mind, she said, 'I love that house, and Jacob and Sarah will too. I can't wait to move in. Thank you for letting me have it.'

'It's my job, one of them,' he said but the heartfelt way she spoke touched him. A run-down house with peeling paint and an overgrown garden. She was easily pleased.

'What else *do* you do? Simon said you're the Mr Big of Flynn's Crossing.'

Gone was the tentative anxious girl. Was she teasing him? Flirting? No, not Antonia. She didn't flirt. She was asking because she wanted to know, not because she had ulterior motives—concerning him. Get a grip! Ignore the fact she was sitting there, pretty in pink with a light perfume addling his brain and her...

'I own the pub and a bit of land here and there and the real estate office. I'm also chairman of the town council.'

'Do you live in the pub?'

'I have an office there but no, I have a house on the other side of town. Someone manages the pub for me. Donna.'

'How long have you lived here?'

'Eight years.'

'Where were you before that?

'Here and there. I moved around, went overseas for a bit. I started out in Toowoomba.'

'Is that where your parents are?'

'They were, but now they live in Fremantle.'

'Gosh, that's a big move.'

She'd been firing questions at him but he didn't mind, he liked that she was relaxing in his company, that she was interested in him.

'Yes, my mother came from there and they went back to visit her parents and decided they liked it better in the west.'

'Why did you come here?'

'Same reason as you. I liked it.' He slowed for the entrance to the cooperative. 'Have you met the others here?'

'Only Lauren.'

Flynn parked the BMW outside Simon's A-frame, but before he and Antonia could walk to the door Simon came out with an enormous grin and a big umbrella.

'Hello. Welcome.' He kissed Antonia and shook Flynn's hand. 'Lauren's here, and Georgia.'

As usual, at the cooperative meals the smells coming from the kitchen were fantastic. Everyone seemed to be a good cook and they all contributed to communal dinner gatherings. They weren't vegetarian but vegetables and fruit naturally played a major role in meals.

Simon introduced Antonia to Georgia, a wiry tanned woman in her fifties who'd started the venture ten years ago with husband Aidan and their friend Rufus. He had to hand it to them; they'd worked bloody hard and made it into a profitable business, supplying cafes and restaurants in a wide radius.

'Aidan and Rufus will be here shortly,' she said. 'Bernie's had to stop overnight in Mungaree. The truck broke down.'

'Sit down,' said Simon. 'Drinks?'

Flynn and Antonia handed over their wine.

Lauren sat next to Antonia on the sofa while Flynn took a chair.

'How are you liking Flynn's Crossing?' asked Lauren. 'Bit small for you?'

'I like it,' Antonia replied. 'Flynn found me a house and I've just started with Cath and Len at the Paragon.'

Simon gave a beer to Flynn and handed her a glass of wine. 'Well done!'

'That was fast work,' said Georgia.

'I'll have to go back to Sydney to pack and collect Sarah and Jacob but I hope to be settled within a week.' The smile on her face was pure joy and it made Flynn smile too.

'Sarah and Jacob? Who are they?' asked Lauren.

'My children.' Antonia glanced at Simon.

'And mine,' he said.

Chapter 4

'Yours?' Lauren shot off the sofa as though her bum was burning, her face a study in shocked outrage. Flynn figured his was probably similar, total surprise without the outrage. Only Georgia took the announcement in her stride.

'Yes, mine.' Simon held out his hand to Antonia and she took it, holding onto him like a life preserver. He sat on the arm of the sofa next to her.

'How old are they?'

'Five,' said Antonia.

'Did you know?' asked Flynn.

'No, well I knew she was pregnant but...' Simon looked at Antonia.

'We were seventeen. My parents took charge and told him I was having an abortion,' she said. 'Your parents never knew, did they?'

Simon shook his head. 'They're very religious.'

'So, what happened?' asked Flynn, trying very hard to keep his voice level and non-confrontational. No wonder these two were so close. 'You obviously didn't have an abortion.'

'No. I changed my mind.' She met his gaze fearlessly and he held it for a moment before Lauren spoke, breaking the link.

'Why didn't you tell me?' She glared at Simon.

'I didn't know. I only found out this morning. You saw Tonia arrive.'

'So are you going to set up house with her?'

'Lauren...' Simon looked at her helplessly. Totally bewildered. Flynn could have laughed at his expression if the situation had been different. If Antonia wasn't involved. But the same question lurked at the back of his mind. Had she come here to move in with Simon?

Georgia stepped in. 'Calm down, Lauren. Simon hasn't seen Antonia for years. That's right, isn't it?'

He nodded. 'Since we were seventeen.'

'I thought my children should know their father and he has a right to know them,' said Antonia. 'I have no intention of forcing anyone to do anything. I don't want...' Her lip trembled, close to tears. Flynn wanted to put his arm around her but this wasn't his business.

'And you're perfectly right,' Georgia said. 'You were brave coming here on your own. Did you know what Simon would say?'

Antonia moistened her lips. 'Not really but I had a pretty good idea. My parents were worried but they didn't know him like I do ... did.'

'And if he'd said go away?' asked Flynn.

She looked at Simon. 'He wouldn't.'

He leaned down and kissed her cheek. 'No, I wouldn't. I'm proud to be a father. Twins! How about that?' He beamed around at everyone.

How about that, indeed. Lauren remained tight-lipped, hurt, and in *her* eyes, betrayed. He'd seen that look on a girl's face before. Not his fault this time. Flynn raised his beer. 'Congratulations, mate.'

Antonia glanced at him, looked away just as fast, and smiled.

'What are we celebrating?' Aidan and Rufus clumped in.

'Simon has twins,' snapped Lauren.

'Twin what?' Rufus asked. 'Lambs?'

'Children,' said Simon. 'Antonia's and mine.'

Aidan, stocky, solid as a brick, laughed and shook his head. 'You kept it quiet. How did you manage that?' He switched his attention to Antonia. 'Sorry. I'm Aidan. This is Rufus. How do you do, Antonia?'

She shook hands with them both, eyeing Rufus's numerous tattoos. Hard to tell what she thought about the bearded, long-haired, tough biker look.

Rufus went to the fridge and came back with two beers. 'So what's happening?'

'Antonia and I knew each other in high school. She ... we ... got pregnant, her parents kept it quiet and told me she was having an abortion. I didn't see her again until yesterday.'

'I came to see Simon so he could get to know the twins,' she said.

'I'm a twin,' said Rufus. 'Identical.'

'Really? You never told us that,' said Simon.

'Aidan and I knew,' said Georgia.

'Liam died when we were little. He had heart problems.'

'I have a boy and a girl,' said Antonia softly. 'I'm so sorry about your brother. You must miss him.'

Rufus nodded. 'Yep. It's like I have a gap inside me. Crazy really, because we were about two when he died so I never knew him. Not really.'

'Sorry, mate, but this is a depressing conversation,' said Aidan. 'Antonia. How long are you staying?'

'I'm not sure. For a while.'

'We should serve this food or it'll be dried out.' Lauren went to the small kitchen, bad vibes emanating in waves.

Simon grimaced and stood up.

'I'll go and help her,' said Antonia and sprang off the couch.

'But it's my...'

'It's okay.'

Lauren had her back turned when Antonia approached, chopping something and adding it to a large bowl of salad that looked full to overflowing already.

'Anything I can do?' she asked.

'Take the casserole dishes out of the oven.'

Antonia picked up two oven gloves and opened the oven door. 'Hmm, it smells delicious. What is it?' She carefully removed a large cast-iron baking dish.

'Moussaka and the other dish has baked vegetables. They can go on the table.'

Still she didn't turn around. Antonia took the dishes to the big wooden table. Lauren brought the salad and went back to the kitchen. Antonia followed.

'Lauren, I'm not here to steal Simon from you,' she said softly so no one would overhear. 'Honestly. I've had ... a ... bad experience and...' To her astonishment and embarrassment, a couple of tears ran down her cheeks. 'Sorry. I'm sorry. I don't know why I'm crying.' She sniffed hard and quickly wiped her eyes and cheeks.

Lauren touched her arm gently, concern in her eyes. 'No, I'm sorry. I'm not usually so rude. It's just that ... well ... Simon, you know?' She shrugged lightly, confirming Antonia's impression from the morning.

'He was never very cluey. He had very religious parents who thought everything to do with sex was a sin. We could never figure out how they managed to have him.' Antonia smiled.

'But as far as I'm concerned, he's yours. If you can get him to understand.'

'How did you manage it? I mean you must have...' Lauren's cheeks turned pink. 'Sorry...' She giggled.

'He was pretty cute back then. I guess my desire to make him sin outweighed his not to. I was very adventurous. And he *was* a seventeen-year-old guy...'

Lauren burst out laughing. 'Right.' She looked across to where the others sat deeply engrossed in some agricultural discussion. 'He still is cute.'

'He was always incredibly good-natured and loyal,' Antonia said. 'My parents didn't want me to come here but I was positive Simon would want to meet his children. I just knew he'd love them and it's not fair to keep them all apart. Is it?'

Lauren shook her head. 'No, it's not.' She picked up a pottery flask with Salad Dressing written into the glaze. 'Thank you for explaining.'

'Is it ready yet?' called Rufus. 'We're starving over here.'

'Yes. Let's eat.'

With the tension diffused, the mood around the table was relaxed and comfortable and for the first time in years Antonia felt safe with strangers. These people were honest and hardworking, striving to produce the best crops they could while living in as natural a way as possible. The contrast with where she'd been held captive was stark.

Mealtimes had been fraught. The women and children in his 'family' were silent unless specifically addressed. The children were almost too frightened to eat and subsequently were yelled at for not finishing their food. The women prepared and served and cleaned up afterwards, always in the knowledge one or other would be chosen to share his bed and the humiliation and violence that went along with that honour.

'Are you okay?' Simon touched her arm gently.

She blinked and focused on her hand with a forkful of food poised over her plate. All eyes were upon her. 'Sorry. I zoned out for a minute. Tired I guess. It's been a big day.' She offered a bright smile round the table, skating past Flynn who was watching her with a slight crease in his brow and a question in those blue eyes. 'This is a lovely dinner.'

'Simon's a good cook,' said Georgia.

'Did you cook? I thought Lauren did.' She turned to him, surprised.

'I like cooking.' Simon squeezed her arm gently. 'It's so great you came.'

'I'm pleased I did.'

Flynn raised his glass. 'Here's to Antonia. Long may she stay in Flynn's Crossing.'

This time Lauren's smile was as welcoming as the rest.

***

In the car going back to the motel, Flynn asked, 'What did you say to Lauren in the kitchen? She was pretty pissed off with Simon, I thought. Next thing you were laughing together.'

'She was surprised. Like everyone else. Like you.' No way was she betraying Lauren's trust by gossiping with this man.

'I'll admit it did surprise me, but now I think about it, it makes sense your coming here. I should have guessed.'

'Didn't it make sense before?' What did he mean by 'he should have guessed'?

'Not really. I mean, I don't know your parents, but they sound supportive and I wondered why you would choose to live so far away from them on your own. Now I understand.'

Antonia didn't know how to reply. What business was it of his what her motivation was? Flynn didn't press his point. At least he knew when to be quiet, which was a mark in his favour.

When he drove into the motel driveway she said, 'Thank you for the ride.'

'No worries. I'll see you tomorrow.'

'Yes. What time should I come to the office?'

'After lunch suit you?'

'Okay.' She had the breakfast shift at the Paragon, finishing at ten-thirty, so she'd have a couple of hours to fill. Maybe she'd visit Simon again or explore the area. She opened the car door.

'When are you going back to Sydney?'

'After I sign the lease.'

He nodded.

She got out but bent to say, 'Thank you. Goodnight.'

'See you tomorrow.' He lifted a hand and his teeth flashed in the dim interior light.

She closed the door and walked towards her room. His car hadn't moved. She stopped and turned. Why was he waiting? To see which room was hers? A chill ran up her spine, the hairs on her neck rose. She changed direction and forced herself to walk not run towards the reception office where a light still showed. An older grey-haired woman was on duty tonight, she'd seen her on the way out.

Flynn's car tyres crunched on the gravel as he turned to go. She slowed her pace so his tail-lights had gone before she reached the door to the office. Her breathing slowed. The door to reception opened and a young man in shorts and a yellow fluoro shirt came out carrying a backpack.

'Hi,' he said.

'Hello.'

He walked over to a bike propped against the wall and wheeled it down the path in the opposite direction to her room. Normal people doing normal things. She had to get used to that fact. She turned and went the right way. But why had Flynn waited in his car?

She unlocked her door. There could be any number of reasons. Texting? Answering the phone? Fiddling with the radio or choosing a CD? Or maybe he was just waiting to see she got in safely. Her dad did that when he dropped her friends home after some event, waited till they opened their door and a light came on. Caring and courteous.

She tossed her bag on the bed and went to the bathroom. She must stop being paranoid. Her car was parked right outside her door. Flynn could easily guess which was her room.

But before she hopped into bed, she put the safety chain on.

***

Simon couldn't concentrate. He must be driving the others nuts; but in their typical easygoing manner, one or the other would collect the rake he'd left in the garden, or the half-full barrow of compost and wheel it to the shed, collect the eggs he'd forgotten all about and generally tidy up after him and remind him of a chore.

Over the evening beer on Aidan's front verandah, two days day after Antonia had left Flynn's Crossing to collect his children, he apologised for the twentieth time.

'You're right, mate,' Aidan said. 'We all know what's going on. It's a big thing, meeting your kids.' He stretched his long tanned legs out and slapped at a hovering insect.

Georgia came out with a dish of assorted nuts and sat down. 'She's a lovely girl.'

'Yes she is. She showed me a picture of the twins. They look like her and they're beautiful.'

'She must have had a rough trot there for a while,' said Aidan.

'Yeah, I reckon.'

'And you had no idea she'd kept the babies?' asked Georgia.

Simon shook his head. As he looked at Aidan's weather-beaten face with the kindly grey eyes, and Georgia's equally calm and non-judgemental hazel ones, the urge to tell what had really happened was strong. These people were like family; in fact, they were more like parents than his own had ever been—more loving, more caring and far more understanding of life and all the odd issues and troubles that living threw at people.

Rufus was the same, although Simon suspected he'd had a chequered career before he came to Flynn's Crossing with Georgia and Aidan, and had probably had more than a tussle with drugs along the way. Rufus didn't say, Simon didn't ask. If he wanted to mention something from his past he would. Like Antonia. Like the twins thing.

So he had to respect Antonia's wish to keep her past private, as difficult as that may be.

'What are her parents like?' asked Georgia. She knew what his were like.

'Separated, both remarried. I knew her mother was, but Tonia said her dad is going to marry someone who was a teacher at school. Her music teacher.'

'Is Antonia musical?'

'She used to learn the flute. I don't know about now.'

'That'll be good,' said Aidan. 'I'll pull out the old fiddle and we can play a few tunes.'

'She might not like Irish folk tunes,' said Georgia in a dampening voice.

Simon smiled and caught her eye. The odd occasions when Aidan had played his violin for them had been excruciating for the audience.

'She can learn. What's not to like?' He took a swig from his stubbie.

'Will the parents come up to help her settle in?' asked Georgia.

'She texted me today and said she didn't want her mother to see the house until she'd got it fixed up a bit. Her dad and his fiancée, Jax, are both working but her dad might take a few days off to come up.'

'What does he do?'

'Landscape gardener.'

Aidan nodded. 'Nice. He'll be interested in having a look at this place.'

'Probably. He's a good bloke. He used to be pretty strict but for the right reasons. Her mum's a bit hysterical at times. Her brother's starting uni this year.'

Rufus wandered along with a sixpack under his arm and joined them. Aidan and Georgia's house was the original large sprawling weatherboard home on the fifty-acre block of land they'd bought ten years earlier. The Big House had naturally become the meeting place for business discussions, celebratory get-togethers and after-work beers on the verandah. Rufus had converted what had been a tumbledown abandoned servant's cottage but the other houses, like Simon's, were kit homes, built new by whoever came to live at the cooperative.

'She's even more beautiful than I remember,' Simon said. 'She was always pretty. Really vivacious and confident. The sort of person you thought could do anything.'

'Having twins must have knocked that out of her,' said Rufus. 'I wouldn't say she was full of confidence now.'

Simon drank some of his beer and rolled the chilled bottle between his palms. 'She's changed.'

'Did she finish school?'

'I don't know.' She couldn't have. Poor Tonia.

Georgia shook her head. 'It's so unfair. The girl is always left with the responsibility of bringing up the children and wrecking her career opportunities. She's lucky her parents were onside and helped her.'

Simon sat up straight, bristling. 'I would have helped her if I'd known. If they'd let me near her.'

'I'm not criticising you, but you were seventeen, what could you have done?'

'He could have offered emotional support,' said Aidan. 'They were both involved.'

Georgia nodded. 'That's true. It's just so unfair that a girl's life is completely altered by that one event, usually for the worse, yet very often the man just swings along doing his thing. Moves on to a new girl and doesn't give a hoot about his children.'

Her words stabbed like a knife to the heart. 'I'm not like that. I want to make it right. I want to be a proper father, a good father and I want us to be a family.'

'Marry her, you reckon?' Rufus cocked an eyebrow at him.

Simon frowned as the idea took root in his head. He hadn't thought far, hadn't had time but Tonia had bowled him over when he saw her walking towards him and it wasn't just because of who she was, it was because she was a very attractive, very desirable woman. He'd loved her once, there was even more reason now for that love to be rekindled.

He grinned at Rufus. 'Maybe. I won't say no.'

Georgia exhaled loudly, slapped her hands on her thighs and stood up. 'Excuse me, boys.' She picked up an empty bottle and went inside.

'Is she upset about something?' asked Simon.

Aidan shrugged. 'Probably. What are we going to do about the tractor? We have to make a decision. And Bernie said the truck's going to be a few days while they get parts in from Sydney.'

'Bugger. We'll have to use the van for deliveries. That'll take twice as long.'

***

While Antonia was away, Flynn went round to the Tracey house and replaced the pieces of rotting wood in the verandah. The guttering would need fixing at some stage but the roof didn't leak so the place was habitable. He couldn't rent out a house that was unsafe to anyone, let alone Antonia and her children.

Josef from next door tottered in on his gammy legs to see what he was up to and made himself useful by holding a new verandah rail in place while Flynn wielded the hammer.

'What's she like, the new neighbour? I saw you bring her in the other day. Looks young. On her own, is she?'

'She is young but she has twin five-year-olds. She'll fit in okay.'

'I miss Jean, you know. Made beaut scones and the best marmalade I've ever tasted. Still got a few jars stashed away. Mango chutney too.'

'We all miss Jean.'

'Five-year-olds.' He grunted.

'She reckons they're well behaved and quiet. She is too. You won't have to worry about that.'

'Yeah, well. We'll see. Reckon she'll mind if I take a few mangoes?'

'You'll have to ask her.' Flynn whacked the last nail into place and straightened. 'Reckon that'll do for the front.'

'You gunna paint it too?'

'I'll put a weather seal on it but the whole place needs painting.

'Jean's niece won't come at that. Stuck-up bitch, she is. Barely said hello when they were looting the place. Wouldn't have minded a memento of Jean. She was a good mate.'

'You got that right.' They'd been neighbours for about fifty years. Josef's wife Greta had died twenty years ago in a car crash and the Tracey's had kept him from giving in entirely to his grief.

'Maybe this new girl will do the painting herself.' Josef eyed him slyly. 'With a bit of help.'

'I'm only doing this so she won't have an accident.'

'Never known you put yourself out before for a tenant. You usually hire Tony to do your maintenance work.'

'This wasn't worth bothering him with. I could do it easily. I like doing odd jobs.'

Josef cackled, displaying teeth stained brown from years of tobacco and tea. 'Yeah, she's a pretty girl all right.' He hobbled down the steps. 'Lawn needs mowing too, while you're at it. See ya later.'

He headed for the gate laughing like a loony, and scooped up a couple of mangoes on the way.

After applying the weather seal on the new wood, Flynn walked around to the rear of the house. The lawn did need mowing but he wasn't sure what state Jean's mower was in. If he remembered rightly, one of the neighbours used to come in to take care of the grass, but whether he used her mower or not he didn't know. The shed was a relatively new metal one, unlocked luckily; although people rarely locked anything in Flynn's Crossing, especially the older residents. But Jean's great-niece wasn't a local and would probably raise hell if a hammer went missing.

A wave of superheated stuffy air hit him in the face when he opened the door, but a cursory inspection revealed plenty of old rusty tools: two hoes, a couple of shovels, a leaf rake, clippers, shears, saws and old boxes and packets of garden maintenance stuff like snail bait, but no mower. He'd have to come back with his own.

He went inside and flicked the light switch in the laundry. The power was back on. In the kitchen the fridge hummed and water flowed from the tap, albeit a bit spluttery and brown for the first few moments. The stovetop worked, as did the oven and presumably the power points. If not she could let him know.

He flushed the toilet, turned the bath and shower taps on and off. The washing machine in the laundry was almost as old as he was, but when he pressed a few buttons, water flowed and the spindle turned.

All in all, the place was liveable. She'd need beds, more chairs and dressing tables but that wasn't a problem. She hadn't given him a date for her return and really she didn't need to because she had the keys already. Technically, he needed her permission to come in but he preferred to see it as doing an agent's inspection. Josef was way off beam with his insinuations. Silly old goat.

He locked up carefully on his way out. Roly-poly Bron on the other side was out the front trimming some plants. Still good-natured and friendly even while rearing five noisy boys, she waved and came over to his car in the driveway.

'G'day, Flynn. I'm glad Antonia's moving in. It'll be good to have someone in the place again, specially with young kids.'

'Do you know her?' How could they have met?

'We had a natter when she called in the other day. She came in for a cuppa before she headed back to Sydney. Nice girl.'

How come Josef hadn't mentioned it? He didn't miss much but maybe he'd been asleep, or listening to the radio with the volume on full blast, the way it had been the day he showed Antonia the house.

'Did she say when's she's moving in?'

'She wasn't sure but she's pretty keen, so as soon as she's organised I'd say.'

'Yes, she really likes the house.'

'Be great if she bought it. I reckon she'd like to but I don't think she's got much money.'

'Do you know who used to do the lawn for Jean? I was going to give it a once-over but there's no mower in the shed.'

'Kev did it usually.' Her husband, the local mechanic. 'But sometimes Gary or Stuey did.' They were the middle two boys. The older ones had left home, the youngest was about to start high school. 'I'll send one of them over.'

'Thanks. Give whoever does it this.' He handed her a twenty.

'Ta.' She laughed and stuffed the note in her pocket. 'I might do it myself. I told her I had odd job boys and babysitters on hand but she said she was keen to do stuff herself.'

'She seems that way.' He opened the car door.

'She doesn't say much, does she?'

'City girl,' he said. 'They're not used to everyone gossiping.'

'It's called community support,' she said with a grin. 'She'll figure it out soon enough. She looks like she needs some.'

Flynn drove home, turning over Bron's comments in his mind. She hadn't mentioned Simon at all. Antonia had kept that information quiet. Of course, it wouldn't stay quiet for long when Simon started visiting and taking the twins around town, but still...

Antonia had deeply hidden aspects to her personality. She was the most interesting, intriguing woman he'd ever met. No wonder Simon was bowled over by her, and judging by the glances they exchanged and his little intimate touches of hand on arm, or kiss on cheek that she didn't discourage, she felt much the same. She was comfortable with Simon in a way he doubted she would ever be with him, no matter how much he tried to get her to relax and how gently he treated her. Sure, she and Simon had known each other for a long time, and intimately at one stage, but he couldn't shake the feeling there was more going on.

Something in her manner made him feel that deep down she was constantly on alert, wary and afraid even among the most non-threatening of environments. Or was that only when he was there?

Chapter 5

Antonia grew more and more nervous the closer Flynn's Crossing came. Her father followed her car in his light truck, loaded with the numerous bits and pieces that represented her and her children's lives, including a new chest of drawers wrapped tightly in a tarpaulin, for the twins' room. Ultimately she was glad he'd insisted on coming with her but she couldn't help the fluttering nerves in anticipation of his reaction when he saw the house.

A landscape gardener wouldn't be impressed by the neglected yard or the peeling paint and he'd be worried by the rotting boards on the verandah. The power should be on by now but what if the wiring was shonky and nothing worked? What if the place had burned down in her absence? That was silly. Flynn would have told her. If nothing else, she had no doubts he was an honest businessman. In a small town like this he couldn't afford not to be.

'I'm hungry,' Jacob called from the back seat.

'Me too,' came the predictable echo.

'You'll have to wait. We're nearly there.'

'No we're not,' Jacob said boldly and Sarah giggled.

Antonia smiled to herself. She loved how they were discovering they could be cheeky and a bit naughty without being locked in their room or yelled at randomly for saying almost anything. They were testing the limits, the therapist said, and she should be careful not to let them turn into obnoxious little brats. Not that she phrased it exactly like that but it's what she meant. As far as Antonia was concerned they were a long way from brats because strangers immediately turned them mute and clingy, but her family spoiled them rotten and the twins learned quickly that Nana, Grandad, Frank, Jax and especially Uncle Damien were pushovers. Kindy would be good for them.

Half an hour later she turned into the driveway, drove alongside the house into the carport and switched off the engine. The truck pulled up behind her.

'The Mango House, the Mango House,' Sarah sang loudly while Jacob unclipped his seatbelt.

'Everybody out,' Antonia said. 'Here we are at last.'

She helped Sarah out of the car. Jacob had already scrambled out and run to his grandfather who was stretching his arms over his head and straightening the kinks in his spine.

'Look at the mango tree, Grandad,' yelled Sarah.

'The yard doesn't look too bad,' Connor said as he walked across to where Antonia stood. 'It needs a bit of weeding and trimming but the basic design and plant layout is good. Someone knew what they were doing.' Both children raced around, examining the tree and the shrubs.

Antonia looked about, puzzled. Something was different. The grass had been cut. Who did that? Flynn or one of Bron's tribe of boys? Whoever it was had made the first good impression on her dad.

'Can we go inside?' Jacob bounded up the steps onto the verandah.

'Careful,' Antonia called. 'Some of the boards might be rotten. They're very old.'

Connor, following close behind Jacob who'd disappeared around the corner of the verandah, ran his hand along the railing. 'It's been replaced, and so have a couple of boards.' He inspected the floor at his feet. 'Done a good job too.'

Flynn?

'Let's go in.' She unlocked her front door and stepped inside, with the twins pushing and shoving their way past. Someone had aired the house out. The closed-up smell had almost gone, the layer of dust on the remaining furniture had disappeared and the power was on because the fridge hummed from the kitchen. Two wooden chairs she didn't recognise sat against one wall.

Connor surveyed the living room, nodding. 'Looks better than I expected. Needs a coat of paint but that's easy enough to fix. Let's have a look at the rest.'

Antonia took him on a guided tour, her heart pounding with a mixture of excitement and dread that his good impression might suddenly evaporate.

Sarah tested the toilet. Antonia waited apprehensively for the flush, hoping the plumbing functioned properly. It did.

'Where's our room?' Sarah said when she came out.

'Wash your hands,' said Antonia.

Sarah darted into the bathroom and water splashed and gurgled for a minute or two.

'Here,' shouted Jacob from the room at the rear of the house. 'Mummy said this is our room.'

Sarah ran to find him. Connor continued out the back door through the laundry to the garden. Antonia followed like a child anxiously waiting for a good report.

'What do you think?' she asked when she couldn't stand it any longer.

Connor put his hands on her shoulders and kissed her cheek. 'Sweetheart, it's fine. If you're happy to live here that's all that counts. The vegetable garden is great and you'll never run short of mangoes. The twins have plenty of room to run around and the house is pretty much what I thought it would be. Old but solid and a good size for you.'

Tears sprang to her eyes. 'Thanks, Dad, I was really worried you'd hate it.'

'Have faith in yourself.' He pulled her into a hug. 'You know what's best for you and the twins. You're an intelligent woman and a good mother. Trust your judgement.'

He let her go and she walked over to the riotous zucchini plants climbing out of the garden bed. 'The last decision I made for myself was pretty crap,' she said. 'It's hard to forget that, hard to believe I can do something right.'

Understatement of the century. Her self-confidence was hanging on by a fingernail, completely undercut by years of being told no one wanted her except 'him', no one cared and he was the only one who'd bother with her. And the kicker underlying the whole thing was she'd brought it on herself, a fact he wouldn't let any of his 'family' forget. 'You chose to come here,' he'd tell them and hammer it home with a backhander to the cheek. What did that say about her judgement?

'Not many of us make intelligent decisions at seventeen, but you're not that girl anymore.' Connor came to stand beside her. 'Finding Simon was right, renting this place was right and getting yourself a job was right. Start from there. Don't forget we're standing behind you ready to help when you need it.'

'I know, Dad. Thanks.'

'Let's get the troops some lunch, then come back and unload the truck. Can we walk to a cafe from here?'

'I'm not sure. It's so hot it's better to drive until I know my way around.'

***

Flynn was coming out of the pub when Antonia drove by in her red car. His heart bumped and added a few extra beats before he steadied his pulse with a couple of deep breaths. Had she been to the house or had she just arrived? He forced himself to stroll down the street in the same direction, barely stopping to say hello when people greeted him and making sure he maintained visual contact with the red car. As he'd hoped, she swung in close to the Paragon.

He'd been thinking of having lunch there today. That's what he'd tell anyone who asked. 'Just dropping in for a bite to eat, Cath. Oh hello, Antonia, didn't realise you were back in town.'

She had a man with her, an older man who must be her father, and the two littlies being herded into the cafe would be the twins. Two dark-haired little cuties, the girl with a red ribbon in her hair. He slowed his pace and went in to the real estate office. Brandon was on the phone. He looked up and smiled.

'Just nipping over the road for some lunch,' Flynn told him and he nodded.

Now it wouldn't look like he'd chased after her down the street and into the cafe.

Her group was in one of the booths along the wall, Antonia with her back to the door. The family resemblance between the four was unmistakeable.

'G'day, Flynn.'

Cath waved him to a table for two in the middle of the room. His usual spot on a stool at the counter was taken. He sat down and studied the blackboard menu on the wall. Antonia was in his peripheral vision. She must have heard Cath greet him but maybe they'd all been talking and she hadn't noticed. A movement caught his eye. Antonia was sliding out of the booth. He returned his attention to the menu.

'Hello, Flynn,' she said.

'Hello! Welcome back.'

'Thanks. We've just been to the house. Did you mow the lawn?'

He shook his head. 'One of Bron's boys.'

'What about the repairs to the verandah?'

'Guilty. It was a bit dangerous. I didn't want my rep as an agent to suffer if you had an accident.'

A frown appeared momentarily, as though she wasn't sure what to think about that remark.

'Would you like to join us? Dad wants to meet you.'

Dad did? Not Antonia? She issued the invitation like it was a duty. Flynn glanced across at the big man chatting with his little grandchildren. 'All right.

Thanks.' He stood up and followed her to the booth.

The children's faces underwent a startling transformation when he approached the table. One minute they were both giggling, the next wide-eyed with an expression akin to panic. The girl, sitting next to her grandfather, snuggled as close as she could. He slipped an arm around her.

'Scoot over here next to me, Jakey. Then Flynn can sit with your mum.' The little boy scrambled around to the other side of the table and nestled under his grandad's other arm.

'It's not personal. They're a bit shy with strangers,' Antonia said. 'Dad, this is Flynn. Flynn, Connor.'

The hand Connor held out was rough and work worn, his face showing the wear and tear of outdoor life. Flynn realised with a jolt of surprise the man was a similar age to himself. A few years older but no more than ten he'd guess. Maybe Antonia's parents had been teenagers when she was born and knew how hard it was to raise children at such a young age, which was why they reacted the way they did.

Something must have made them change their minds. Antonia?

Antonia slid to the far side of the bench seat and Flynn sat down. Two pairs of dark brown eyes stared at him.

'Hello,' he said. 'My name's Flynn. What are your names?'

'Sarah,' whispered the girl, and the boy said, 'Jacob,' almost at the same time.

'Do you like your new house?'

'Yes,' they said. It was slightly unnerving, the way they responded; quickly, as if they were terrified of giving a wrong answer or being late with their reply.

Cath saved him from more awkward attempts to befriend them. She appeared with her notebook and her usual face-splitting smile. 'What will it be? What takes your fancy, little ones?' She directed the grin at the twins who both gave her a tentative smile in return—more than they'd offered him. 'I bet you like milkshakes. I make the best ones in the whole of Australia.'

'Do we, Mummy?' Sarah asked.

'Try one and see,' said Connor. 'What flavour would you like?'

'If it's your very first one it has to be chocolate,' said Cath. 'Try my Unearthly Junior Chocolate Machine. Special kids' size.'

The twins nodded. 'Yes, please,' they said in unison.

Orders taken, Cath went off to the kitchen.

'Thanks for helping Antonia with the house,' Connor said. 'I appreciate it. I suppose she's mentioned that her mother and I are a bit worried about her leaving Sydney and heading off on her own up here.'

'I'm not completely on my own, Simon's here,' Antonia put in quietly.

'Flynn's Crossing is a good place to live. She'll make friends quickly and we tend to look out for each other.' He turned to Antonia. She was running a strand of long silky hair through her fingers. Nervous. 'You've already met Bron, haven't you?'

'Yes.'

'Her husband Kev is the local mechanic so you won't have to worry about your car, she has five sons, three still at home and good for odd jobs, and Bron herself will give you the shirt off her back if she thinks you need it.' He stopped, aware he might be doing an oversell.

Connor's face was impassive. 'I don't doubt any of that,' he said. 'It's this pair. We'll miss them and they'll miss us. It's a long way to visit and they don't have other relatives.'

'You can stay with us, Grandad,' said Sarah.

'I know, sweet pea, and Jax and I will.'

Jax? Who was Jax? Had her parents separated and Connor remarried?

'It may not be permanent,' said Antonia. She stopped playing with her hair and leaned her elbows on the table. Her fingers had no rings, no nail varnish. They were hands that had done outdoor work of some kind, tanned and with a small scar running across the base of one thumb. 'Just for a while. If someone buys the house we'll probably have to move anyway.'

Flynn nodded despite the unaccountable disappointment her words evoked. When she left a week ago she was talking about staying permanently. 'I don't think the house will sell very fast, and even if it does the new owner may choose to rent it out.'

Cath placed two milkshakes in front of the twins. Flynn smiled at the delighted astonishment on their faces. Even the kids' serve was a monster. Cath's version of a milkshake involved a tall glass filled with chocolate milk, ice-cream, whipped cream, marshmallow and chocolate pieces, all topped with chocolate syrup.

'You'll be sick if you eat all that,' said Connor with a grin.

'No we won't,' said Jacob shaking his head. He already had the straw in his mouth and the spoon in his hand, ready to dive in.

'Haven't had a sick customer yet,' said Cath.

'We love milkshakes,' announced Sarah, after a long suck on her straw.

'Yes we do,' said Jacob.

'Are you staying in the house tonight?' asked Flynn. The milkshakes had diverted the children's attention away from his alarming presence at the table, although one or the other shot him a wary glance every now and then, in between mouthfuls of chocolate and ice-cream.

'No, the beds and mattresses aren't arriving until tomorrow,' said Antonia. 'The shop promised.' She cast an anxious look at Connor.

'They'll turn up, don't worry. And if they don't, we'll stay another night at the motel.'

Cath brought the rest of their order. 'Bon appétit.'

'I might not be able to come in for a few days yet, Cath, I'm sorry,' Antonia said.

'That's all right. Just let me know when you're ready. I've managed to twist Aunty Gail's arm into helping out for the lunch shift.' She nodded towards the corner where Gail was chatting with Arnie and Barb from the old dairy farm. 'The trouble is she talks more than she works.' She shook her head and went away laughing.

'Is Gail really her aunt?' asked Antonia.

'Yes, she's Len's sister,' he said. 'If you want to know anything about anyone in town, Gail's your girl. She's better than the internet for information and can spread the word faster than any communication system known to man.'

Antonia grimaced and glanced at her father. 'What does she know about me?'

'As much as anyone does, I imagine, which isn't much. You haven't been here long enough.' Why had he blabbed out that inanity? He knew she liked her privacy.

'She sounds terrifying.'

'Don't worry, sweetheart.' Connor reached over and squeezed her hand.

'Gail couldn't be kinder,' said Flynn hastily. 'She just likes to talk. Don't tell her any secrets, that's all,' he added as a joke, hoping to lighten the mood his information had sunk into gloom.

'I won't.' Her tone was grim.

What were her secrets? That she had one or two Flynn had been sure of; didn't everyone? But her reaction to his offhand remark suggested there was something dark in her past she desperately wished to keep hidden. Something her father knew all about. And Simon too?

Gail eventually found an excuse to bustle up to the booth and say hello, but really to give the newcomers the once-over. Today her hair was a violent shade of orange with matching lipstick, which clashed horribly with the red-checked staff apron.

'G'day, Flynn,' she said, and not waiting for Flynn's greeting, picked up Connor's empty coffee cup. 'Can I get you something else? More coffee?' Her eyes travelled over the group, lingering on the twins and coming to rest on Antonia. 'Aren't they just darlings? Hello, Antonia. I'm Gail. Lovely to finally meet you. Cath was delighted when you walked in wanting a job. Flynn'd already told her you were on the lookout. News travels fast in this place.' Her cheery laugh accompanied the statement.

'Nothing more, thanks,' said Connor.

Her attention swung to him like a searchlight. 'You must be Antonia's dad. Helping her move in, are you? That's nice. Families should always pitch in and help out. Some don't, but then some families are in a real mess, aren't they? Don't talk to each other because they're always on their silly electronic gadgets, don't have meals together ... that's not being a family is it? What chance do young folk have growing up in a home like that? Well it's not a home is it? It's a ... a...'

She paused to search for the next word. Flynn was about to leap in and derail the Gail Express when Antonia said, 'You're right. I want my children to have a home like the one I grew up in. That's why I came here.'

'So your two little darlings can be near their dad. Aren't they adorable? That's wonderful. You came to the right place, Antonia.'

To Flynn's amazement, Antonia smiled. 'Thank you.'

'Simon's a very nice young man,' Gail said, clearly ready to start on another dissertation.

'Well! I think we should make a move if everyone's finished eating,' said Connor in a man-of-action voice. 'Could we have our bill please, Gail?'

'Of course.' She took a couple more dirty plates and went away.

Flynn stood up. 'I'll get this.'

'No,' Connor and Antonia said at the same time, but he waved away their protest.

'Call it a welcome to Flynn's Crossing.'

'Thank you,' said Connor. 'That's very kind.'

She said nothing but offered a little smile.

Out on the street, while Antonia loaded the twins into the car, Connor shook Flynn's hand. 'Thanks for helping Antonia. Having met you and Cath and Gail, I'm feeling happier about her staying now.'

'You don't need to worry. If you ignore the Gails of the town, people are genuinely ready to help a newcomer. We want young people to move into the area or we start to lose amenities like the school and the post office and so on.'

'Is that likely here?'

'Not yet, but soon. The population is in decline—ageing, and the kids tend to head for bigger towns or the cities. There's not a lot for them here after they leave school. I think the answer is in promoting tourism and we're looking at ways of doing that. We have some good hiking and camping areas but Flynn's Crossing isn't really on the map yet.'

'It's certainly a beautiful area.'

'We could do a lot more to bring people in, I think. I have a few ideas.'

Connor nodded. 'Good luck. I'd better make a move. We have a truckload of stuff to unload.'

'Need some help?'

'I think we'll be right, thanks. It's mainly suitcases and boxes of toys and books, the kids' bikes. The heavy stuff is coming tomorrow. Simon's coming over soon to meet the twins so...' He didn't need to finish.

'Okay.'

Connor climbed into the driver's seat. Antonia called 'goodbye' and got in beside him.

Of course Simon would want to meet his children as soon as he could. Lucky bastard, having a readymade family like that one fall into his lap. A woman like that. Flynn crossed the road to the office, mouth set in a hard line. He shouldn't be jealous but he was and he didn't know why. He'd had a few opportunities along the way to settle down and make babies, but no matter how sexy and loving the current woman was, he could never bring himself to make that commitment. Deep down he knew he didn't deserve to be part of a happy family.

***

'He's a good bloke,' her father said on the way back to the Mango House. A newly minted name courtesy of the excited pair in the back.

'I thought you'd like him.' She twisted round in her seat. 'Did you enjoy your milkshake?'

Silly question. They'd scraped their glasses clean and eaten their sandwiches as well. The novelty of food in all its varieties still hadn't worn off. She didn't want to discuss Flynn. Something about him unsettled her. His eyes were too blue, too penetrating for comfort, as if he could see inside her head. Sometimes he looked at her the way a man looks at a woman he's interested in, which was unnerving in a whole different way. She had no skills to deal with that.

'We always want milkshakes,' said Sarah. 'We love them.'

'They'll be a sometimes treat,' said Antonia. 'I'm going to be working at that cafe soon so you'll be able to try other things too.'

'We only want chocolate milkshakes.'

'Goodness,' she murmured.

Connor chuckled. 'They're happy,' he said. 'And they deserve to be.'

'I don't want them to be spoiled, that's all.'

'They won't be. They'll settle down when they go to school and make some friends.'

'I should call in to the school.'

'Do it tomorrow. By the sound of it they'll already know you're coming. Gail's a force of nature, isn't she?'

'Hmmm.' She lowered her voice. 'Do you think anyone knows ... anything?'

'I doubt it. It may not have even made the news up here and we were lucky the political travel rorts scandal pushed us off the front page in the first place. The police did a pretty good job keeping the details out of the papers and the twins were never photographed. People's attention span isn't very long these days. I doubt anyone would recognise you, or me for that matter, and if they did they wouldn't necessarily know why.'

Antonia nodded. 'I just hope ... I couldn't bear it if the whole town started talking about it ... me ... and especially them.' She inclined her head towards the twins but they were busily discussing milkshake flavours and weren't listening.

'More than they are already, you mean?' Her dad laughed. 'You're a novelty. Simon is one of their friends so of course they're interested in you. It's a pretty interesting scenario by anyone's standards, you turning up with twins he didn't know about.'

'I suppose. But what about the trial? That will be in the news won't it?'

'Yes, but we can deal with that when it happens. No date's been set yet. It could be a year away. These things take a long time. Try to relax, sweetheart. I like it here. Jax and I might come up and visit, do some hiking.'

'Simon takes beautiful photographs of the bush.'

'Flynn told me he has ideas for boosting tourism in the area.'

'What for?' What an awful thought. Busloads of people with cameras wandering around, traffic clogging the streets.

Her dad looked at her, surprised. 'Because these little towns can't survive if the population drops too much.'

'But that's why I like it here. Because it's quiet.'

'I'm just telling you what Flynn told me.'

'You know why he's so keen? Because he owns the real estate agency and lots of property in the area. He's greedy and wants to rake in a few millions selling holiday houses. Maybe he wants to build some gigantic ugly resort.'

'That's a very cynical view and a bit unfair,' he observed. It was harder to provoke him now than when she'd been growing up. Then, she knew exactly which buttons to push to set him off. 'It could be that he genuinely cares about the town and wants it to survive.'

'Maybe, but it won't be the whole reason,' she muttered.

'Is that Simon's ute?' her father asked.

An old white ute was parked in the street in the shade of the mango tree.

'Yes.' She licked her lips. 'Simon's already here,' she said to the twins.

'Simon who is our real daddy?' asked Jacob.

'Yes.'

'Is he a nice man?' Sarah doubted that such a thing existed but she'd accepted her grandfather, her Uncle Damien and Frank, so she was beginning to understand that at least a few males were kind.

'He's a very nice man and he really wants to meet you.'

'He's our daddy, Sarah,' said Jacob. 'Our secret daddy.'

'He's not a secret anymore,' said Antonia, but still her heart pounded in anticipation of the meeting. Was this the right thing to do? Were her babies ready to meet yet another strange man in spite of the fact they'd heard about this mythical secret daddy all their lives?

Her father gripped her hand. 'It'll be fine,' he said.

***

Simon heard the car pull up in the driveway and walked around the verandah to the front of the house. He'd arrived early but he couldn't wait at home a minute longer. The morning had dragged like a cast-iron chain. He'd finished his chores by ten-thirty, having given up trying to sleep when his eyes popped open just before dawn. After a lingering morning tea, which turned into brunch, he cleaned the bathroom and vacuumed the house. Then he wandered along to chat to Rufus about the fence on their southern boundary, which had been pushed down yet again by next door's cattle.

The land was for sale and the absentee owner wasn't interested in upkeep. If they had enough money they'd buy the place, but the asking price was ridiculously high and Flynn said the owner wouldn't budge. The bloke had bought the property eight years ago after the original owner died at ninety-five, with ideas of being a city dweller with a rural retreat. Turned out to be too far from the city, and too expensive and awkward to get to easily. The house needed a ton of work, which he'd started doing but stopped. Another idiot who thought farming was easy.

Antonia texted just after one to say they'd arrived and were having lunch first at the Paragon, meet him at the house at two.

He crossed the grass, eyes fixed on Antonia's red car. She got out and came forward to greet him. He kissed her cheek lightly.

'Hi.'

'Hi. Simon, I ... I'm...'

'So am I,' he said all in a rush. 'I'm terrified they'll hate me.'

'No, they won't hate you but they'll be very shy. Don't be put off by that. They know all about you and who you are.'

He nodded, but how could he not be terrified? These two small people held his heart in their tiny hands.

Connor got out of the driver's seat. A large man, greying hair around the temples, smiling and friendly. He hadn't been when last they met. Then his brown eyes had been suspicious, filled with anger and pain. His daughter had disappeared and he thought Simon had something to do with it. He'd been right.

'Hello, Simon. It's been a long time. How are you?' He held out his hand. Simon shook it firmly.

'Not too bad.' His gaze flew to the car where a small face stared out at him. Jacob. His son. The breath jammed in his lungs.

Antonia opened the car door. 'Come on.'

The little boy came first, standing close by Connor's side, gazing at him with a worried expression. Simon drank in the sight of him. Dark brown hair, big dark eyes, smooth pale skin. The most beautiful child he'd ever seen.

'Hello, Jacob,' he said.

No reply.

'This is Sarah.' Antonia's voice broke his focus and he turned from Jacob to his sister. The same dark hair and pale skin, the same anxious manner but in a sweetly feminine version. Equally beautiful. Astonishingly so. He wanted to sweep them into his arms and hold them close forever, never lose sight of them again.

'Hello, Sarah.' He managed to control his voice with a superhuman effort, but his body was shaking and his throat clogged with tears. He mustn't cry in front of them, they'd be even more alarmed. Sarah buried her face against Antonia.

'Shall we go inside?' said Connor. 'You two can show Simon the house.'

He took Jacob's hand and led the way to the front steps.

Antonia smiled at Simon. 'Come on, Daddy.'

Sarah peeked at him then hid her face again, but not before he glimpsed a tiny smile. Heart bursting, he followed his family into the house.

Chapter 6

Flynn couldn't concentrate. His mind would not stay away from the Tracey house and how Simon and the twins might be getting on. It was none of his business. He kept telling himself that but it made no difference. Antonia had been tight-lipped about the whole thing and her father didn't give anything away either. Why was he so concerned about them?

The phone rang, and in an effort to occupy his rogue thoughts he snatched it up before Brandon could make a move.

'Flynn, Margie.'

'Hi Margie. What's up?'

She always spoke in shorthand. Margie was a fellow town councillor with big ideas for the area. A retired lawyer, she and her husband had moved to Flynn's Crossing four years ago and built a big house on their block. Barry did something high up in the finance industry, a job that involved a lot of travel, but he loved retreating to their mountain home when he had the chance.

'I think I've found us an investor.' She spoke calmly but he could tell she was excited.

'Really? Who?' He sat up straight.

Brandon sent him a questioning look and he said, 'Margie, I'll call you back in a few minutes.'

'Come over here where we won't be interrupted.'

'I'll be there in ten. Have you called anyone else?'

'Not yet. I'll get onto Phil, see if he's free.'

'Yep, fine. See you soon.'

'Council business,' he said to Brandon as he went out.

Between them, Margie and Barry knew most of the movers and shakers in the moneyed classes. He wouldn't be at all surprised if she announced the investor as Richard Branson or James Packer.

The house was on a ten-acre block just north of town. They'd built on the crest of a hill to take advantage of the sweeping view down the valley; the home itself was unassuming, carefully designed to be so, but Flynn knew great care had gone into making the place eco-friendly and virtually self-sufficient, relying on wind and solar power, rain water tanks and biodegradable sewerage. When Barry had explained all the details of the design, Flynn had been incredibly impressed. If only the whole town could embrace those methods!

Phil's ute followed him up the driveway to the house and pulled up next to him. Phil levered his bulk out of the cabin. If he wasn't careful he'd keel over with a heart attack one day. He already puffed and wheezed like a leaky tyre.

'G'day, mate.'

'G'day, Phil. How's it going?"

'Can't complain. Has Margie said anything about this mystery man?'

'Nope. My money's on Richard Branson.'

Phil guffawed. 'I was thinking Rupert Murdoch.'

Flynn grinned and knocked on the door.

'It's open,' she called.

Inside, the slate floor of the entry foyer lowered the temperature immediately. Margie, neat and trim in knee-length navy blue shorts and a sleeveless white blouse, appeared at the end of the passage.

'Hello, come through.'

The open-plan living, dining and kitchen area was the feature of the house Flynn admired most. Long floor-to-ceiling glass folding doors almost the length of the room led onto a paved terrace, one end of which was shaded by a grapevine trailing over a roofed outdoor barbecue area with a wooden table and chairs.

She'd put a jug of iced water and glasses on the outdoor table, along with a folder.

'I'm pleased you could come so quickly,' she said. 'Take a seat.'

'Whose arm have you twisted?' asked Phil.

'No one's,' she said, but she smiled. 'This person came willingly to the table. He's interested in the whole concept and wants to expand into hiking and adventure holidays—the mountains. He already has a couple of coastal resort hotels.'

Flynn nodded. 'That sounds good. Who is it, Margie?' Enough of the teasing.

'Sean Baldessin.'

Phil grunted. 'I've never heard of him. Who is he?'

'He's very wealthy and he owns two resorts in Queensland which are very well run and successful. He's smart and he's honest and has a good reputation. Most importantly, he cares about environmental issues and wants to use this as a pilot project in sustainable and responsible tourism.'

'Sounds ideal,' Phil said. 'What sort of control does he want? I mean, what's the deal? Do we have any say in anything?'

'That's what we need to negotiate. This is very early days but I think he's exactly the sort of partner we've been looking for.'

'In theory,' said Flynn.

'Exactly. We need to tread very carefully. A lot of people in town will be deadset against this idea, and a couple of our fellow councillors already are, as we well know.'

The older, longer-serving members of the council—Judy, Bill and Walter. In their eyes, any change to the way Flynn's Crossing operated was out. Aidan from the cooperative hadn't committed either way yet and could well be the deciding vote if it came to the crunch. Flynn had no idea which way he might go. On the one hand, he was in favour of eco-friendly initiatives and another market for his produce; but on the other, he and the others in the place had come to Flynn's Crossing for the quiet rural life, not to be swamped by tourists and all they brought with them.

The perfect land for the development was on the boundary of the cooperative, which would mean improving the access road, at the moment not much more than a dirt track, and months of building right next door. The best spot to build the accommodation would be right up in their closest corner, in Flynn's opinion, and that might be the decider when it came to Aidan's vote.

***

Simon helped Connor unload the truck and carry the heaviest items indoors, where Antonia directed their placement. Distracted by all the activity and the excitement of setting up their new bedroom, Sarah and Jacob gradually relaxed and stopped falling silent when he appeared in the doorway holding a box of toys or books and asked where it should go. Sarah even went so far as telling him which corner her bed would be in when it arrived the next day.

'My bed goes there.' She pointed to the window. 'So I can see the flowers.'

Encouraged, he said, 'I can come over and help Mummy in the garden. We can plant more flowers.' His reward was a smile, which melted his heart.

By six the house looked more like a home, even with empty packing boxes stacked on the verandah. Antonia celebrated by brewing the first pot of tea in her own house. Simon drove to the shop for milk and biscuits, and by the time he returned the table was set with mugs and an old-fashioned floral china teapot, which Antonia had bought in an op shop on the way back to

Sydney on the first trip. She had been surprised to find assorted mugs and plates on the shelves and cutlery in the drawer.

'Cath said she'd ask around for stuff but I didn't think she'd actually do it.'

'Why not?' asked Simon. 'People here are happy to help out if they can.'

When everyone was seated round the red formica table, Connor pulled out his phone. 'Photo for Jax and Rob,' he said. 'Twins, scoot closer to your dad.'

To Simon's surprise, they slid off their chairs and came to stand one on either side of him, with Antonia smiling behind Jacob.

'Perfect.' Connor put the phone in his pocket.

'Thanks for helping, Simon,' Antonia said.

'No problem.' In an obscure way, her words hurt. Why wouldn't he help her move? These were his children, she was an old friend if nothing else, and she was a person he wanted to know much, much better. He'd loved her when he was a boy and he doubted he'd ever really stopped. All she needed was time to let herself relax and learn to love him in return. There was plenty of time, and patience had always been one of his virtues.

'We should head back to the motel,' said Antonia, 'It's getting late and we have to find dinner somewhere.'

'There's the Chinese,' said Simon. 'Or the pub has decent food.'

'That sounds better. These two are used to plain and simple,' said Connor.

Much as he would have loved to have stayed with them, Simon reluctantly waved goodbye and got into the ute when the family were ready to go. No one had suggested he eat with them, which was disappointing, but they were here to stay and he'd see his children every day from now on. And Antonia, beautiful, strong, admirable Antonia, the mother of those two precious little people. Loving her was as easy as breathing.

***

'What did you think of Simon?' Antonia asked her father later, after the twins were asleep in the connecting room.

'He'll be a good father. You were absolutely right about him and I don't mind admitting I was wrong all those years ago.' He sighed. 'I made a lot of mistakes when you were growing up.'

She laughed softly. 'So did I, and I think I win that contest hands down.'

He smiled. 'But you survived, sweetheart. Look at those wonderful children you raised. You're an amazing woman and I'm incredibly proud of you.'

'I think the twins kept me going while I was there. I was determined we'd get away one day, and when we finally did, I didn't want that man to shape the rest of our lives. It's hard but I don't want him, or the memory of him, to control me. He's finished doing that.'

Her hands ached and she grimaced as she looked down and saw them curled into white-knuckled fists gripping the arms of the chair. 'I guess I've a fair way to go though.' She shook her hands to release the tension.

'Make sure you contact that therapist in Kurrajong,' he said casually, but the underlying concern was there.

'I will. Doctor Barlow said she was very good.'

He nodded. 'I think Flynn's Crossing will be a great place for you to start out. Cath is very laid back and understanding, and Simon will back you every step of the way. So will Flynn, I think. I like him.'

'So you said.'

'Don't you?'

'I suppose ... he's been helpful.'

'But?' He frowned. 'He hasn't ... bothered you, has he?'

'No, no not in the way you mean. No, he's...' What could she say? Flynn had done nothing wrong, quite the opposite. 'He makes me uncomfortable.'

'Why? In what way?' He leaned forward eyes alert. Dad was not going to let this go and she had nothing specific to say.

'I don't know. It's nothing I can pinpoint. Sometimes he looks at me ... he has a very intense gaze ... his eyes are really blue.'

He relaxed, crossed his legs, leaned back in the chair and studied her. She had the feeling he was trying not to smile. 'Are they? I hadn't noticed.'

'Well, I did. It's like being under a laser beam.' Her skin prickled. The room was hot. 'His eyes are like that actor's in that old movie you like. *The Great Escape.*' 'Steve McQueen. Maybe he likes the look of you. You're a very pretty girl.'

'You're biased. And I doubt that very much. He's not interested in me other than as a client for a house he can't sell.' She got up to wind the window open a little more. The cool air caressed her overheated face and neck.

But lying in bed later, his comment rolled around in her head. Was Flynn interested in her as a woman? Simon was, she knew that. But his interest was only because she'd crashed back into his life with his children in tow. The novelty would wear off soon enough and she wasn't inclined to revitalise their teenage affair. She'd broken it off in the first place because he was too naive and passive, and he hadn't changed. Lauren was the woman for him.

Was Flynn her type? She had to admit he was good looking, but a man would need to prove himself in more ways than that to stand any sort of chance. And he'd need to be very, very patient and not want to have a family, because after the traumatic birth of her babies and the subsequent violence associated with the attempts at sex, the thought of being touched intimately made her skin crawl.

No man would be prepared to accept her under those conditions.

***

Connor left for Sydney the next afternoon after hugs and kisses and a few tears. Antonia stood on the nature strip with the twins, waving until his truck disappeared round the corner. Alone. She felt the loss immediately. Her father had been a large, solid, unwavering presence ever since he'd appeared at that house near Coalcliff and fought to save them all. Now it was up to her to prove what she'd been saying, that she was ready to make a life for herself and the twins.

'When will we see him again?' asked Sarah.

'Not for a while, but we can phone him and Jax, and Nana and Frank every day if we want to.'

'We do want to,' said Jacob.

'Let's walk along to the school and introduce ourselves,' said Antonia. The sign said Term 1 was starting the following Monday so she assumed the teachers would be there today preparing, it being Thursday.

School would be a massive step for the twins, having been isolated from other children all their lives, except for the two older girls in the house and a baby. They'd eventually enjoyed the preschool they'd been to at the end of the previous year but were wary of the adults in charge. With any luck, their first kindy teacher would be a woman.

She ran back into the house for her purse and keys then grasped a little hand in each of hers. 'Come on. This will be our next adventure.'

'Can we be together at school?' asked Sarah.

'Yes.'

'All day?'

'Yes.'

'We might like it,' said Jacob. 'They'll have toys to play with.'

'They will. And books to read.'

Antonia cut across the playing field, the dry grass crisp under foot. Large trees shaded the asphalt assembly area in front of the white-painted weatherboard buildings and a few cars were parked in the parking area.

'They have a playground. Look, Sarah.' Jacob pointed to a brightly coloured climbing frame and monkey bars. 'Can we play, Mummy?'

'After we've been inside.'

She walked across the quadrangle to the main door. A sign said 'Welcome to Flynn's Crossing Primary School'. Two tubs of pink petunias sat at the bottom of the wide shallow steps, scenting the warm air.

A corridor led right and left but directly opposite was a reception area with a grey-haired woman staring at a computer screen. She looked up, smiling, and came to the sliding-glass window.

'Hello, how can I help you?'

'I'd like to enrol my children in kindergarten, please. They're both five.'

'Twins? How lovely. We already have a set of twins in third grade. Identical girls. What are your names?' She looked at Sarah and Jacob, who were studying her carefully while clutching Antonia's hands.

'Sarah and Jacob,' said Antonia. 'They're very shy with new people.'

'I'll let Mrs Birdie know you're here. She's the Principal. Your name is...'

'Antonia Farris.'

She made the call. 'She'll be here directly.'

'Who teaches kindy?' asked Antonia.

'Kate Armstrong. She's just joined us this year too, so you can all get to know each other and the school together.'

Thank goodness it was a woman, although the chances of a male kindy teacher were slim.

'Is it a big class?'

'Your two make eleven, so quite small this year. We usually number about one hundred and fifteen students in the school.'

Small was good. Much less overwhelming than the city school they would have attended with its overcrowded classrooms and limited play areas, the traffic noise and the people. All strangers.

A tall thin woman with short black hair and wearing a black and white striped dress stepped out of a room farther down on the right.

'Here's Mrs Birdie.' Magpie flashed into Antonia's mind and stuck there.

Mrs Birdie shook hands with a strong grip from a cool bony hand.

'Welcome, Antonia. And children.'

'Hello. This is Sarah, and Jacob.'

'Come in to my office and we can have a chat. Thanks, Louise.' When they were all seated, Mrs Birdie said, 'Have you just moved to town, Antonia?' 'Yes, we finished unpacking this morning. We're from Sydney but I'm renting a house just behind the school.'

'With a mango tree,' said Jacob unexpectedly.

'How wonderful. I like mangoes. Do you?' Mrs Birdie smiled and he actually smiled back.

'Yes, we do,' he said.

'How about you two have a look in my special box of interesting things,' she said. 'While I chat to Mummy.' She indicated a large yellow-painted box in the corner.

'Go on,' said Antonia and they both went wide-eyed to investigate.

'And is the children's father here with you?'

'He lives on the cooperative. His name is Simon Leith but the children are Farris.'

'Is he allowed to see them?'

'Oh yes, absolutely. He'll be very involved in their care.'

Mrs Birdie nodded. 'That's good. Have the children attended preschool?'

Antonia had prepared for these questions. 'Only for a term, last year. We lived in an isolated area before, so they haven't had much opportunity to meet other children. They're learning ... and they're very shy with adults at first. Particularly men.'

Mrs Birdie's keen eye lighted on her face. Was it her tone, her words, or was Mrs Birdie very experienced in reading between the lines? 'Was it an abusive relationship you were in?'

Antonia nodded. 'But it's over now and it wasn't Simon. He didn't know. And the children weren't ever hit.'

'That's something at least. So you've come here to heal.'

The understanding and sympathy took her by surprise. 'Yes.'

'Our school community is small but very strong,' she said. 'I think you've come to the right place.'

'Mrs Birdie, I'd like to make a clean start. I have the name of a counsellor in Kurrajong for us to see, and we will, but I'd like to keep my past private.'

'Of course. Nothing you say to me will be repeated without your say-so, but Kate Armstrong will need to know some details in order to help the children.'

Antonia nodded. 'I understand.'

'Make sure to see Louise on your way out. There are some forms to fill in. Do they have any medical issues? Allergies and so on?'

'No, they're very healthy.'

'Are they up to date with their inoculations?'

'Yes. I have their records.' The poor twins had received a number of jabs since their rescue, but exposure to other children after being isolated since birth meant they'd be wide open to any germs.

'That all sounds perfect. Now Antonia, do you have any skills you can offer us at school?'

'Skills?'

She laughed. 'No need to be alarmed. We're always on the lookout for things our parents can bring to the school in the way of knowledge. We don't get the support city schools get in a lot of ways. Languages and music, for example. Can you speak a foreign language, sing or play an instrument?'

'I can, as a matter of fact. I learned the flute all through high school and I took it up again last year.'

Mrs Birdie's smile was of pure delight. 'We have a piano teacher in town so some of our children go there for lessons after school. Would you be prepared to take on our recorder ensemble? Or perhaps offer flute lessons if anyone's interested?'

'I hadn't thought of that ... I could take on the recorders I suppose.' Teach flute? Who would want to learn in this little town? But Mrs Birdie was so keen...

'Wonderful. Anything else? A language, painting, sports coaching?'

'No. Sorry.'

'The music will be a wonderful start. The arts are so important. One of our town councillors comes in and takes the seniors for photography sessions during the year. They produce some amazing work.'

'A councillor?'

'Flynn, you must know him, he would have rented you the house.'

'Yes, of course.' Simon mentioned Flynn liked photography. 'Simon is a good photographer.'

'Really, I didn't know that. I don't know him very well, Rufus is the one who comes in and teaches the children about gardening. We have quite a thriving vegetable plot once the year gets underway. And we have hens.'

'Goodness. It sounds very comprehensive.'

'We try,' she said. 'Now, let's go and meet Kate.'

'Before we do can I ask you, please ... I didn't finish my last year at high school. Is it possible to enrol for my

Higher School Certificate somewhere? Not right away; later in the year.'

'Absolutely. I'll look into it for you. There's a TAFE in Kurrajong, but also online courses.'

***

Simon arrived that evening. He stood on the verandah with an overflowing box of vegetables at his feet and a shy smile on his face. He held a framed picture.

'I just picked them,' he said. 'I thought you might not have much food in yet. And I brought you this as a house-warming gift.'

He turned the picture so she could see. One of his beautiful photographs, this one of a waterfall splashing down a fern-laden gully, cool and green.

'Simon, it's beautiful. Thank you. I love it.'

He shrugged. 'I have plenty and there's a whole national park full of subjects right next door.'

'Thanks, that's wonderful. Come in.'

He hefted the box and followed her to the kitchen where Jacob and Sarah were doing colouring-in at the table.

They both stopped, pencils poised. 'Hello,' he said. 'I brought you some lovely fresh veggies from my garden.'

Two pairs of eyes moved to the box.

'Want to help me unpack it?'

Jacob nodded but Sarah stayed put.

Antonia lifted the photograph to show them. 'Simon brought this for our house.'

The twins studied it, then Simon.

'It's pretty,' said Sarah.

'Did you take that picture?' asked Jacob.

'Yes.'

Antonia propped the photo carefully on the kitchen bench.

'I'll have to decide where to hang it,' she said.

Should she invite him for dinner? She opened the fridge, which was empty save for milk, eggs, butter and a jar each of vegemite and strawberry jam, Sarah's favourite. Enough to cover breakfast and scrambled eggs for dinner, in other words.

Simon had brought lettuce, celery, shallots, tomatoes, potatoes, corn, zucchini, carrots, lemons, parsley and a jar of honey. 'It's not much but it will get you started,' he said.

'Simon, it's brilliant. I was going to make do with eggs and toast tonight but now I can add salad and do a frittata.'

He squatted with Jacob and together they transferred items to the fridge, handing Antonia the lemons and tomatoes to put on the bench.

'I need a proper fruit bowl.' She reached for a plastic container.

'We should go to the markets in Kurrajong. They have all sorts of stalls, craft as well as food and produce. There's a great chocolate and fudge maker who comes regularly.'

'Can we, Mummy?' Sarah piped up.

'When is it?'

'Second Sunday of the month, so the Sunday after this one.'

'Sounds good.'

'We went to school today,' said Jacob.

'Did you? What was it like?'

'I like the playground things.'

'The climbing frame? I always liked the monkey bars best but I wasn't very good at them.' Simon straightened and closed the fridge. 'My best friend could swing across really fast. He was like a monkey. I could hang upside down by one leg though.'

'Don't try that, Jacob,' said Antonia swiftly. Simon pulled a face at Jacob, who laughed. 'I enrolled them. Mrs Birdie is very nice and so is the kindy teacher.'

'Miss Arms,' said Sarah and giggled.

'Miss Armstrong.' Antonia caught Simon's eye and laughed. 'Mrs Birdie asked me if I'd teach the recorder group because I told her I used to play the flute.'

'Great. You'll meet lots of people really quickly.'

'I'll have to ask Jax how to go about it. Lucky I've got her as a resource. Mrs Birdie said Rufus helps with the garden.'

'Yes. They have chooks too. You should get some.'

'I thought of that. We had them ... before.'

'I'll come over and build a run. Jacob will help, won't you?'

'Yes.'

'A good strong one so foxes don't get in.'

Jacob nodded with a serious expression. 'You have to shoot bloody foxes,' he said.

'We don't say bloody, Jakey,' Antonia said. Would she be able to override that man's influence? Simon's gentleness would help. And school. Kate Armstrong wouldn't be impressed by five-year-old swearing. 'We had trouble with foxes before—but we won't shoot them.'

'No, we'll just build a strong fence,' Simon said. He picked up the empty vegetable box. 'Would you like to stay and eat frittata with us?' she asked. 'Thanks, I'd love to. Do you need anything extra? I can take a run to the shop.' 'I can only offer tap water or milk, so if you'd like something else to drink you'll have to get it. And more eggs, please. And a clove of garlic.' Simon smiled. 'I'll be back in ten minutes.' When he'd gone, Sarah said, 'Is he coming back?' 'Yes. Is that okay?' 'I s'pose,' she said. 'He's our daddy,' said Jacob, as if that settled the matter. 'Yes, he is but if he worries you he doesn't have to stay.' 'We like him,' said Jacob. Sarah nodded and resumed colouring. Five minutes later, someone knocked on the door. Simon must have forgotten something. Antonia went to open it, calling, 'Come right in. You don't need to knock.' The door swung wide on Flynn. 'Hello,' he said. 'I thought I should knock seeing as how it's your house now.'

Chapter 7

She was obviously expecting someone. Simon? Who else would she greet that way? Her total surprise was better than annoyance, but pleasure would have been nice. Delight even better.

'Hello,' she said.

'Hello. I came to see how you were settling in and to check everything was working okay. I brought this as a house-warming gift.' He produced the bottle of wine he'd held half hidden by his side, chosen specially because she'd enjoyed it at Simon's dinner.

'Oh. You didn't need to...' She made no move to accept it.

'I know but I did.'

She relented and took the bottle awkwardly. A pink flush appeared on her cheeks and she ducked her head. 'I'm sorry. Thank you very much. That's kind of you.'

'It's nothing. Have you got everything in place? Did the furniture van turn up?'

Was he babbling, trying to fill the awkward spaces with noise? He'd embarrassed her, and was busily embarrassing himself. Being uncomfortable was uncomfortable—unfamiliar and downright unpleasant.

'Yes, right on time. We moved my things in yesterday. I don't have much so now we're all set. I just need to slowly build up my kitchen equipment and maybe buy some ornaments and things. Did you bring in the extra chairs and the plates and cutlery?'

'I brought it here but Cath put the word about.'

'That's so kind of everyone. Thank you. Simon is taking us to some markets soon. He said some really good craftspeople take their things there.'

As she spoke, the tension left her body and what he suspected was the real Antonia shone through, a happy, excited, confident young woman setting up a home for herself and her children. Thank God for that. She could easily have shut the door in his face. For a nasty moment he thought she might.

'The Kurrajong markets?'

'Yes.'

'You'll enjoy them.' The perfect family day out. He never went. Not by himself.

'We're looking forward to it. I'm hoping to find some decorative bits and pieces.'

She lifted a slim hand to push a strand of smooth dark hair behind her ear and he had to stop himself reaching out and smoothing it down, running the silky lengths through his fingers. He swallowed, shifted his focus and her deep brown eyes locked with his for a heart-stopping moment.

Breath rushed back in suddenly and he blurted, 'Would you like a photograph or two of the bush? I have a couple you could have. They'd just need framing.' Shut up!

By the look on her face he'd overstepped some mark.

'But you'd probably prefer to choose something yourself,' he said quickly to spare her the awkwardness of refusing.

'No, it's not that.' The flush was back, deeper and pinker. 'Simon brought us one of his.' A worried wrinkle appeared on her brow.

'Right. Okay.' He should get out of here before he made a total idiot of himself ... even more of a total idiot of himself. 'I'll leave you to it then.'

He stepped back on to the verandah. Antonia stayed in the open doorway.

'Thanks for coming by. And thanks for the wine.' She sounded anxious, the flustered girl again.

'No worries. If anything goes wrong let me know. With the house I mean.'

'Yes. Thanks. I will.'

'See you later.' He strode down the steps without looking back, intensely conscious of the fact the door hadn't closed and he knew she was watching him go. Thinking what? He didn't want to know.

He slammed the car door and backed out of the driveway like a man with a deadline to keep, and accelerated much too fast. As he shot past the school, a white ute rounded the corner heading in the opposite direction. Simon. Of course. He belonged with his children. She'd welcome him in, eager for him to build a relationship with them. And with her?

His jaw ached and he had to consciously relax and grimace to relieve the pressure. How could he be jealous? He barely knew Antonia, and Simon was a friend.

He knew nothing about her, not really. But rationalising the situation didn't help. He had to face the fact he was infatuated with her. Like a fifteen-year-old with a crush. He laughed.

'God, what a fool,' he said aloud.

The only thing to do was ride it out. Crushes didn't last, infatuations faded. He hadn't had a girlfriend for some time now, so this Antonia thing was simply the result of a bit of a drought in that department. In a week or two he'd be back to normal. In the meantime he could distract himself with a weekend away. If he left tomorrow he could make it a three-day jaunt. Or go bush—couple of nights camping with his camera and the beautiful bush to keep him company. That would be cheaper and very enjoyable.

Except he'd be alone with his unrequited passion. Bloody hell! What he needed was distance and attractive female company. He could drive to Brisbane late on Friday afternoon and catch up with Lou. She always had something going on or could hook him up with one of her friends.

At home, Flynn pulled out his laptop and booked a room in his favourite hotel for Friday and Saturday nights. Lou was more than happy to hear from him and thought she could wangle an invite to a function she had to attend on Saturday.

'Bring a suit,' she said. 'It's a work thing, boring as batshit, but they always turn on a good feed and plenty of booze. After that we can have supper somewhere and hear some live music.'

'Sounds perfect.'

He hung up, well pleased. All he had to do was put Antonia out of his mind and enjoy the few days with Lou and when he returned the little emotional hiccup would be over.

***

'Was that Flynn?' Simon asked when he came in with the groceries.

'Yes.' Antonia took the eggs from the bag.

'Why didn't he stay?'

'I don't know. He seemed in a hurry.'

'What did he want?' He unpacked milk and two cans of beer.

'He was checking that everything was okay in the house. He brought a bottle of wine as a house-warming.'

Simon shut the fridge door. 'You should have invited him in.'

'I ... I didn't think of it.'

Simon shook his, smiling. 'Tonia, relax, he's a nice guy. He was being friendly and welcoming, that's what he's like.'

Antonia grimaced. 'Will he be offended?'

'No. Now, twins, look what I got for dessert.'

He held up the final item. A tub of ice-cream. 'To go with our mangoes.'

'Yummeeee.' Sarah clapped her hands together.

'Bathtime first,' said Antonia.

Simon chopped garlic and zucchinis while Antonia ran the bath. When she returned to the kitchen, he'd turned on the oven and was cutting potatoes for wedges.

'I need some more baking dishes too,' she said.

He pointed to the biscuit tray on the bench. 'I found this, it'll do. Are they all right in the bath on their own?'

'Go and check if you like.'

He grinned and put the last of the wedges on the tray, sprinkled olive oil on top and slid it into the oven.

She broke eggs into a bowl and began whisking. Shouts of laughter and splashing came from the bathroom. Coming here was definitely the right thing to do. Those three were meant to be together. Jacob, especially, needed a decent, kind, normal male role model. Connor's influence had already made its mark, now Simon could take over.

Flynn's face flashed into her mind. She should have invited him in. She'd been unbelievably rude but he'd been gracious as ever. Why did that happen whenever she ran into him? Some internal switch seemed to be tripped to off in his presence, the one that moderated her behaviour. It wasn't because he was a stranger, a man as threat, because she knew he wasn't. Basically she liked him. Liked him a lot.

Not the way she liked Simon. She loved Simon the way she loved her little brother Damien.

She liked Flynn but at the same time he made her jittery and unaccountable for her words. Better to avoid him. That wasn't going to be easy in this small town but once she had a routine going, their paths wouldn't cross very much and she'd be able to relax. That's what it was. Her whole life was settling after months of turmoil and Flynn was on the receiving end of her adjustment. She owed him an apology. Tomorrow morning she could take the twins to school to buy their uniforms from the clothing pool, then go to his office. She would say her piece, and her conscience would be clear.

'Are you three nearly ready?' she called.

'No,' shouted Jacob.

'We're having fun.' That was Sarah, giggling like a loony.

She tore leaves from the lettuce and chopped another tomato for salad.

'I'm starting cooking the frittata now. You've got ten minutes.'

'Okay,' called Simon. 'We'll be there.'

Sitting at the table with Simon opposite and her two freshly bathed sweet-faced cherubs on either side, Antonia raised her glass of Flynn's wine, drunk from one of her four wine glasses, a gift from Jax. Simon had opened it for her saying it was a special occasion, which made her feel even more guilty.

'Here's to our new home,' she said.

'Your new home,' said Simon and clicked his beer can against her glass. 'I hope you'll be happy here. You deserve to be.'

'Thanks. So far so good.'

'When do you start at the Paragon?'

'On Tuesday. Except for the Saturday shift, it's perfect. Cath will let me leave at three to collect these two.'

'I could have the twins on Saturdays if you like, and if they wanted to, of course.'

She looked at the children. Sarah had stopped eating. Jacob had his worried face on. 'That would be ideal and I'd love them to spend time with you but, well ... it's early days. We have to get settled at school first.'

'Of course.'

'I don't want to rush them.'

'No, of course not. I'm sorry. But we can still build the chook pen together, can't we, Jacob? With Mummy helping.'

Jacob nodded and Sarah resumed eating.

She'd have to be careful. Just because Simon was their father and keen to be part of their lives didn't mean they were ready to accept him wholeheartedly. When it came to the crunch, Antonia was their rock and the one they relied on to keep them safe. At that man's house, Hannah and her two girls had been the other caregivers they trusted. More recently their grandparents had widened the circle and the preschool teacher last term had been a model of patience and understanding. Regular counselling had helped a lot. Connor, however, had been the only man they were happy to be left alone with and that was in part because he'd saved them all, he was a hero in their eyes. Superman. How many men would be able to match that?

***

Flynn was on the phone with a buyer for a rural block near Kurrajong, focused on the file on his desk and discussing fence lines, when the office door opened. Brandon was out, dammit. He glanced up.

Antonia! He smiled and waved her to the chair opposite, brain in a flurry. The client on the line had asked another question, which he'd missed completely.

'Could you repeat that, please? I didn't quite catch...'

The man burbled on about getting the surveyor's report by tomorrow and a building inspection done on the house in case of asbestos insulation, despite a certificate stating it was clear of the stuff.

'Of course we can organise that for you, but it won't be done by tomorrow. It's Saturday.'

He finally managed to finish the call.

'Sorry about that, Antonia. How are you?'

She hadn't taken the chair but remained standing, looking at the pictures of properties for sale on the wall by the window. He had a moment to drink in the sight of her before she turned. Glossy brown hair falling over her shoulders, slim bare legs, blue denim skirt over a neat rear end, and sleeveless white blouse. Simple and beautiful, fresh as the sparkling streams that flowed down the cool fern filled gullies in the mountains.

When she faced him, her expression held a shadow of apprehension, as though he was a headmaster and she'd been sent for punishment of some transgression. Before he could attempt to set her at her ease, she said, 'I've come to apologise for being rude to you yesterday. I'm sorry.'

'Rude to me?' That, he hadn't expected. Had she been rude? Not that he'd noticed. On the contrary, she'd been beautifully flustered and then unusually talkative. For a few moments.

'Simon said I should have invited you in. I didn't ... I'm sorry. I thought you must be busy and ... anyway I didn't and I'm sorry if you thought I was rude. I didn't mean to be.'

Flynn stepped forward involuntarily, anxious to close the gap, to reassure her, to prevent her worrying about something so trivial, so sweetly nothing.

'You weren't rude,' he said gently, falling into the soft deep brown of her eyes, wanting to touch her and pull her into his arms. Kiss her.

She blinked. Her gaze dropped to his shirtfront, then up again. 'Really?'

He nodded, unable to speak.

A little smile hovered on her lips and he couldn't resist. He leaned forward and brushed her soft mouth with his, light as a butterfly wing. She gasped.

He drew back. 'Sorry. *That* was rude.'

Her face was a kiss away, frozen. He waited, barely breathing. Those beautiful brown eyes gazed into his for a long, long moment, then the tiny smile reappeared.

'No,' she said so quietly he barely heard her. 'It wasn't.'

He couldn't stop the smile that burst spontaneously across his face. 'I guess we're even then.'

And to his delighted amazement, she laughed. 'Yes, we are.'

He moved back towards his desk, putting distance between them, just in case. 'Antonia,' he said. 'I don't know what you may have experienced in your life and this may be way off beam but I get the feeling you might have been in an abusive relationship...'

Her expression darkened. 'Did Simon say anything to you?'

'No, no ... it's just ... a feeling. And if I'm right, I want you to know that you never need to feel frightened I'll react in a violent way to something you've said or done. It doesn't matter what, I won't ever hit you or abuse you. Or anyone else, for that matter.'

Her eyes widened but the import of his words sank in. 'Thank you,' she murmured. The sheen of tears glistened but she smiled again. 'Thank you.' More strongly. 'I'd better go. I left the twins over at the cafe.'

'With milkshakes?'

'I hope not. I said they could have an ice-cream.'

He laughed and it was relief and joy and pleasure all rolled into one. He took the plunge. 'Have a coffee with me?'

She hesitated but only for a split second. 'Okay. Now?'

'Yes, it's coffee time. After you.'

He flipped the 'back in ten minutes' sign and pulled the door closed behind them. So much for keeping away from her. Here he was fuelling his stupid crush like a madman. Still. Sharing a cup of coffee was a normal thing to do and meant nothing. It wouldn't mean a thing to her anyway and avoiding someone in this small town was virtually impossible.

He stood beside her, waiting for a couple of cars to go by.

'You know, if you're thinking of painting the house it's best to do it before you get too much stuff in there.'

'Hmm. I don't think I can afford to do anything like that for a while. I won't have time either. It's not too bad.' She added grimly, 'I've seen worse.'

'Simon would help, wouldn't he?'

'Yes, probably, but I also don't want to spend money on paint when the place might be sold. The owner won't pay for it, will he?'

'She, but no, not this owner. You don't think you'd be in a position to buy?'

'My parents would say yes, but I won't ask them. They've done plenty for us already.'

She stepped on to the road and he followed her across to the Paragon. The twins were in a booth towards the rear where Cath could watch them from the counter. Gail wasn't in yet, fortunately. Flynn didn't want her beady-eyed and ultimately wildly embellished assessment of the situation. Whatever this situation with Antonia was.

'Morning, Cath.'

'Good morning,' she called as she went into the kitchen.

'We've got ice-cream with strawberry flavouring, Mummy,' announced Sarah.

'Lucky you.' Antonia slid in beside her.

'What would you like?' Flynn asked.

'Flat white, please. I should be taking the order. I work here.'

'Not yet you don't. Enjoy it while you can.'

He sauntered across to the counter to wait for Cath to reappear. Antonia leaned across the table, speaking to Jacob. Flynn was too far away to hear what she said but he assumed it was to do with Flynn having to sit beside him on the bench seat. The boy didn't seem too concerned, more interested in spooning pink ice-cream into his mouth.

Order placed, he went back to the booth. 'Okay if I sit here?' he asked Jacob, and received a nod.

***

'I thought chocolate was your favourite flavour,' he said to Sarah. She had a pink ring around her mouth and drips down her T-shirt front.

'Cath said we should try all the flavours,' she said.

'Good idea. So what's best so far?'

'Chocolate.'

'I like caramel. You should have that next.' He'd plucked that at random, remembering he'd liked it as a kid.

'Caramel? Really?' Antonia pulled a face.

'What's wrong with caramel?' He pulled his own face back at her and Sarah and Jacob giggled.

'What's wrong with caramel?' echoed Sarah.

'It's so sweet. I didn't have you down as a sweet-toothed person.'

'I have hidden depths. What's your favourite?'

'I don't have a favourite. I don't eat ice-cream much. I like fruit.'

'You'd like fruity gelatos and sorbets. There's a good gelato shop in Kurrajong. The owners are Italian and make their own the traditional way.'

'Can we go there?' asked Jacob.

'We might. How big is Kurrajong?'

'It's the regional centre. That's where our high schoolers go. There's a TAFE too.'

Cath appeared with the coffee. 'How's the house?' she asked.

'Fine. We like it,' Antonia said. 'I'll have to get into the garden and clean up the vegetable patch.'

'If you need a hand, give me a call,' he heard himself say.

'I want to start a compost heap. Where can I get one of those bins?'

'Have you asked Simon?'

He'd be the best person to ask about gardening gear but for some reason she was asking him. Making conversation? Maybe.

'I don't want to rely on him for everything,' she said.

'There's a hardware store and a couple of garden centres in Kurrajong. They're your best bet.'

'Okay.'

'You seem to know a bit about it,' he said. 'I'm not much good at gardening but I can do the heavy lifting.'

'Mummy had to grow the vegetables and we had to help,' said Sarah.

'Look at the mess you're in, you grub.' Antonia took a paper serviette and began dabbing at the pink blobs on Sarah's T-shirt, effectively preventing any further revelations.

Had to grow the vegetables? Five-year-olds included? Was that as bad as it sounded? Where had they been living and with whom? One look at Antonia's face told him she wasn't going to elaborate and the way she was fussing over Sarah meant the subject was closed.

'I'm off to Brisbane for the weekend,' he said.

Antonia brightened. 'Any special reason?'

'Bit of R and R. Catching up with friends.'

'That'll be nice.'

'Yes.' But it wouldn't. He'd much prefer to stay in town, go shopping for a compost bin and help pull out weeds in her garden.

***

Friday night in Brisbane. Flynn didn't contact any of his other friends, he had dinner and went to the latest Bond movie. Saturday loomed empty but again he made no calls, preferring to wander about the city centre, the Botanic Gardens, visit the Queensland Art Gallery, linger over lunch and go back to the hotel early to lie on his bed and read one of the books he'd picked up while idling away time in a bookshop.

He met Lou at the venue, wearing a suit and tie as instructed. She kissed his cheek and tucked her arm in his as they walked into the hotel foyer.

'How come you look better each time I see you? It's not fair,' she said.

'You look great, what's your problem?' She might've gained a bit of weight but it suited her. She claimed she fought a running battle of the bulge, which was idiotic because in his opinion she'd always been on the skinny side.

'Age,' she said. 'Grey hairs, extra poundage, you name it. First floor, Garden Room. Stairs or lift?'

'Stairs. For God's sake woman! Stop with the weight thing. You look terrific. Very sexy.' Male heads always turned when she walked by. He'd always enjoyed being out with her and tonight she looked stunning in a simple black figure-hugging cocktail dress with a diamond feature nestled in the vee of fabric at her cleavage. She'd rolled her dark hair into a loose bun and clipped it in place with a sparkling silver clasp. Silver drop-earrings caught the light as she moved.

'Do you mean that?' The staircase was a sweeping affair with annoyingly wide shallow treads.

'Of course I mean that. Sexy has nothing to do with weight and everything to do with personality and confidence. A few curves help, and a great smile. You've got all that.'

'Why have I just been dumped then?'

'Because whoever it was is an idiot.'

'Actually, I think you're right. I was going to dump him but he got in first, which is a bit of a bummer.'

'Forget him. You have me now.'

'Only for this evening, I hope,' she said in mock alarm. 'I don't want you on a permanent basis. We tried that and failed, remember?' She turned right at the top and headed for an open doorway with a sign indicating the event in progress.

He laughed and kissed her cheek. 'Thanks very much.'

'You're too young for me. I want a man my age at least.'

'I'm only five years younger. I'm not a child.'

'I was starting school and you were a newborn baby.'

'Okay, I resign. What's this thing you've dragged me to?'

'It's a meet and greet for our clients and people in power. Government ministers, heads of departments and so on. Federal and state.'

She took a name tag for herself and one marked 'Gate Crasher' for him. 'It's our little joke,' she said. 'For guests like you.'

Lou said it would be boring but Flynn's interest level picked up as he scanned the name tags on the table. If these people turned up, he could do a bit of schmoozing of his own. Networking was the best way of putting Flynn's Crossing and the proposed development of the area on the map. None of these people would have heard of the place but if he could get the ear of a few of them, particularly the local state ministers, he might be able to do some good. Name-dropping might be an in—Margie and Barry Cunningham for example. Barry had worked in the finance industry for years, he must have mates in the business.

***

Flynn arrived home midmorning on Sunday and immediately phoned Margie and Phil.

'Can you come over this afternoon? I have news,' he said.

Flynn took his visitors through to sit in the garden rather than the house. The refreshing breeze made a pleasant change to the stifling heat of the previous week.

'I met Sean Baldessin last night at a function in Brisbane.'

'How did you manage that?' asked Phil. He took a long drink of the cold beer Flynn had furnished him with. No beer for Margie, she was happy with iced sparkling water and a seat in the shade. The front of the old wood-framed house had the view. The back was his own little corner of rainforest. Lush, fragrant and cool.

'I went along with a friend as her guest. She works for the company that gave the reception. It was full of government heads of department and state ministers. All the big names. It was pure luck. But I introduced myself to him. He sends his regards to you and Barry, Margie.'

'Thanks, I like Sean. Not at all what you expect from someone in his situation.'

'He's very approachable.'

'Was Tegan there? His wife?'

'No. Anyway, as Margie already knows he's really interested in the proposal and wants to visit and have a look at the area. He's coming on Thursday. We'll give him lunch at the pub.'

'Fantastic!'

'So when do we get the other councillors on board?' asked Phil. 'We're not going to be able to keep his visit quiet.'

'I thought about that,' said Flynn. 'This is still in the very early stages so we're not committing ourselves to anything, just discussing ideas. I'll phone and invite them to lunch and say a verbal proposal for a development on that block has been put forward to the council and we're meeting with Sean to hear his ideas. It's no secret that we're in favour of some sort of economic boost to the town.'

'Sounds okay,' said Phil. 'Margie can email everyone with her information so far and you can tell them exactly what you just told us.'

'Fine with me.' Margie nodded.

Flynn raised his glass. 'Okay. Let the battle commence.'

It would be a battle, there was no doubt about that.

***

Antonia walked the twins to school on Monday morning for their very first day. Both were excited and very proud to be wearing their new uniforms of black shorts and red T-shirt with the school logo. They'd adapted to being left at preschool surprisingly quickly so she was hoping this would be a similar experience for them. As the therapist said, it was easier for them as twins and they'd learned to be resilient living in that house. Antonia wasn't always with them and they were often minded by Hannah or another of the women, or locked in their room for long periods. As long as they were together they'd be okay.

Miss Armstrong welcomed them with a warm smile. Today was for the new students to get their bearings, tomorrow was for everyone to return, she said. Two sets of kisses and hugs and promises to be back at three and the twins joined the small group of kindy children settling down on the mat in front of Miss Armstrong. Antonia waited for a while with the other mothers, a grandmother and two fathers, watching for signs of a meltdown, but all eyes were on Miss Armstrong who was asking everyone to introduce themselves to the class. All the children except Sarah and Jacob already knew each other so much giggling ensued.

Antonia withdrew quietly and walked down the corridor. Her babies would be fine. Two mothers walked with her.

'How are you feeling about leaving them?' one asked.

'It's weird not having them with me.'

'I'm Cheryl and this is Di.'

Cheryl was the tall one with short dark hair and a toothy smile, Di was short and plump with blonde hair in a ponytail.

'I'm Antonia.'

'We know. You're in Jean's old house, aren't you?' said Di.

'Yes. I love it. The twins call it the Mango House.' She wouldn't get anywhere wondering what else the townspeople knew. She needed to make friends and fit in. 'Would you like some mangoes? We can't eat them fast enough.'

'Love some.'

'You could come across now if you like.' She made the suggestion tentatively. These women would be busy.

'Okay, thanks,' said Cheryl.

'How many children do you have?' Antonia asked as they set off across the playground.

'I have three. Seth in fifth grade, Bella in third and my last, Aaron, is in kindy; Di has two.'

'Fiona in third grade and Erica has just started,' said Di. 'We're going to celebrate our freedom at my place. Why don't you come along with us after we get the mangoes?'

'Are you sure?'

'Of course. A few others are coming too. You can meet them.'

And so half an hour later Antonia sat with new acquaintances Helen and Mary, Hugo and the grandmother whose name she didn't catch, drinking cheap sparkling wine in Di's house and toasting their newfound hours of freedom.

She'd prepared herself for an inquisition but everyone already knew the basics of her situation, even down to her father's assistance with the move. Di was also a single mother. Her husband had deserted the family a year ago and not been heard of since.

'Good riddance,' she said. 'He gambled away everything we had except the house.' Now she worked as a cleaner at the pub and the motel, juggling shifts to fit around the school day. 'It's hard but it's better than when he was around. At least I'm in charge of every dollar I make.'

Cheryl's husband drove trucks and was away a lot. 'I'd like to get a part-time job but there's not a lot around here,' she said.

'Mrs Birdie said I should give music lessons,' said Antonia. 'And she wants me to take the school recorder group.'

'That'd be lovely,' said the grandmother, whose name no one repeated. She and her invalid husband minded her son and daughter-in-law's two children before and after school because they commuted to Kurrajong for work. 'Music is very important. What instruments do you play?'

'Flute.'

'How nice. I must tell my son. I'm sure he'd be keen for my granddaughter, Olivia, to learn.'

'I play guitar a bit,' said Hugo. Untrimmed beard, dreadlocks, blue singlet, sandals and loose tie-died Indian cotton pants. He couldn't look more like a leftover from the sixties if he tried, and he had a pungent unwashed odour. He lived with several other families on a commune on the other side of town.

'Have you told Mrs Birdie?' Antonia asked.

'No, I don't do a structured thing. I just play from the soul.'

Behind him, Di rolled her eyes as she topped up glasses from a second bottle.

'Have you heard what the council is thinking about doing?' The grandmother looked around the group with raised eyebrows.

No one had.

'They want to bring in a developer to put a massive holiday resort on that land out next to the cooperative. They want to buy Aidan out and use that whole section for a golf course and Lord knows what else.'

'Whose brilliant idea is that?' demanded Helen among the amazed chorus of reactions.

'Flynn's.'

'They can't do that! It hasn't been approved, has it? No one's heard anything about it.'

'I never liked Flynn,' said Mary. 'He's always on the lookout for number one. Doesn't give a damn about the town. You can bet he's set to make a nice profit out of any deal that goes through. No doubt he'll be handling the land sale.'

'He's the real estate agent, of course he will,' put in Cheryl. 'Flynn's a good bloke.'

'He's been very kind and helpful to me,' said Antonia.

Hugo smiled with an unnerving gleam in his eye. 'Because you're a very pretty young woman.'

'She is, but that's not the reason,' said Mary with a reproving glare. 'Guys like that cultivate everyone just in case there's an angle they can use.'

'I won't be any use to Flynn.'

'You don't know. You're connected to Simon and he's part of the cooperative...'

'That would put Antonia on the other side of the fence to Flynn, wouldn't it?' asked Di.

'Are there sides to this?' asked Cheryl.

Mary shrugged. 'I don't know, I'm just saying. Flynn's a wheeler-dealer. He owns half the town already.'

'Really? I thought he just owned the pub,' said Antonia.

'He has the house out on Majura Lane, one in the main street and he used to own the place next door to you.'

'Bron's house? I thought they'd always owned it.'

'Them and the bank. She and Kev had some financial trouble a few years back. He lost his job and they moved here because a mate offered him the job running the garage. They were renting from Flynn but he sold it to them. Probably at a good profit.'

'Anyway,' said Helen. 'We don't even know if this thing about the resort is true yet. Who told you that, Gwen?'

The grandmother was Gwen.

'Stuey heard it in the pub the other night.'

'If it does turn out to be right, we need to be prepared,' said Mary. 'And organise a protest group. The last thing I want is Flynn's Crossing turned into some tacky holiday destination for cashed-up tourists. Imagine the traffic. And the people. We don't have the roads or the facilities. The council hasn't even got our public toilets built yet.'

'I'm with you,' said Hugo. 'And the others on the commune will be too. We came here to get right away from the crazy, commercial, capitalist society.'

***

Antonia walked home with a head buzzing from drinking in the morning. But Di and Cheryl had been very friendly and welcoming, and whether they meant to or not had taken the edge off her first morning without the twins. She had the feeling it had been deliberate. Maybe for their own sakes as much as the others in the group but whatever the reason, Antonia was grateful. And she'd made friends. With Di and Cheryl more than anyone else, and Cheryl in particular for her easygoing cheerfulness.

The gossip made her uncomfortable, but learning more about Flynn was interesting. He'd never said a word about Bron's house, which meant he didn't discuss other people's business. That was reassuring.

Did Simon and Aidan know about the council's plans? They must have heard the rumours, surely? As a newcomers it wasn't her place to get involved, but her sympathies did lean towards Mary's and Hugo's. Would Flynn really railroad his friends into selling their thriving business to be turned into a golf course?

Chapter 8

'So what's the story, Aidan?' asked Lauren on Monday evening when the group convened on Georgia and Aidan's verandah for drinks. She had a determined set to her jaw Simon had never seen before.

'About the developer? Yeah. It's all over town.' Rufus's usually relaxed manner was belied by the sharp way he looked at Aidan.

'What's happening?' Simon asked. Lauren and Rufus obviously knew something he didn't, something that pissed them off. What did Aidan know and about what?

Simon's attention had been otherwise occupied the last few days. Antonia and the twins consumed his free time, and his thoughts all the time. The more he saw them the more he fell in love with his family. Sarah and Jacob welcomed him with smiles now and accepted he was part of their lives, especially after an afternoon clearing weeds in their vegetable plot and planting the lettuce seedlings he'd brought. They called him Daddy, which thrilled him, but he wasn't sure they fully understood the concept. They would.

'Flynn and the council want to develop the block next door,' said Rufus. 'Word is that the resort company owned by Sean Baldessin is interested.'

'Nothing's decided yet,' said Aidan with a pull at his beer. 'It's just an idea at this stage. Everyone knows the council is generally in favour of some sort of development in the area.'

'I've never heard of them or him,' said Simon.

'He's a millionaire,' said Lauren with a sour twist to her mouth. She made millionaire sound like paedophile. 'Made his money in technology but now owns a bunch of resorts along the coast.'

'What sort of resorts are they?' asked Georgia. 'I mean, what sort of thing do they want to build here? We're a long way from the coast.'

'Who knows, who cares,' Rufus said. 'How come you didn't tell us, Ade?' Again the intent focus. Rufus was seriously annoyed.

'Because it was council business and still under discussion. Not all of us are keen on this idea but we can at least meet the man and see what his proposal is. Anyway, it's only just come up. Flynn was in Brisbane over the weekend and ran into him at some function he was invited to.'

'I bet,' growled Rufus. 'I reckon he's been cooking this up for ages and knew that bloke was going to be there.'

'He's coming to Flynn's Crossing on Thursday and we're having lunch with him at the pub. I'll be able to tell you more after that.'

'Let me get this right,' said Lauren. 'The council is talking to Baldessin about putting some kind of resort next door to us? Are they sure that block is big enough for him? It's only fifteen hectares with two boundaries on the National Park and some of that is pretty steep and rocky. I bet our land is on the table too. We're on a much better block, level and with the river running through.'

'Flynn wouldn't let the council do that to us. They can't force us to sell.'

'Grow up, Simon,' Lauren snapped. 'Of course he'd apply pressure if it made the difference between doing the deal or not.'

'What about my vote?' said Aidan. 'I'm on that council. And Simon's right. No one can force us to sell. 'Our land aside, it's next door that's up for grabs. Can you outvote Flynn and Margie? She'll be all for it given her and Barry's background. And they can be very persuasive.' Rufus clunked his empty bottle on the table.

'Will the owner sell, do you reckon?' asked Georgia

'Sure to, and we can't match the price a big developer would pay.' Aidan sighed. 'We'll just have to wait and see what Baldessin has to say and what he's proposing. Margie says he's very eco-friendly and into sustainable development and you know what she thinks about that. You only have to see what she and Barry have done on their place.'

'That's true,' said Georgia. 'But this won't be a private house. This will be a much bigger project.'

'At least they'll fix the fence,' said Simon. 'And the road.'

Lauren groaned and it wasn't an amused sound.

'It could mean a new market for our produce,' said Aidan. 'And jobs for people.'

'Sounds like you've already decided,' said Rufus.

'No, I haven't, but I want to give the bloke a fair hearing before I do decide, not dismiss it out of hand.'

'I would have thought that's exactly what you would do,' said Lauren. 'The last thing we want is a massive tourist development over the fence from us. Somewhere else, fine, but not here.'

'So you're a NIMBY.' Georgia smiled. 'Not in my back yard,' she said guessing correctly when Simon opened his mouth to ask what that meant.

'Damn right I am in this case,' said Lauren. 'And I'm amazed any of you are even giving this idea brain space.' She stood up. 'See you in the morning.'

Simon watched her stride across the grass to her own house, back rigid, head up. He'd never heard her so vehemently opposed to something.

Usually she was calm and cheerful. Unflappable. He didn't know her at all.

'Wow,' he murmured.

'She's right.' Rufus stood as well. 'Night all.' He disappeared into the gloom.

Simon looked from Aidan to Georgia in surprise. 'I didn't expect that. They're really upset.'

'I did,' said Aidan. 'Especially from Rufus. He hates those corporate types.'

'So do I,' said Simon. 'That's why I love this place and the town so much. But Flynn does too. I can't believe he's as bad as Lauren makes out. Is he?'

Aidan shrugged. 'Have to wait and see.'

'Would Rufus stay if this thing goes ahead?' Simon frowned. 'This is our home. We've all worked really hard...'

'I know, but we don't know yet what scale his idea is on. It might be quite small and not affect us at all.'

'I doubt that,' said Georgia. 'It wouldn't be worth his while and given the land, the best area to build is right on our boundary.'

Simon stared blindly out into the gathering dusk. If the group began to break up over this his world would crumble. This was his home, these people were like family; he'd planned on being here for the rest of his life. But of course, he had a real family now—Antonia and their children. They were a little beacon of hope for the future. He would always have them and if the worst came to the worst they could move and set up again somewhere else. A proper family unit.

***

Antonia looked up when the cafe door opened. The customer met her automatic smile with one of his own. Flynn. Her welcoming smile faded to confusion as a rush of conflicting emotions swamped her: pleasure at seeing him combined with a niggling feeling of mistrust, mixed with curiosity about the friend in Brisbane he'd been visiting, a woman, for sure, according to the grapevine. And her neck was hot. Flushing like a teenager under the weight of those stunning blue eyes.

'Good morning.' It came out relatively normally. She gave the counter another wipe over and tidied the already tidy pile of menus.

'Hi, how are you?' He glanced around and nodded to a couple of people, receiving vague acknowledgements in return. Did he realise he was the topic du jour? He'd probably revel in it.

'Fine, thank you. Take a seat.'

'Thanks. Long black, please.' He chose one of the four stools at the end of the counter, which meant she was right under his eye.

Cath came out from the kitchen with two of her super milkshakes for the young couple in the corner booth.

'G'day, Flynn. The usual?'

'Thanks.'

Antonia took the milkshakes. She hadn't learned the art of using the espresso machine yet but each time Cath made an order and she wasn't busy, she watched carefully. Len would teach her, he said. She would learn a lot from him. Her dream of opening her own cafe or restaurant one day was still alive. Not that she'd shared it with anyone here.

'You're the talk of the town,' Cath said to Flynn. 'Socialising with millionaires.' She concentrated on making the coffee.

Antonia glanced at him as she took the order to the booth. He gave nothing away. The other customers sat with ears flapping, not even pretending they weren't listening.

'Hardly socialising,' he said. 'It was a business function and I went with a friend because she invited me. I wasn't going to pass up an opportunity like that.' So it was a woman. One of the exes he never kept in contact with?

'What sort of opportunity are we talking here, Flynn?' called a middle-aged woman seated in a booth with two friends. They'd been there for an hour dissecting the marriage of a fourth woman and the reasons for her constant visits to Kurrajong—definitely not for shopping—and showed no sign of moving or ordering anything other than the one pot of tea between them. Annoyed the heck out of Len.

'A good one for Flynn's Crossing,' Flynn said.

'Says who?'

'Nothing's been decided, Glenda. The council will listen to what he has to say, that's all at this stage.'

'Do we get a say?'

'Of course. Any proposal the council considers viable will be put up for public comment. It's a long process.'

'I can tell you right now what my comment will be.'

'You're entitled to your opinion but so is everyone else and we need to hear them all.'

'And we know how that works out, don't we? Money talks.'

Flynn turned back to Cath, who had placed his coffee on the counter in front of him. 'Thanks.'

Antonia went to serve another couple who hadn't joined in but sat listening at their table by the window.

'Sounds like a hot subject,' the man said.

Antonia nodded. 'It is. I'm new in town so I'm not as involved.'

'Yet,' said the woman with a smile.

'Are you locals?'

'No, we're on a driving holiday, heading to Darwin eventually.'

'Gosh. That's a long way.'

'Jeff's on long-service leave so we decided to see Australia. We're from Canberra.'

'I went there once on a school trip.' Another lifetime, another world where she was a carefree child in a secure loving family. 'What would you like?'

Antonia took the menu and went to place their order.

'Did you get the weeding done?' Flynn asked.

'Heaps. Simon came and helped.'

'He'd be good at it. How's he getting on with the children?'

'Sarah and Jacob call him Daddy now.'

'That's nice.'

He picked up the coffee but didn't drink. A muscle twitched in his jaw. The altercation with Glenda must have unsettled him. The three of them were still there muttering together like Macbeth's witches. She wracked her brain for something to say.

'They started school yesterday.'

'How did it go?' No smile. Was he really interested?

'They loved it. We were a bit restricted with learning activities before.'

She paused. No reaction from Flynn. Was he even listening? 'They're pretty independent when they feel secure.'

A frown flicked across his brow and suddenly the blue eyes locked on hers. 'Are they? They didn't strike me that way.'

She lowered her voice. 'It's not personal, Flynn. They're just unsure around men. The teacher is a woman. They're used to being with other women and kids when I'm not there.'

'But they've accepted your father and Simon.'

'They're *starting* to accept Simon, yes. And Dad...'

Flynn was waiting for her to finish the sentence but she couldn't tell him Connor had saved them all without opening up that whole mess she wanted so desperately to put behind them.

'Dad ... is just Dad,' she said. 'How could they not love him? We lived in his house for the last eight months. It took them a bit of time though.'

He nodded. 'So you reckon they might accept me one day?'

What was he saying? Why was that important to him? He wanted reassurance. The realisation smacked her in the head. 'Yes, of course.'

Some of the tension left his face. 'Good. I don't want everyone in town to think I'm a monster, including little kids.'

'I don't. They don't. Lots of people don't.' So it wasn't concern for acceptance by her children, he liked to be liked by his townspeople regardless of age. How disappointing, She didn't think he was as much of a politician to the core as that.

She also didn't think he lacked confidence. Quite the opposite, but his question had exposed a surprising vulnerability before he covered it with the glib remark. Was he unsure of himself underneath the easy manner? Or was it all acting? He was a master of charm while she was groping in the dark when it came to establishing adult friendships. Men like Flynn were a foreign land to her. Filled with unknowns and incomprehensible situations and attitudes.

'What do you think about this proposal?' He eyed her squarely now, all traces of self-doubt gone and proving how right she'd been about her lack of understanding.

'I don't have an opinion, I haven't been here long enough but I know Cath and Len are in favour of bringing more tourists to town.'

The door opened and a couple of young women in hiking gear came in, faces shiny with heat and sweat.

'Excuse me.'

She grabbed a menu and went to greet them. When she returned, Flynn had finished his coffee and counted out coins for his bill in a neat pile.

'They're the sort of people we want to encourage,' he said softly.

'Hikers?'

He nodded. 'The National Park is a wonderful area for nature lovers, hikers and photographers and hardly anyone goes there. There are some spectacular views, waterfalls, orchids, rainforest areas ... native animals ... all right on our doorstep.'

'I'd love to see it.'

'I can take you in. There's a walk the children could manage that goes to a very pretty waterfall. It's a nice place to swim and have a picnic too.'

'That sounds lovely.'

'We could go this Sunday.' His manner was offhand, as if he didn't care one way or the other whether she accepted.

'All right. They can't swim yet though.'

'That's fine. There's a little shallow area they can paddle in. I'll pick you up at eleven.'

'Thank you. We'll bring the picnic.'

'Mangoes?' He laughed, relaxed for the first time this morning. She must have taken his mind off those women.

'What else?'

'I'd better go and do some work. See you later, Cath.'

'Got a date?' Cath asked after he'd gone.

'It's not really a date. He's just showing us...' She stopped when the grin on Cath's face turned into laughter. 'I suppose it is, sort of. But not like you think.' Hot neck and cheeks again.

'And is that what Flynn thinks?'

'No. My kids are coming. I'm not the sort of woman he'd date. He's just being nice.' He'd go for the upmarket Brisbane girl who invited him to glamorous functions and introduced him to useful, interesting people. Wealthy people with power and influence.

'Maybe.'

'He wants to show me the rainforest and a waterfall.'

'It's a lovely walk, that one. Easy.'

'You know what I think? He's campaigning to get me onside for his resort plans. I said I had no opinion and the next thing he invited me to see how beautiful the area is and how it should be used more.'

'I reckon he's right. But I also think that's not why he asked you.'

Cath went to clear the table that Glenda and her cronies had finally left. Could she be right? No way. Cath was teasing her. Flynn was being quite attentive but she was new in town, a novelty, and she had nothing to hold his attention for much longer. Not if he had a high-flying girlfriend in Brisbane for personal activity. What did a single mother of twins have to offer? She had no money, not much education, and if he ever found out about her past it would kill any interest stone dead.

No, her first instinct was right. He wanted her onside in the upcoming stoush over the development. Which was a relief because she didn't want to have to deal with personal approaches from him.

***

Unsurprisingly, Thursday's meeting attracted a crowd of townspeople who loitered about the pub waiting for a chance to waylay Sean Baldessin and tell him what they thought of his resort plans. Not knowing what those plans actually were was no deterrent to the likes of Glenda Foley and her ilk.

Flynn *was* surprised to see Rufus and Lauren from the cooperative standing in the shade of a street tree. He'd arranged that Baldessin would meet him and the councillors in the bar first and then have lunch in the courtyard garden, which had been closed for the private function. It would probably be better if they bypassed the bar and went straight through to the courtyard, given the mood outside. Although that would give rise to all sorts of conjecture and charges of secrecy.

Not that any of it worried him. Antonia had agreed to go on a picnic and the image of her smile as she said yes would buoy him through any unpleasantness yet to come. It was his secret talisman, held close to his heart, giving him strength.

Three of the councillors were at the bar already—Aidan, Margie and Judy. Margie and Judy perched on stools with untouched glasses of white wine while Aidan leaned against the bar, arms folded. Most of the tables were full, not unusual this close to lunchtime, but the low murmur of voices replaced the more normal chatter, giving the room a brooding air of unease. Young Martin moved about collecting empties while Sal delivered plates of food.

'Hi, boss,' she said as she passed.

'G'day.' He crossed to the bar with eyes boring into him.

'Where's this bloke?' asked Judy by way of greeting. She was economical with words, very popular in the area, having been born and raised on a dairy farm, which she now ran, and didn't have time for fools or people she considered gasbags. Flynn liked her but on this issue predicted she'd be very conservative.

'He's not due till twelve. It's only ten to,' said Margie.

'If he doesn't show up on time I'm going. Got better things to do than wait around for some city suit.'

Flynn smiled. Judy had worn a dress with small blue flowers on it, white low-heeled sandals and done her hair up in a bun. Her regular attire was jeans and an old checked shirt with the sleeves rolled up. He wouldn't have put it past her to turn up straight from the cow paddock in manure-caked gumboots. Perhaps the prospect of meeting a millionaire had softened her.

'You look very nice,' he said. 'Blue suits you.'

She gave him a flinty-eyed look but he signalled to Donna for a beer. Phil and Walter arrived together; Phil, puffing and wheezing as though he'd run all the way, Walter, the epitome of a country storekeeper, his usual thin pale self with wispy hair neatly combed and rimless glasses perched on his beaky nose.

'Is Bill coming?' Flynn asked when the newcomers had drinks in hand.

'Should be,' Phil said. 'Where's the guest of honour?'

Where indeed? Flynn looked at the clock over the bar. Two minutes before twelve. If Baldessin stood him up he'd look a fool. A gullible fool. Aidan hadn't said a word yet beyond greetings. He'd refused a drink and Flynn had no idea what he was thinking. Lauren and Rufus must be against any sort of development, judging by their presence outside and the stern set of their faces. Was Aidan here to block any chance of a deal on the land next to his?

A group of people came through the door, Bill included. He marched straight to the bar while the others milled about looking for a place to sit. Bill gave the impression he'd been in the army, but he hadn't. He was a retired public servant who'd worked in the State Government Revenue Office.

The entrance had caused a stir. All heads turned, expecting Baldessin to appear. Did anyone know what he looked like apart from Margie and himself? They might if they read financial or business magazines, but he didn't feature in gossip columns or social pages online or in newspapers.

'Hello, Sean.' Behind him, Margie's delighted voice cut through his musings.

'Margie, how lovely to see you again. You look great.'

Flynn turned to see her receiving a kiss on the cheek from a dark-haired man in tan shorts and a white Polo shirt. Sean Baldessin. Where had he sprung from? Not that it mattered, the man had turned up, thank God. No wonder he'd walked in unnoticed. He looked like any other tourist stopping off for lunch in the town.

'Flynn. Good to see you.' His hand was grasped firmly. 'Thank you for inviting me. Nice place you have here.'

'Hello, Sean. I'm sorry, I didn't see you come in.' He'd forgotten the man's soft Irish accent. That should count for something with Judy, her surname was O'Boyle.

'I've been here for a while.' He nodded his head towards the far corner.

Spying? Checking up? Making a preliminary survey, taking stock and doing his own appraisal? A smart man.

'Right. Let me introduce my colleagues on the council.'

Sean's appearance had taken everyone by surprise. The people in the bar who cared hadn't realised who he was, the rest weren't interested anyway. Those waiting outside to quiz him on the way in would be disappointed.

'Shall we go through to the courtyard?'

Flynn signalled to Donna and she nodded and disappeared into the kitchen to warn chefs Linda and Karl.

When everyone was seated at the round table under the vine-and-flower-covered pergola, drinks replenished and Sal had taken orders, Sean said, 'Let me just say how delighted I am to be here, regardless of any business we may undertake. This is a beautiful area and I truly think Flynn's Crossing is a town you should all be proud of.'

'We are, don't worry about that,' said Judy. 'And we aim to keep it that way.'

'I'm sure you do and I certainly don't want to come in here and change things.'

'What do you want to do then?' asked Bill. 'Why are we here?'

'Perhaps we should eat first and talk business later,' suggested Flynn.

'I don't see why,' Judy said.

'Neither do I,' said Sean. 'We all have things we want to say so I reckon we should get on with it.'

Bill and Judy exchanged glances. Surprised? He hoped so. Sean had surprised him in Brisbane, and again today.

'How long have you been in Australia?' asked Phil.

'Since I was a teenager. Still haven't lost the accent.' He smiled. 'I'm a proud citizen and my wife is Australian. She grew up in Sydney.'

'Can we get back to why we're here?' asked Bill.

'Of course. I'm here because Flynn thought I might be interested in putting a resort in the area. I'm very interested in sustainable living and eco-friendly development so this would be an experiment, if you like. My idea, and this is purely an idea at the moment, is for a development in stages. Stage One would be lodge-style accommodation and camping for hikers and climbers and so on with a restaurant, cafeteria, information office, rest rooms and facilities for day visitors. Stage Two would be luxury accommodation. Perhaps cabins with a boutique hotel attached. I'm not sure. I'm thinking solar panels for power, eco-friendly methods of water conservation and waste recycling.'

'That block you have in mind, Flynn, would never take all that,' said Aidan.

'I agree,' said Sean. 'I went out there this morning and had a look. Much too small and the National Park forms a barrier to expansion. The ideal place is next door. It seems to be a market garden from what I could see—I didn't go in, of course—but according to the land division maps I looked at, the block is fifty hectares. That would be perfect. The river runs through it as well.'

'It is perfect and I'm a part owner,' said Aidan. 'Unfortunately we have no intention of selling at the moment. Or subdividing.'

Sean nodded. 'I understand. We may be able to come to some future agreement.'

Flynn looked at Aidan. He sat unmoving, still with that impassive expression. He picked up his water glass and downed half in one swallow.

'I reckon it sounds brilliant,' said Phil. 'Not taking over the co-op,' he said hastily, 'But the lodge idea. There's nothing like that here at the moment and we have the most spectacular scenery hardly anyone can enjoy. We don't even have a decent camping ground.'

'There's a fair bit of land for sale in the area,' said Walter. 'You should have a look around for somewhere else.' Most of it was farming land too far from the National Park to be attractive to Sean, or in parcels too small to be useful.

'I plan to,' said Sean. 'I think Phil is right. And Flynn and Margie agree with us. This town could really benefit from my proposal.'

'And who would benefit most?' asked Judy.

'Me, of course,' said Sean and burst into a rich, genuine laugh. To Flynn's amazement, Judy joined in with her own cackle. Even Bill and Aidan smiled.

'At least you're honest,' she said.

'You can say and think whatever you like about me but I'm an honest man, you can rely on that.'

'And one who gets his own way,' added Bill.

'Usually. Flynn's Crossing is my preference but there are other areas I'm considering. On the far side of Kurrajong for example—the town of Whiterock has a very nice site but access to the National Park isn't as good.'

Flynn met Margie's eye. He knew exactly what she was thinking. No way would they sit back and let the Whiterock residents benefit from what was originally their own idea.

**

Mrs Birdie phoned Antonia on Friday afternoon to pin her down for the recorder group.

'When are you available?' she said, happily assuming Antonia hadn't had a change of mind since her initial enquiry.

'It would have to be on a Monday because I'm at the cafe on the other days.' And she had her first appointment with her new therapist, Anita, at ten on Monday morning.

'Oh good. Shall we say Mondays straight after lunch for forty minutes? That's one-thirty. You'll be able to use the hall.'

'How many children will there be?'

'I'm not sure. I'll be sending notes home about it and letting them all know you're available to teach recorder, and flute as well. We'll only offer it to the seniors at first. You can do that either at the school or at home after school. Which would you prefer?'

'At home, but I could take some at school on the Monday.'

'All right. Can I give them your phone number?'

'Yes.'

'We'll aim to start the following week.'

'All right. Thank you.'

'Thank you, Antonia. I'm very excited about this. Music is so important.'

Antonia hung up with far less excitement than Mrs Birdie and the feeling she'd been railroaded by a very skilful operator. She'd never taught anything in her life. She had no idea how much to charge for lessons and where she could get hold of music; her own teacher had used the standard flute books, which had given her a thorough grounding and still had. She'd have to talk to Jax and soon. It had slipped right out of her mind.

But even though the ensemble at school would be voluntary, the lessons wouldn't be. Even a few students would put welcome extra dollars in her pocket.

All in all, their first week at school and work had been very successful. Sarah and Jacob loved Miss Armstrong and had already made friends with their classmates who regarded twins as an extremely interesting phenomenon. As she'd told Flynn, Simon was becoming a natural part of their lives and they accepted him as their daddy. She knew they discussed things in bed at night and on this had come to a unanimous decision—they liked him. Having a proper daddy was important for them at school. She'd overheard Sarah telling one of her new friends that her daddy grew yummy vegetables and had showed her how to do it.

The picnic with Flynn had a mixed reception. The idea of a picnic was fun but Flynn was still a vague quantity, not actively disliked or feared but not accepted wholeheartedly.

'Can Daddy come too?' asked Sarah.

'I don't think so. Flynn asked us. He wants to show us the waterfall.'

'I like picnics,' said Jacob. They hadn't been on a picnic until last year when Connor and Jax took the family to the beach. Sitting on a blanket, eating food from a basket, was the biggest novelty of their lives to that point and an outing they'd begged to do again and again.

'We're in charge of the food,' said Antonia. 'What should we take?'

'Cake,' said Sarah. 'Make a chocolate cake.'

'Ice-cream,' said Jacob.

'We'd need an esky to take ice-cream but we don't have one.'

'Chips.'

'Sausages.'

'Chocolate biscuits.'

'Lollies.'

The suggestions came pouring out amid escalating giggles until Antonia put up her hands. 'Okay. Enough silliness. I'll do the picnic food but there'll be yummy things for you to eat.'

'Goody.' Sarah clapped her hands.

'Can we go on a picnic with Daddy another day?' asked Jacob.

'Of course we can. We're going to the markets with him soon. Remember?'

Why did the thought of a picnic with Flynn give her little shivers of anticipation and delight, whereas going to the markets with Simon, while pleasurable, would be like going out with her brother?

The markets! When were they held? Hadn't Simon said the second Sunday of the month? That would make it this coming Sunday.

Who would be the easiest to turn down? Which outing would she prefer?

Chapter 9

Flynn drove to Antonia's house on Sunday with an unusual fluttery sensation in his stomach. Nerves coupled with the notion that this really was the wrong thing to be doing. Apart from any misgivings on his own behalf; namely, that he'd decided not to indulge this ridiculous crush and had completely failed, Antonia was Simon's friend and the children were his children. What would his thoughts be on Flynn taking the family out for the day? A niggling voice kept insisting Antonia had agreed and not only that, she'd seemed happy to accept the invitation so whatever Simon thought didn't matter. But it did. Poaching another man's girl was never right and in this town at this moment in time it could be disastrous.

Simon's views on the development project would necessarily influence Antonia and his views were sure to be in line with Aidan, presumably Georgia and definitely Lauren and Rufus.

He really shouldn't be taking Antonia out. The thought crossed his mind yesterday to phone and cry off. But he didn't. And he didn't pick up the phone this morning either, which proved his long-held belief that a person can justify anything to themselves if they tried.

He pulled into the driveway. The twins were on the verandah and as soon as they spotted him, raced indoors with a crash of the screen door. Was that a good sign or a bad? They were either excited and waiting for him or didn't want to go and rushed to tell their mother the enemy was nigh.

The fluttering turned to drunken elephants rampaging through his middle. He got out of the car and approached the house. Voices came from inside and the thud of feet on the bare floors. He knocked on the screen door.

'Hello, anybody home?'

'Come in.' Antonia's voice floated down the hallway. 'We're nearly ready.'

Flynn stepped inside and let the door close on his sigh of relief.

'Where's your hat, Jacob? Have you been to the toilet?'

More thudding feet and a small body shot into view and out again just as quickly at the far end of the hallway.

'Do you need a hand?' Flynn asked in the general direction of the rear of the house.

Antonia came out of the kitchen carrying a large basket, a blanket and a plastic carry bag. Flynn hurried to take the basket and blanket and received a heart-stopping smile.

'Thanks,' she said. 'Sorry. Hello.'

'Good morning.' He desperately needed to kiss that smiling mouth but Sarah was right behind her mother, dressed in pink shorts and top and holding a pink backpack.

'Hello, Sarah,' he said.

'Hello.' Not so shy now. School must have helped with that. 'Mummy has yummy food but she won't say what it is.'

'That sounds very interesting.' He caught Antonia's eye but she looked away quickly. She wore her short denim skirt and a green blouse that emphasised her dark hair and eyes. So beautiful his breath caught.

'Where's Jacob? Come on,' she called.

'There's no rush,' Flynn said. 'The waterfall's not going anywhere.'

'Yes it is,' said Sarah. 'It's going over the cliff.'

Flynn laughed. 'Clever girl. You're absolutely right. It is.'

She giggled.

'And you know what else is going somewhere?' he asked.

She shook her head, dark brown curls bouncing around the sweet smooth-skinned face.

'The path that goes to the waterfall,' said Antonia.

'And us. We're going to them both,' said Sarah.

Jacob came out of the bathroom.

'Let's go,' said Flynn.

Antonia locked the front door and herded the children to the car. Flynn stowed the picnic gear in the boot, along with the esky he'd brought for the drinks and the waterproof ground cover to sit on.

'Can I put these in your esky, please?' Antonia took two plastic containers from the basket.

'I brought water, juice and soft drink,' he said as he packed in her items. 'No alcohol. Is that all right?'

Antonia laughed. 'What do you think I am? Of course it is. I brought a thermos of coffee too.'

He opened her door then hurried round to the driver's side.

'Seatbelts on?'

'Yes.'

'We're all set.'

'Let's go, Joe,' called Jacob.

'Who's Joe?' said Flynn with a surprised laugh.

'Let's go, Flo.' Antonia looked over to the back seat, smiling.

'Let's go, jumbo,' said Flynn. Word games, he could play.

'Let's go, flamingo,' said Antonia.

'Let's go, bingo,' said Flynn.

'Let's go, tomato,' said Jacob.

'Let's go, mango,' said Sarah and both twins collapsed in giggles.

Smiling, Flynn said, 'Smart.'

Antonia nodded. 'They both are. They're excited, they love picnics.'

Driving with the children in the back seat and Antonia by his side, Flynn's nerves gradually settled to a hum of anticipation for the day ahead. His greatest fear had been allayed by the obvious excitement of the twins, the silly wordplay and Antonia's reassurance.

'I saw the waterfall walk in a brochure at the motel when I first arrived,' she said after a few minutes. 'I thought it might suit them.'

'It will. There's another one that's longer and goes up and down a bit but they'd probably manage. We could go another day. If you like.' He threw her a sideways glance but she was looking out her window.

'That sounds nice. I haven't explored the area much yet. I've never been on this road.'

'It comes out past the cooperative. You can take the road to Simon's but this is a better surface until we turn off into the National Park.'

'How did that meeting go?' she asked suddenly. 'With the developer?'

'What did you hear?' Working in the cafe would give her the gossip firsthand.

'Not a lot. I don't think the councillors had much to report to the grapevine. As far as I can tell, nothing's been decided.'

'That's right.' Everyone had liked Baldessin and given him a fair hearing, which was all he'd wanted and expected at his stage. 'We're having a council meeting about it on Tuesday.'

'Did he seem interested? The millionaire? I don't know his name.'

'Sean Baldessin. Yes, but it's a matter of finding the right site. Flynn's Crossing isn't the only place he can set up his development.'

'I don't know much about that sort of thing.'

'What do you mean?'

The way she said it made him look across at her curiously. She was an intelligent, aware woman yet she spoke as though she wasn't clever enough to understand. She was.

'Business,' she said. 'Finance. Investment. That sort of thing.'

'Don't know or aren't interested? They're different things.'

'I don't know about any of it. I don't know about anything much.'

'But you're a very intelligent woman. What did you do when you left school?' As soon as he'd said it he knew it was a stupid question. She'd been a pregnant teen, what could she do?

'I ... raised my children,' she said.

'By yourself?' One question too far. Her face had closed into that blankness he'd seen before. Shutting him out.

Where was that abusive husband? When had her father stepped in to put an end to her torment? Connor wasn't the type of man to stand by and allow his daughter and her children to suffer. All indications were it had been a fairly recent intervention. What the hell had happened to her? Where had she been living?

With the two in the back seat, this wasn't the time to press for answers.

'Sorry,' he said. 'Not my business.'

'I'm sorry,' she murmured, just loud enough for him to hear.

He forced a smile. 'We're even. Again,' he said, hoping she'd remember the reference to her last apology. When he'd stolen a kiss.

The pink flush that glowed on her cheek proved she did. Could she be more beautiful, more attractive, more lovable? Not likely.

They drove in silence until he turned off the road onto the rougher dirt track that led to the parking area for the falls walk.

'Mummy, there are lots of trees,' said Jacob. Flynn looked at Antonia, frowning. The boy sounded frightened.

'It's okay, Jakey. This is where we're going for our picnic.'

'Is the waterfall in the big trees?' asked Sarah. Timid all of a sudden. Where were those giggling, excited, little kids?

'Yes, it is. We have to walk on the path between them for about ten minutes.'

Flynn parked in the clearing and opened his door.

'Everybody out,' he said.

Jacob and Sarah didn't move. Antonia got out and leaned into the back, talking to them in a low voice. What was wrong?

He walked around to her side. 'Everything okay?'

She straightened and moved away from the car. 'They're a bit frightened of walking in the bush. They—we—had a bad experience last year.'

'You should have told me. Were they lost?'

She hesitated. 'Sort of. It was very frightening for them. I'm sorry. It never entered my head they might not want to ... I'm so stupid. I should have thought ... I should have known it would worry them.'

'Does it worry you?' he asked gently.

She looked around at the trees, drew in a deep breath of warm air, heavy with the aroma of flowers and moist earth and vegetation. She shook her head. 'No, it's different up here. It's beautiful.'

'Maybe they'll see that too.'

'Maybe.'

'We can have our picnic here in the clearing. There's a table over there by the stream just down that slope.' He pointed. 'Will that be all right?'

'I think so. Thanks for understanding, Flynn.'

'I don't really but I'm hoping you'll tell me one day.'

He walked to the car. 'Hey Jake, do you know how to skim stones?'

'No.' Interest sparked in the brown eyes.

'Come and I'll show you. We'll have a go down at the creek.'

'Where's the creek?'

'Just down there past the picnic table.'

'I'm pretty good at skimming stones,' said Antonia. 'Come on. We can do that then have our picnic here in the clearing.'

Both children scrambled out of the car and stood staring around at the towering green giants. Flynn took his camera out of the boot and snapped off a few quick shots of the family. Both little faces were incredibly photogenic and had strong elements of their mother, but Jacob in particular had something of Simon in his mouth and eyes.

Flynn lowered the camera and led the way to the grassy area where the single old wooden table provided the picnic facility. The ground sloped gently down to the banks of the creek, which widened into a shallow pool before continuing on to join the river a few miles downstream. A fading sign pointed to the right, indicating the track to the waterfall.

'Listen.' Flynn put his finger to his lips. 'What can you hear?'

'The wind,' said Sarah after a moment.

'Birds,' said Antonia.

'Insects.' Sarah again.

'Splashy water,' said Jacob.

'That's the waterfall,' said Flynn. He walked down to the sandy creek bank and began looking for suitable stones. He selected a few and showed them to Jacob and Sarah. 'We need flat ones like these.'

The twins scurried about, searching.

'Watch this,' said Antonia. 'I'm the champion.'

She bent down and sent her stone skipping and bouncing across the water.

'Four skips,' said Flynn. 'Pretty good.'

'Told you. And I haven't done this for years.' She grinned. 'What can you do?'

Flynn hefted a stone and made a show of preparing. His stone did six bounces and crashed into the far bank.

Sarah and Jacob clapped.

'Show me,' said Jacob. Antonia gave him a demonstration and he managed one hop before the stone sank. Sarah's stone went straight under but they both took to it with a passion that surprised Flynn.

'I didn't think it would be that popular,' he said to Antonia as they stood watching and encouraging the skimmers. He took more shots as they played, capturing their laughter, their intent faces and their enthusiasm.

'There's a lot that's new to them,' she said with a touch of sadness in her voice. 'They didn't have much opportunity to play before.'

He didn't dare ask why.

'Can they paddle here? Is it very deep?' she asked.

'In the middle it'd be up to their chests, but if they stay fairly close to the bank it'll only be knee-high on them.'

Antonia was already kicking off her sandals. She waded into the creek and splashed about. 'Ooh, this is so lovely and cool.'

'Can we come in too?'

Flynn sat on the bank and took photos as the trio paddled about, skimming stones and exploring the creek bed. Who would have thought a picnic with two five-year-olds would be so much fun? Luckily, during his experience with the children doing photography at the primary school, he'd discovered that basically kids loved to learn and the more hands-on the better. His own life would have been quite different if someone had ignited a passion for learning in him at that age. But it was what it was and the best he could do was try to make amends in his own private way, in spite of having paid the legal penalty for his actions. The guardians of society might count his debt as paid but he doubted he ever would.

Eventually they straggled back and sat with him on the grass to let their feet dry.

'Shall we eat first or go to the waterfall?' asked Antonia.

Sarah and Jacob looked at each other. 'We're hungry,' Jacob said.

Lunch was a casual, noisy affair and one of the most enjoyable meals Flynn had eaten in years. Antonia and the children were relaxed and happy, laughing over how much chocolate cake was a reasonable amount to consume in one sitting, arguing with Flynn over who got the last piece of cold grilled chicken and exclaiming in delight when he produced a tub of ice-cream from the esky.

Antonia poured coffee from the thermos for Flynn and herself while the twins scoffed ice-cream and mango slices.

'Great meal,' he said. 'Thank you.'

'It was your great idea and you brought the best bit in their eyes. Ice-cream.'

He raised his mug to her. She smiled across the table, her eyes linking with his, shutting down his brain, stifling his breathing. His pulse thudded in his ears, he couldn't move. She had him pinned to the rough wooden bench, coffee mug raised, eyes locked on hers, pulling him in, devouring him whole. She was speaking but he couldn't understand what she said.

'Sorry, what did you say?'

'I hope the coffee is all right.'

He took a quick mouthful and swallowed. 'Fine.'

'Good. I know you like espresso but this is from a plunger pot.' Still so worried about doing something wrong or arousing his displeasure.

'I'm not fussy. As long as it's drinkable.'

Antonia began packing the dirty plates and bowls back into the basket and putting lids on the containers.

'Do you two want to walk to the waterfall?' she asked.

Another silent communication. 'No,' said Jacob.

'We don't like the big trees,' said Sarah. 'But we like the picnic.'

'And the creek,' added Jacob.

'We can come another day when you feel like walking,' said Flynn.

'We want to skim more stones now,' said Jacob.

'Okay, we'll watch from here. Don't go in the water,' said Antonia.

'We won't.'

Both children rushed down to the creek and began searching for flat stones.

'It's only early, what would you like to do now? We could go somewhere else.' Flynn poured himself more coffee and topped up Antonia's mug.

'Do you have the time?' she asked.

'Of course I do, it's Sunday. What about the markets in Kurrajong? Didn't you say you wanted to go there?'

'I do. Simon suggested it.'

'Were you supposed to go today with Simon?' Great. This outing was already causing a problem. How did Simon feel about being ditched?

'Not really. I'd forgotten which Sunday it was so when he phoned I told him we couldn't go. I was going to call him but he rang first.'

'But we could have changed our picnic day.'

'I'd already told you we'd come and they were really looking forward to it.'

Flynn shook his head gently, mouth tight. 'Antonia, you can easily alter plans if you want to. I'd understand. Was Simon upset?'

'Not upset … disappointed maybe.'

'So we'd better not go to the markets today, had we?'

'Probably not.'

Flynn sighed. 'I think this should be our last outing.'

'Why?'

'I don't want to cause trouble between you and Simon.'

'Why would you be causing trouble?'

She sounded so genuinely bewildered Flynn had to smile. She had absolutely no idea how he felt about her and no idea how Simon did either.

'He might be jealous.'

'Jealous? Simon? Of what?'

'Another man taking his family out,' he said lightly, keeping the smile in place.

'But that's...' She looked around as though trying to gain inspiration from the clearing and the parked car, the towering trees, the creek. 'That's archaic. The twins are his but I'm not.' Her expression hardened. 'I don't belong to anyone and I'll never belong to a man. Never.' Her eyes turned flinty when she held his gaze. 'This is my life and I make my own decisions about who I talk to or spend time with.'

'Okay,' he said carefully. Somehow he'd tapped into a deep well of resentment against, presumably, the man who had abused her, and the effects of which had tainted her view of all men.

'But that doesn't mean I want to deliberately hurt Simon's feelings.' The rage had subsided as quickly as it had arisen.

'I understand that.'

'Or anyone else's.' He took that to mean his own feelings, which at the moment were staggering under the realisation that Antonia was not only uninterested in him but she also wasn't remotely interested in a relationship at all, with anyone. The question was could he turn that around? Should he try? And was Simon aware of the depth of her antipathy? He was in for a rude awakening if he wasn't.

But for now the twins were happy playing about on the bank of the creek; and if that satisfied them, so be it. Flynn was more than happy to laze with Antonia, watching them.

'Friends?' he asked

'Friends.' But she sounded doubtful.

The silence stretched out, slowly changing from mildly tense to something comfortable and easy.

'How come you don't have a wife and kids?' she asked suddenly.

'Didn't we have this conversation before?'

'Did we?'

'You asked me if I had a girlfriend.'

'And you said no. Why not?' If she hadn't already stated how vehemently opposed she was to starting up a relationship he'd think she was flirting.

'Haven't met the right person,' he said lightly.

'It must be hard ... to meet the right person. How do you know?'

He considered his reply very carefully. 'I assume when it is the right one, you just know.'

She frowned. 'I always thought Mum and Dad were right for each other but now they've split and they're both with other people.'

'I suppose circumstances can change how couples view things and each other.' He shrugged helplessly. 'I'm the wrong person to ask.'

'But if you keep waiting, the right person might go off with someone else.'

'Doesn't that mean they weren't the right person?' He smiled.

'There could be more than one, I suppose. Dad loved Mum and now he loves Jax.'

'Maybe.'

More silence. Where had that little burst of questions come from? He felt like her father trying to answer them, as if she were a teenager wanting his wise advice. The advice of an older person. He wasn't that much older!

'You're very good with children.'

'I like them in general and yours are great.'

'Thank you for not pushing them. It's such a shame you don't have any of your own. You'd be a great father.'

'No, no. I'm happy to borrow other people's for a while.' He shook his head and stared away across the creek into the deep green of the forest where the shadows and sunlight shifted with the breeze in a constant interplay of light and dark. A family of his own. A dream he could never fulfil.

'But don't you want your own family?' Why was she persisting with this?

He sucked in a deep breath and said what he'd never said out loud to anyone. 'I don't deserve to have one.'

Why he chose Antonia to confess to he had no idea, but the instant the words were out he regretted it. She had enough problems of her own without his to think about, and anyway he barely knew her.

Maybe that was why. She was a private person, didn't gossip, didn't know anyone in town well enough to pass on information. And in a weird way, maybe he wanted her to know he would be no good to her if she ever had thoughts in that direction, Stop her, cut off any hint that something might develop between them. Make it very clear. Friends.

'Why?'

He couldn't meet her eye, couldn't continue.

'Flynn, you're kind, you're decent and you like children. As far I can see, that qualifies you to deserve a family. I should know.' The bitterness in her voice spoke volumes. 'The man I was with...'

He turned then, stretched across to take her hand in his. She didn't pull away. 'I'm sorry,' he said. 'I must sound petty and self-pitying but you don't know ... I just...'

She smiled and her fingers curled over his for a moment. 'It's okay. I understand. Some things need to be put away and not spoken about until it's time. If ever.'

He nodded. When it's time. Would she tell him the things she wanted to keep locked away in her past? Would he ever tell her his?

'If I ever do speak about it, it will be to you,' he said. Deep in his heart he knew that was the truest thing he'd ever said.

'Mummy, we need to do a wee.'

Antonia's hand slipped from his. 'Are there toilets here?'

'No. Just go behind a tree.' He smiled at the twins. 'Find a wee tree.'

Sarah giggled. She was such a delight.

'Come on.' Antonia led the way into the trees.

***

Antonia's routine settled over the following weeks. Jax had express-posted music and advice to get her ensemble started and she tried to wrangle seven small recorder players into shape on Mondays. Two sixth graders had begun flute lessons also on Mondays at school, which gave her a little bit of extra money to boost the wages from the cafe.

Her new counsellor, Anita, was serious and attentive, willing to see her when required but encouraging her to establish herself in the new life. 'Do what you feel is right,' she said. 'Trust yourself and your instincts.' Antonia hadn't brought up the awkward question of Flynn yet.

Sarah and Jacob were happy with Miss Armstrong and were slowly making friends, although neither wanted to play separately from each other yet or visit someone else's house. Simon came to visit three days per week, collecting the twins from school and they'd all been out to the cooperative several times.

Flynn dropped in to the cafe for coffee or sometimes lunch once or twice a week at most. He hadn't invited the family out again, which wasn't surprising but just a tiny bit disappointing. The picnic had been very successful and she thought he'd enjoyed himself. Maybe he had but it was a one-off thing and he meant what he'd said about getting in Simon's way. Or he'd discovered she wasn't a very interesting companion after all.

He certainly didn't linger when he came to the cafe.

From the gossip she picked up from customers and at school, the resort proposal had gone off the radar. The council hadn't announced anything beyond a vague statement saying they were looking into all the angles and no decisions had been made. It was early days.

Bron, next door, was friendly and always ready for a chat if they saw each other but she was busy, as was Antonia. The old man on the other side was virtually a recluse. Bron said his name was Josef Popovic. He played classical music loudly in the afternoons, which she quite enjoyed when she and the children came home after work and school but she hadn't spoken to him, and both times she went over to introduce herself he didn't answer her knock. She'd left homemade shortbread on the step the first time and it had disappeared when she looked later, so presumably he'd eaten it and knew it was from her. She'd only seen him once through the side window, tottering out with his bin on garbage collection day, a white-haired figure in a blue cardigan with stick-like legs in baggy grey pants.

Despite running out to say hello, she missed him again. It occurred to her he might have heard the screen door bang and run himself—back into the house. The bushes on the fence screened her driveway from his so she couldn't verify her suspicion.

She'd been to Cheryl's with the twins and they'd had cups of tea while the children played. Cheryl had invited her to join the local book group but she'd had to decline because of the baby-sitting problem. The twins weren't ready to stay at home at night with someone else, even Simon.

Six weeks after she'd first come to Flynn's Crossing, on a slow Tuesday morning at the cafe, her phone rang. Her dad? Mum? Private caller.

'Hello.'

'Hello, Antonia, how are you getting on? Keith McBride here.' The detective she didn't know existed until last year but who had spent much of the previous five years trying to find her.

Hoping she'd covered the surprise, she glanced at Cath. 'Hello. I'm fine, we're doing well. Hang on a minute.'

Cath raised her eyebrows. She'd think there was a family disaster because no one ever called her at work. Antonia covered the phone with her free hand. 'Sorry, I have to take this.'

'Anything wrong?'

'No, nothing like that. But...'

'Go on.' Cath grinned. She'd think it was Flynn. For some reason she harboured the belief there was something going on between them. There wasn't.

She went out the back to the small yard where the bins were kept. Detective McBride wasn't ringing to have a friendly chat. Something had happened.

'Sorry, I'm at work. What's up?'

'The prosecution is preparing to go to trial and want to interview you.'

The trial. Antonia's chest tightened. Face him? Have his eyes on her while she spoke? She had to. She swallowed. 'Okay. And Dad and Jax?'

'Yes. The prosecution will call on all of you. I phoned to give you a heads-up. Someone from their office will be contacting you soon. Probably Michael Hodge.'

'I'd rather go there than have him come here.' Impossible to keep a visit like that private. Speculation would run riot about the big city man in a suit who came calling.

'That's fine. You can arrange that when he calls.'

'Have they set a trial date yet?'

'No, they've had a preliminary hearing to charge him but the trial won't be till later this year, or even early next year. There's a lot of evidence to gather. He's charged with a variety of things, including the murder of the baby's mother and two other women.'

'Did you find out who she was, Esther's mother?'

'Yes, she was a runaway named Erin Bruce ... we found several bodies buried in the bush. The poor girl was from Wagga.' Sadness mixed with disgust and despair carried through the phone connection.

Her mouth twisted and a rush of salty tears jammed in the back of her throat. It could so easily have been her. And her babies. Hannah had saved all their lives.

She never wanted to think about him again but she knew she had to go to that trial when it came, give her evidence, make sure Murdoch never took a breath in freedom again.

'It won't be pleasant revisiting it all, Antonia, but we want to put this guy away for good.'

'Do you need all of us to testify to do that?'

'The more the better. We have to prove he kept you there by force.'

'He did.' How could anyone dispute that?

'I know he did, but we have to prove it. He'll say you went with him of your own free will and he cared for you and the children for all those years.'

'And Hannah and Izzy?'

'Hannah might be in trouble herself. The prosecution are pushing for her to be charged as an accessory.'

'What? But she was as much a captive as I was. As Izzy was. Without her I could have died in childbirth.' What sort of justice was that?

'They'll argue she assisted him in the abductions over a long period of time. Without her you wouldn't have been there in the first place.'

'She had no choice. None of us did. We had to protect our children.'

'That's what you need to say.'

'Okay. Did you find Billy and his wife?' His cousin and helper, the one who stole cars to facilitate abductions and who ran Jax off the road on her bike—although that was never proven.

'No, they've disappeared without trace. You don't need to worry about them. Without Murdoch, they'll be running scared and are probably in another state by now.'

'I hope so.'

'Stay strong, Antonia. Connor said you have a nice house and that Simon is very happy to have you up there. How are the twins?'

'They're fine. They love it here and they're making friends at school. They're learning to play and be cheeky. Be normal.'

'I'm glad, really glad that it's working out.'

'It is. Thank you.'

Antonia went back inside with emotions churning and her head full of images and memories she thought locked away. Settling in Flynn's Crossing had done what she'd wanted—allowed her to forge a new life. Stupid, really, when she knew a trial would be coming at some stage, but it was in the future, unset in time. She hadn't prepared for the reality of reliving those events in minute detail and being cross-questioned and doubted. Just the thought of going back made her sick to the stomach. And the thought of Billy still on the loose was very disquieting.

'Everything all right?' Len put down the knife and the tomato he'd been slicing.

Should she confide in him, and Cath? She might have to one day. If the trial hit the news as it surely would, her name and her face would appear on TV, online, in the newspapers. How would she explain her silence? She needed to talk to Simon and her father. And Anita.

'I have to go to Sydney for a while, I think. I'm not sure when.'

'Righto, love.' Len resumed his salad preparations. 'Just as long as you come back. We need you.' He gave her a big toothy smile.

'Thanks. I'll definitely come back. This is my home now.'

But how would her new friends react to the news they had a person with her past in their midst? And the twins. They'd be tainted. They'd all be stared at and talked about, maybe pitied; certainly her actions and choices would be dissected by all and sundry. If there's one thing small communities loved, it was gossip.

Antonia went through to the cafe where Cath was putting a slice of carrot cake on a plate.

'Problems?' she asked.

Antonia shook her head.

'Table five,' said Cath, indicating the cake and pot of tea on the counter. 'Then take Flynn's order, please. Corner booth.'

A booth? Unusual. His normal seat was one of the stools at the counter so he could drink his espresso quickly and move on. He had a folder open on the table, which he closed when she approached.

'Good morning.' Blue eyes met hers with a sizzle of awareness but her smile couldn't match his. Not today.

'Hello.'

'Are you okay?' Concern clouded his face. 'Antonia? What's wrong?'

'Nothing ... I ... I have to go to Sydney.'

'Is someone ill?'

'No, it's nothing like that. I'm not sure when.' She forced a smile. 'What can I get you?'

'Coffee and a Mediterranean focaccia, please. You'd tell me, wouldn't you, if you need help in some way?'

'Sure.' Tell Flynn she'd been held captive, raped and abused by that man for years? No way, not in a million years.

Chapter 10

Flynn watched Antonia walk away, her dark hair in a ponytail bouncing like a schoolgirl's as she moved. She'd just lied to him and it was like a stab to the heart. What was going on? Whatever it was, it was something she didn't want to share with him. He knew she didn't feel the same way as he did about her, that she regarded him as a friend; but he'd thought their friendship was developing, based on a measure of trust. He was wrong.

He opened the folder and stared blindly at the sheet of words and figures Baldessin had sent in regard to the ideal type of property he was looking for. Antonia would confide in Simon and ask his advice about her problem but she knew him about as well as she knew Flynn, if you discounted that they'd known each other as teenagers. People changed a lot as they matured. They'd both be different now.

He sucked in air and exhaled fiercely. What was he thinking? Why get twisted up about what she thought and did when he knew nothing would come of it? He had a stupid crush that would go away eventually and wouldn't lead to any sort of dalliance in the short term because she wasn't interested. Enough said. Finito!

The papers Sean had sent detailed the first stage project. He had state government interest as well, which made it even more desirable for the town to succeed in attracting his investment. Tourism was a growth industry and the National Park had a lot to offer. If only the co-op could be persuaded to sell off part of their land. Impossible. Rufus and Georgia were deadset against it, Aidan was too but in a less aggressive way. Bernie was against it. Lauren was a recent arrival but she was strongly opposed with a loud voice. Simon? Simon wasn't a fighter but he might be roused to it if the home he loved was threatened. Who wouldn't be?

Antonia slid his coffee onto the table and went away before he could say thank you.

Where did her allegiance lie? With Simon, no doubt. She said she didn't know anything about business but she was happy in Flynn's Crossing and was making this her home. What would she do if the cooperative was sold and Simon moved away? He shook his head and picked up the coffee. Not his concern. This was a business proposition pure and simple. It would benefit the town for many years to some and that outweighed any personal considerations. As head of the council, it was his job to do the right thing by the community as a whole.

The meeting a week after the lunch with Sean had been surprisingly harmonious. At the start. Sean had charmed Judy and impressed Bill and Walter. Aidan had admitted the bloke had some good ideas in regard to the environment, he liked him but there was no suitable land available for the development he had in mind. The government wasn't going to allow a commercial resort on National Park land but had no plans of their own for the area.

'It's a good idea but he'll have to go somewhere else.'

'We don't want Whiterock or anyone else to benefit from our idea and our legwork,' Margie said in exasperation. 'They've done nothing towards it.'

Aidan shrugged, which infuriated her even more.

'Yours is a very selfish attitude, Aidan. You're never going to use three-quarters of the land you own and you know it. Why not let the whole town benefit from it?'

'It's not just *my* attitude,' said Aidan. 'We're a cooperative. We make decisions together. No one wants to sell the land.'

'Not even for the right amount of money?' asked Phil. 'Baldessin has very deep pockets.'

'I'm not going to dignify that with an answer.' Aidan's jaw tightened.

'All right,' said Flynn. 'We're not getting anywhere now. Why don't we say that the block next to the co-op is the only viable area. You never know he might be able to get the government to agree to using a bit of the National Park on the other side.'

'I'm sure he'll give it a shot,' said Judy. 'And he'll probably succeed.

Governments are always amenable to a bit of flexibility where money for them is concerned. Retaining the environment is way down the list when it comes to a lucrative deal.'

'Let's move on,' said Flynn. The uncontroversial and long overdue plans for public toilets in the park had taken up the rest of the meeting. If they could get that project underway quickly, community sentiment would soften towards the council with beneficial consequences for future decisions.

Antonia arrived with his focaccia.

'Thanks,' he said. 'Could I have another coffee, please?'

'Sure. How are the resort plans going?' The Baldessin business name was clearly visible on the papers he'd been reading. He looked about quickly before replying. No one within earshot and the group closest had small, noisy children and couldn't eavesdrop if they tried. But he kept his voice low.

'So-so. Got an opinion yet?'

A flicker of a smile appeared. 'Simon said Baldessin wants to buy their land but they won't sell.'

'Sort of true. He'd like to have that block because it's in the perfect position and the one for sale next door isn't big enough.'

'What do you think?'

'The resort would be really good for the town.'

'About the co-op?'

'It's their decision.'

'But you think it's wrong.'

'I can see their point but Baldessin doesn't want the whole block. They have fifty hectares, they only use a small part of that and he'd buy half at most.'

'The half closest to that fenceline. Where the houses and gardens are.'

He nodded. 'That's the problem.' She knew the score and he'd bet Simon and the gang had more than impressed their views on her.

'I'll get your coffee.' She picked up the empty cup.

Still no indication of her thoughts on the matter. When she returned a few minutes later, he asked, 'What does Simon think?'

'He loves that place.'

'If the resort goes in next door, regardless of whether they buy co-op land or not, would he stay there?'

She frowned. 'I don't know.'

'If he goes would you go?'

'Flynn, I ... it might not happen. Baldessin might give up and go somewhere else.' Something akin to fear flickered in her eyes. Guilt for pushing her swamped the desire to know her feelings.

'I'm sorry. You're right. It might not work out. It's your business, not mine, if you stay in Flynn's Crossing or not.'

'I want to stay here. I like it and my children are happy. That's the main thing. I'm more worried our lovely house might be sold from under us.'

'Perhaps you should make an offer on it.'

She laughed softly. 'Sure. Do you think she'd take a few hundred for it?'

'There are ways to borrow money.'

'I couldn't get a loan. I'm a terrible credit risk.'

'I thought you knew nothing about finance.' He cocked his head and raised an eyebrow.

'I'm not a complete idiot.' She sighed. 'But I'd love to own the Mango House.'

'Talk to your parents.'

'Uh-uh.' The ponytail swished from side to side.

'They could go guarantor or take out a loan you repay.'

'Uh-uh.' Another firm shake of her head.

Stubbornly independent. So was he. Sometimes it was good, sometimes not.

She went to serve someone else. He took a bite of the neglected food on his plate. Antonia was changing. She was stronger and more confident, less wary of him, more ready to have a conversation without the fear of offending him or saying the wrong thing, progress that gladdened his heart. It didn't sound as though she'd blindly follow Simon if he left, so if he could convince her to buy the house she'd have even more reason to stay in town.

He stopped mid-chew. The smart thing to do was buy the place himself. In secret. That way she wouldn't be evicted on the whim of the Tracey woman and the house wouldn't be sold to anyone else. It wasn't a great investment and he'd have to borrow but he might be able to beat her price down a bit. The pub was only just breaking even and the rent on the house in Vernon Street wasn't quite enough to cover itself. He couldn't possible raise the rent on Sharon and her kids.

Making money to be rich wasn't the point of the exercise, and contrary to the beliefs of some townspeople it never had been. The point here was Antonia and her children. Flynn gobbled down the rest of his lunch, wiped his mouth, collected the folder and paid Cath at the counter.

'In a rush?' she asked.

'Things to do,' he said. 'Thanks. See you later.'

He gave beautiful Antonia a brief wave as he left, smiling to himself at the security he was about to provide for her. Of course he'd never tell her who the buyer was, but as owner he could get the place painted and make a few improvements. Give her some comforts as well as security.

***

Simon said the same thing as her parents when Antonia told him about going to Sydney. The twins were in bed and he sat with her on the back verandah talking and watching the moon slowly glide from behind the hills, a big round silver globe with a dent in one side.

'You have to do it. That guy has to be locked away forever.'

'They'll want you to testify too. You could come with me to see this lawyer.'

Her dad had told her that. He'd been talking to the prosecution lawyer, Michael Hodge, who said Simon's testimony was important in establishing her state of mind before her abduction.

'Fine. Whatever they want, I'll do,' he said. 'We're a family, we stick together.'

'That's what *he* wanted,' she said softly. 'He had this weird idea that we were his family. He wanted all the kids to call him Daddy. I always told the twins they had a real daddy but they had to call him that when he wanted them to.'

'You were incredibly brave.' His fingers curled into fists at the image of his two beautiful children living with that monster of a man. Antonia was an extraordinary woman.

She shook her head. 'I wasn't. I never stood up to him. Not once.'

'How could you? You were a child yourself, and he was violent.' Simon took her hand and squeezed gently. 'After the trial is over, you'll never have to think about him again. We can really start our new life.'

Antonia licked her lips. *Our* new life?

'Flynn asked me today what you thought about the resort development plans.'

'What did you say?'

'That none of you wanted to sell any land.'

'He already knows that.'

'He asked what you'd do if for some reason the resort went ahead next door to you. Would you stay?' She looked at him curiously. What did he think? Would he expect her to pack up and leave if he didn't want to stay?

'Are you asking too?'

'I suppose so. I hadn't thought about it until he asked.'

'The answer is I don't know.' Simon still had hold of her hand. The pressure on her fingers increased. 'Would you come with me if I did leave?'

'I've only just arrived. The twins have just begun to settle. I couldn't uproot them and go somewhere else. I want them to have a proper home, to feel safe and secure.'

'But we're a family. Shouldn't we stay close to each other?'

'Ideally ... I suppose. Yes, but...' What was he asking? How close did he want to be? 'Simon, I'm not going to marry you. Or even live with you. I couldn't do that. I need to be on my own.'

He recoiled momentarily, as though she'd slapped him, but he said, 'I know. But you might not feel that way forever and I'll always be around.'

'I hope you are, for the twins, but don't ignore other chances that might come up in the meantime.'

'What do you mean?' Now he had the totally bewildered expression that made him look about fifteen. In this regard, he *was* about fifteen.

'Other girls, Simon.' Poor Lauren had her work cut out here. 'Lauren, for example.'

'She's a friend.'

'So am I. That's all.'

'Lauren's very angry about the development proposal,' he said. 'I've never seen her so furious. She'll chain herself to a tree or lie in front of the bulldozers if it goes ahead.'

'Gosh.' Lauren never would have let Murdoch beat her up. Lauren never would have gone with him in the first place. She would have confronted her family and taken the consequences. 'She's very strong.'

'So are you but in a different way.'

The phone started ringing inside. Antonia went to answer it, leaving Simon with his thoughts. With any luck he'd have got the message that she wasn't interested in setting up house together. Steering him towards Lauren would be harder than she thought, given the situation. He sounded almost frightened of her. Antonia admired her.

'Hello.'

'Antonia, it's Flynn. Is this a good time?'

'Yes. Why? What is it?'

'There's a buyer for the house.'

'Oh!' She deflated onto the nearest chair. 'Who is it? Will they throw us out?' She was almost too scared to ask. His businesslike tone gave nothing away.

'No. They're happy to rent at the same price. It's an investment for them. I just wanted to let you know so you don't worry about it. Or if you decide to make an offer yourself, you still could.'

'No, that won't happen. Is it a done deal?'

'The contract hasn't been signed but the current owner has accepted the offer.'

'Did she get what she wanted?' Now the news was beginning to sink in. The Mango House was hers for the foreseeable future. A bubble of tension burst inside her, flooding her system with relief.

'Not quite, no.'

'Wow, I feel like celebrating. Thank you for telling me, Flynn. Thanks so much.'

'I thought you'd be pleased.' He sounded happy.

'Why didn't you mention it this morning?'

'It hadn't been finalised.'

'Okay. That's wonderful. Simon's here, I must go and tell him. Thanks again, Flynn. Bye.'

She hung up and danced out to Simon on the verandah.

'Guess what? That was Flynn. Someone bought this house but they're happy to rent it to me long-term. It's an investment property for them.'

Not even a smile. 'Not a very good investment. Who bought it?'

What a miserable response to such brilliant news. By the tone of his voice, he wasn't in the least happy about it. Why not?

'I don't know and I don't care as long as we can stay here.'

'Well that's good then. As long as you're happy.' He stood up. 'I'd better go. Early start tomorrow.'

'All right. Goodnight,' she said to his back as he went down the steps. What had happened? He should be as happy as she was, she'd *expected* him to be as happy as she was.

He went round the side of the house in the darkness to his ute without a word. What was his problem? Flynn understood how she felt about the house. He knew how she craved the security of her own home and the chance to establish roots in this town. He even rang at night, out of business hours, so she would know as soon as possible. How could she have ever thought he was a cold, self-centred man?

***

Simon drove home slowly, keeping an eye out for kangaroos and wombats on the road, but mainly absorbing what Antonia had told him. He'd been operating in a little world of his own, besotted by his children and captivated by the idea of having a family. He'd ignored the fact Antonia may not love him as he loved her. He assumed she'd be thrilled to establish their real family but she'd effectively told him to find someone else to spend his life with. And chosen Lauren as the girl.

He had to be fair. Antonia had endured a horrible situation and it wasn't a surprise she wasn't keen to live with another man. He understood that. What hurt was the fact she wouldn't leave town if he did, evidenced by her excitement over Flynn's news about the house. She'd brought their children to meet him but wasn't prepared to keep them close to him. If he wanted to see them regularly he'd have to stay. And if he stayed she'd expect him to stop regarding her as his life partner.

He shook his head and banged his hands on the steering wheel. He didn't want Lauren, he wanted Antonia and his twins.

Maybe he should pack up and leave regardless of what happened with the land. It would inevitably be very messy and emotional. It was going that way already with the others so vehemently opposed to any sale. Their quiet, peaceful life was no more, the tension palpable between Aidan and Georgia. She wanted him to resign from the council but he maintained he could do more good staying on and providing another opinion, being an insider. Bernie, Rufus and Lauren were implacable in their opposition to the whole proposal and when Aidan put forward the idea of perhaps selling some of their land, Simon truly thought Rufus might resort to violence.

The co-op was no longer the happy place he'd called home. Maybe he should look for somewhere else to live, close enough to see his children regularly but not part of the co-op. Start his own gardening business. Sell tropical plants to tourists. Or do more photography and sell his work in the Baldessin resort shop.

Lauren's light was on when he pulled up outside his house. On impulse, he strode across the rough grass and tapped on her door.

'Who is it?'

'Simon.'

The door swung open. 'What's up?'

'Can I come in?'

'I was about to go to bed.'

He looked at her properly. She had on a singlet top and baggy cotton pants, her dark red hair falling loose over her shoulders. No bra, he realised with a shock that sent an electric current to his groin. He ripped his eyes away from her rounded breasts under the flimsy fabric.

'Sorry. I ... I'll go.'

'You're here now. What is it?'

'I've just been to see Antonia and the twins.'

She waited. The lamplight fell across her face, catching the deep gold and red tones in her hair. Her breath smelled minty; she'd just brushed her teeth.

'So?' she prompted. 'Is anything wrong?'

He turned away before his eyes dropped to the creamy skin on her bare shoulders, and lower.

'Antonia asked what I'd do if the resort project goes ahead.' At a safer distance, he faced her. She hadn't moved, still stood by the door, her expression almost bored, at best he'd say blank.

'And? For God's sake, Simon, get on with it. I'm tired.' Wrong. Not bored or blank, but angry, with none of the usual warmth in her eyes.

'I said I didn't know, but if I did decide to move I asked her if she'd move too.'

'Why would she do that?'

'What?' Was she operating on another wavelength too? The same one as Antonia?

'Why would she pack up and follow you somewhere when she's only just settled herself and her kids here?'

'Because we're a family. They're my kids too and I thought she'd want to keep us all together. She came here so we could all be together.'

'Antonia has raised those kids for five years without you. Sure, they're yours, but she doesn't need you. She only came here out of a sense of moral duty because she thought they should know their dad and vice versa. If you decide to move away from them that's your decision, but you can't expect her to pack up and follow you like some ... puppy dog.'

'But...'

'But nothing. You don't have a clue, Simon. Why did you come here in the middle of the night to tell me this anyway?'

'It's only a quarter to ten,' he said plaintively.

She shook her head and the waves of rich burgundy hair rippled in the light. 'Just go.' She yanked the door open and he had no choice other than to slink into the night. Behind him the latch clicked decisively.

Why was she so upset? He'd dropped in to have a chat as a friend about something that was on his mind and about the changes that were coming. She must have had similar thoughts. Not about Antonia, of course, but about her own future on the co-op. They'd often talked about stuff. Her opinion was important to him. Why was this different?

Lauren wouldn't stay, of that he was certain. She was a much stronger-minded person than he was. She didn't shrink from confrontation. Antonia admired her strength. Weird how those two women seemed to understand each other instinctively right from the start, whereas Lauren said he didn't have a clue and he'd known her for over a year and Antonia for much longer.

It was a good thing he hadn't mentioned to Lauren Antonia's suggestion about getting together with her. In her current mood, she might have whacked him with the rake propped outside the door.

***

'I want to buy that block,' Baldessin said on the phone the following week.

'Isn't it too small?' Flynn flicked through his files and found the information about the property.

'For the whole project yes, but I like the site and we're in negotiations with the Parks Authority. They're pretty keen to make the area more accessible and it's looking good that they might open up a few hectares of the land over the southern fence for the camping and information office, which would leave more room for my commercial activity outside the park boundary. They'd upgrade paths and establish hiking trails to link with the existing network as well.'

'That sounds promising.'

'Let's say I'm quietly confident but I've learned never to celebrate until the deal is done and the papers signed.'

'Yes, indeed.'

'Any problems there with the protesters?'

'No, it's all died down since you were here. Would you like me to get the sale underway or do you want to wait for the other things to fall into place?'

'Go ahead, please, Flynn. Don't want that block snapped up by someone else.'

'I'll let the seller know. Will you meet his price?'

'See what he says and we'll take it from there. But I definitely want that land so if he won't budge, that's the price we pay.'

As soon as Baldessin was off the line, Flynn called the owner who, predictably, knew what was in the wind and stuck to his original price. Flynn closed the deal and phoned Margie.

'Baldessin's just bought the block next to the co-op.' It was hard to keep the jubilation from his voice. 'As good as, anyway. I've only just got off the phone with the owner.'

'So he's in!'

'Yes and he's negotiating with the Parks Authority about shaving a bit off the National Park for an information office and camping ground. He reckoned they were interested in opening up the area more for hikers.'

'Fantastic!'

'It's still in negotiation so we can't tell anyone yet. Strictly between you and me at the moment.'

'I wonder how Aidan's going to react,' she said.

'Not a lot he can do about it, is there?'

'I suppose not but it's going to cause a bit of ill feeling. People will be upset.'

Some townspeople would be but the co-op group would be the most affected. No one else lived close enough for it to be a problem and the local businesses would benefit, as would people in the area wanting work.

Word got around somehow. Flynn had no idea how it happened or who had talked, but by the end of the following day it was common knowledge that Baldessin had bought the block next to the co-op for an exorbitant amount of money—some details were bound to be wrong. But the general tenor was that Flynn had lined his own pocket with a fat commission at the expense of the co-op.

When he ventured into the Paragon for a midmorning coffee, all eyes turned his way. He sat at the counter while Cath made his espresso, hoping Antonia would appear. She didn't.

Cath brought his coffee. 'One of the twins is sick,' she said. 'Antonia's had to stay home.'

'I didn't ask where she was.'

'You were going to.'

He *was* going to. He drank some coffee. Conversations resumed and he could guess what the topic was. Flynn had done a deal with the devil. Too bad. This was business. Anyone could have bought that land at any time and no one would have a say on what the owner did with it.

'So what do you think?' he asked Cath. 'About the land sale.'

'Nothing. Should I?'

'Everyone else seems to have an opinion.'

'You're a real estate agent, that's what you do,' she said. 'I sell food, you sell property.'

'Thanks.'

'For what?'

'Being reasonable.'

'No worries.' She laughed and went into the kitchen.

Flynn drained his cup. Which twin was ill? How bad was it? Maybe Antonia needed some help. Going to the doctor, for example, or getting medicine. He'd better call in.

***

'How's the invalid?' Flynn asked when Antonia opened the door. 'Cath told me.'

'Hello. Come in.' She stepped back to allow him access. 'She has a terrible sore throat, a slight temperature and a runny nose.'

'Poor kid. How's Jacob?'

'He's okay so far. He went to school, which was surprising.'

'That he'd go on his own?'

'Yes. He said they were doing something today he didn't want to miss out on. I think it's to do with Easter.' She smiled.

Flynn handed her the plastic bag containing a tub of double chocolate-chip ice-cream. 'A treat for them.'

Antonia peeked into the bag. 'That's very kind of you, Flynn. Thank you.'

'Is there anything I can do? Any shopping ... medicine to pick up?'

Her eyes widened in surprise. 'You don't need to do that for us.'

'No, but I can easily enough. That's what friends do.'

'Actually, I do need one or two things but I can get them myself.'

'I can do it.'

'No, you can't. It's ... personal ... women's...' A flush crept over her cheeks.

Tampons! She was talking—or rather, not talking—about tampons. Christ! He wasn't going shopping for them.

'Oh right. Okay. I could stay here while you go. Sarah should be okay with that, shouldn't she?'

She bit at her lower lip gently. 'Maybe. I'd be very quick. She's asleep at the moment. I could be back before she even wakes up. I'm not sure...'

'Go.'

'What if she wakes up and panics?'

'I'll handle it. She knows me. Don't worry. Think of it as a trial run.' If she woke up and panicked ... don't think about it. She wouldn't.

'I'll be back as fast as I can.'

Minutes later she was backing her car down the driveway. Flynn sat on the couch and checked his phone for messages.

Sarah's voice wailed from the bedroom, 'Mummeee, Mummmeeeee.'

Chapter 11

Flynn sucked in a deep breath and exhaled slowly as he headed for Sarah's room. He poked his head round the doorframe. 'Hello.'

'Where's Mummy?' Flushed cheeks and a croaky voice, dark curls tumbling messily round the miserable, now alarmed, face.

'Mummy's just nipped to the shops. She'll be back in a few minutes.'

The bottom lip trembled and a look of pure fear distorted her features. She seemed to shrink into the bedclothes, making herself as small as possible.

'It's okay, honey. I'm just here to make sure you're safe while Mummy's out. How are you feeling?'

He remained frozen in the doorway. Any sudden movement might start her screaming.

'My throat's sore.' A whisper.

'Would choc-chip ice-cream make it feel better?' He had no idea whether it was the right thing to give her but he knew she loved ice-cream. And the cold would cool her system down if she had a temperature.

She gave a tiny nod. 'Yes, please.'

'Anything else?'

'Could I have a drink of water, please?'

'Of course, you can.'

At least she wasn't screaming, but this was almost worse. The poor kid was paralysed with fear. The weird thing was she replied with excessive politeness. Too frightened not to answer?

He withdrew to the kitchen, filled a glass with water and found a bowl and a spoon. Antonia had put the ice-cream in the freezer. The laminated benchtops were cracked and stained and needed replacing. So did the floor covering. He'd do that over the next few months.

Sarah lay with her eyes fixed on the doorway and didn't move when he approached with the bowl and water. He put it on the bedside table and retreated. She sat up and reached for the glass, took a few sips then picked up the bowl.

'Thank you.' Another barely audible whisper. She ate a tiny mouthful and then another.

'Is it okay?'

She nodded and ate some more. Crisis point over.

He leaned against the doorframe. 'Did you hear about George Smelly?'

Her eyes flashed to his face. As he'd hoped, a little giggle escaped. 'No.'

'He went to a judge to have his name changed. The judge said, "I understand completely, Mr Smelly, what would you like to change it to?" "William," said Mr Smelly.'

Sarah stared in silence for a moment then started laughing as she sorted out the joke. 'But he's still Smelly. William Smelly.'

'Yes.' Flynn chuckled. Thank God he'd been able to dredge that old joke up from his long distant primary school days. 'You can tell Jacob that joke.'

'Tell another one,' Sarah demanded, face bright now with expectation.

'Gosh, ummm ... where does the king keep his army?'

'I don't know.'

'Up his sleevey.'

More giggles.

'Knock, knock.'

Sarah waited.

'You have to say, "who's there?"' said Flynn. 'Knock, knock.'

'Who's there?'

'Lettuce. Now you say, "lettuce who?"'

'Lettuce who?'

'Lettuce in, it's cold out here.'

Sarah laughed so hard he had to rescue the ice-cream bowl.

'Do another one,' she gasped when she could speak.

'Will you remember me in two minutes?' he asked.

'Yes.'

'Knock, knock.'

'Who's there?'

'Hey, you didn't remember me.'

He couldn't help but laugh with her as she rolled about in the bed, tears streaming down her face.

The car engine sounded outside.

'Mummy's home,' he said. He put the ice-cream bowl on the bedside table and went to meet Antonia.

But it was Simon coming up the steps when he opened the door. He stopped and his eyes narrowed, the normal good-natured expression gone, replaced by a frown.

'What are you doing here?'

'Good morning, Simon. I happened to call in and Antonia took the opportunity to go to the shops. Sarah is sick in bed.'

'I know, that's why I'm here. To see my daughter,' he added with a slight stress on my.

'Come in. She's not too bad. Bit of a temperature and a sore throat.'

Simon grunted and continued on into the house, giving him a scowl as he passed. Flynn hovered in the living room. Should he stay or go? Simon was pissed off to find him here and he'd be pissed off about the sale of the land. Feelings would be running high out at the co-op. He should leave.

He walked down to Sarah's room. Simon was sitting on the end of her bed, listening while she told him one of her new knock, knock jokes but his heart didn't seem to be in it. He looked at Flynn.

'Nice one, mate.'

Flynn frowned a warning. He wasn't going to start up an attack in front of Sarah, was he?

'Not here,' he said.

Simon stood up. 'Say goodbye to Flynn, Sarah. He's leaving.'

'Bye bye, Flynn.'

'See you later, alligator.'

'In a while, crocodile,' she said.

Flynn grinned.

'Outside,' said Simon.

***

Antonia parked in her driveway with a sinking feeling in her stomach. Simon's ute was in the street behind Flynn's and the pair of them were on her verandah. Arguing, by the look of their faces and the tension in their bodies. Couple of bloody idiots! Why did they have to bring their fight to her place? It wasn't her business.

She grabbed her shopping and slammed the door. The pair stopped talking and turned as she strode towards them.

'Hello, Simon. I didn't expect to see you.'

'Obviously.'

'What does that mean?'

'You could have asked me to mind my daughter.'

'I'll leave you to it,' said Flynn.

'No, don't go.'

'But this isn't my...'

'It is. Flynn kindly offered to stay while I went to the chemist, Simon. He dropped in about the house.' He had, hadn't he? 'He's the agent, remember?'

'How could I forget when he's just sold that block of land to Baldessin? And I bet he got a nice cut out of the deal.'

'Why shouldn't he? It's his business.'

'You don't care, do you? You don't care that some greedy developer is going to ruin my home and the area around it.'

'Simon,' Flynn began but was cut off.

'Shut up. People like you always get what they want and they always want more. Nothing is ever enough. All I want is a peaceful life growing vegetables and enjoying the environment, showing my kids the beauty of nature, but you want to destroy that and you want to take my kids as well.'

'That's the most ridiculous thing I've ever heard,' Antonia said. 'Go away, Simon, and don't come back until you can say something sane.' Perspiration ran down her back in an uncomfortable trickle, her hands were shaking. She'd never raised her voice to anyone before, never ordered anyone to go away.

'But...'

'Go.' Blood pounded in her ears. She didn't trust herself to say another word.

Simon pushed past Flynn and marched to his ute.

She dragged in deep breaths and slowly the shaking subsided, her pulse returned to normal.

Flynn said, 'I'll be off too.'

She pulled her brain into gear but her voice quavered when she said, 'Thanks for minding Sarah. Did she wake up?'

'Yes, but it was cool.'

'Really?'

He nodded. 'Are you okay?'

'I'm sorry, I've never been so angry in my life. I don't know where that came from.'

'Stored it up, perhaps?'

'Poor Simon. He didn't deserve that.'

'He said some pretty offensive things.' His eyes still glittered with anger, betraying the mild tone.

'He's wrong about you, isn't he?'

'That I want to take his kids? Of course he's wrong.'

'No, about destroying the co-op and his lifestyle,' she said hastily.

Flynn exhaled noisily and he raised his hands in exasperation. 'It shouldn't make any difference to them. It's more about how they think it will affect the co-op but I reckon they'd do well businesswise with another market for their produce. If they choose to move, it's their decision. They won't be forced out.' He shook his head, still furious. 'I don't see why people think I'd get a bigger commission by selling to Baldessin rather than some other random buyer. It's ridiculous. He paid the asking price, no more, no less. Do they think I'd take a bribe?'

Antonia took a step towards the door, gripping her shopping bag in a suddenly sweaty hand. Flynn wasn't angry with her, she knew that, but his fierce tone and the tension radiating from him triggered a response deep inside her, one that screamed, 'get away. Hide.'

Her fingers fumbled with the latch on the fly screen door and suddenly Flynn was close beside her, voice gentle.

'Antonia, I'm sorry. I'm not angry with you. Don't be frightened of me. Please.'

Head bent, she muttered, 'I'm not frightened of you.' She let her hand fall but couldn't face him. He'd see the panic in her eyes.

He unlatched the door and swung it open. 'Go. Take care of Sarah.'

She scuttled inside and he closed the screen carefully.

'Thank you,' she mumbled.

'See you later,' he said.

Antonia waited until he reached the path then closed the front door. The least she could do was not give him the impression she'd slammed the door shut behind him. Sarah yelled, 'Mummy, are you there?'

'Yes, I'm home.' She hurried to the bedroom.

'How are you feeling?' She placed her hand on Sarah's brow. Still warm but better.

'I had ice-cream,' Sarah said. 'Knock, knock.'

'Who's there?'

'Lettuce.'

'Lettuce who?'

'Lettuce in, it's cold outside.'

Antonia laughed in surprise. 'Who told you that?'

'Flynn. He told me other jokes.'

'Did Daddy come in?'

'Yes but he didn't like my joke very much. He was cross with Flynn.'

'Why?'

'He just was. They went outside but I heard them.'

At least Simon had the decency not to start a fight in front of his daughter. Why was he mixing up the land thing with Flynn's relationship with her and the children? Wasn't she allowed to make friends? He didn't own her and he certainly couldn't dictate who she was allowed to talk to or who was allowed to see the twins. Why was this becoming so complicated?

'I think you need a nap,' she said. 'Snuggle down.'

Flynn wasn't helping by dropping in all the time. Already people were hinting at something more going on between them than there was. Cath had been the first but Di and Cheryl weren't far behind, and Bron next door had a bird's-eye view of his comings and goings. She was bound to be the source of a lot of the speculation.

Why had he come round this morning? She still didn't know, thanks to Simon. Men!

She picked up the empty ice-cream bowl and took it to the kitchen.

When the phone rang, she half expected it to be Flynn but the voice asking for her by name was unfamiliar.

'Michael Hodge,' he said and the penny clanged into place. The lawyer.

'How long will this take, do you think?' she asked when he explained what he wanted.

'Could you stay overnight? I want to be very thorough. The statement you gave the police missed things the defence will pick up on regarding your state of mind, reasons for going with

Murdoch in the first place, why you stayed and so on.'

'Okay. When?' Why she stayed? Basically because she was locked in and threatened with violence if she tried to leave.

'As soon as you can manage would be good.'

'I'll need to arrange a few things.'

'Of course. Just call and let me know when you're coming.'

'All right. Do you want Simon to come too?'

'Not necessarily. I can talk to him later.'

'Okay.'

'Antonia? Don't worry. We've more than enough to lock this guy up for life but we don't want any holes he might crawl through.'

'Good. That's good.' His confidence was reassuring.

'I know how hard it is for people to relive the trauma of this type of experience but the more you talk about it the better you'll manage when it comes to the trial.'

'Will you need to talk to my children?'

'No, and if for some reason we do need them to speak we'd use video. One of the older girls has said she wants to give evidence.'

'Which one?'

'Lucy.'

Brave Lucy. Now fourteen. Since they'd escaped, she'd grown in stature and confidence with a toughness honed by her life in the house. Although at first she and Hannah clung together, and sharing a house had worked for a while, both of them realised they weren't willing to continue when the reality of their new freedom took hold. They were too different, wanted different things from their lives. Antonia moved in with her mother as her parents had wanted all along. But again, not for long. She wanted her own life, her own home.

'Are you charging Hannah?'

'No, I don't think we could mount a strong enough case. Her evidence against him will be very useful.'

'If it hadn't been for Hannah I probably wouldn't have survived the birth of my babies.'

'You were one of the lucky ones, Antonia.'

'I know. Hannah did her best for the other girls but...' A sob broke free. 'He wouldn't let me help, he wouldn't ... let anyone help.'

'He's going away for life, you can count on that.'

'I just want to forget it.'

'You will.'

He sounded nice, sympathetic. Antonia made lunch, pondering when she could go to Sydney. If she went on Sunday and came home Tuesday afternoon, met Michael on Monday and Tuesday, she'd have to cancel her teaching but would only need one day off from the cafe. Next Monday then.

She rang Connor.

'Don't drive to Sydney. Leave the car at Brisbane airport and fly down,' he said. 'The twins can stay with your mum while you're busy. She'll love it and so will they. I'll book your tickets. Don't worry about the money.'

'Thanks, Dad.'

As he predicted, her mum was thrilled. 'We miss you all so much,' she said. 'Why don't you stay the whole week?'

'I have a job, Mum, and the twins have kindy. They love it.'

'Are you happy there, darling?'

'Yes, I am.' Despite the tension with Simon, she *was* happy. Happier than she'd been for years. 'We love the Mango House. It was sold recently but the new owners will rent it to me as long as I want to live here.'

'That's lucky. Are they locals?'

'I don't know. Flynn didn't say.'

'Connor told me about Flynn.'

'They liked each other.'

'So he said. How's Simon getting on with the twins?'

'Very well. They love having a proper Daddy.'

'What about you? Are you interested in him at all?'

'Mum, no!'

'Okay. Just asking. What about him?'

'Actually ... he's a bit...'

'What?'

'He's becoming a bit possessive. He seems to think he has the right to tell me who I can talk to.'

'Ant, don't let him get away with that!'

'It's not like ... like before. I don't mean that. It's more that he seems to expect me to ... well for example there's a thing going on here with a property developer and half the town is against the proposal, Simon and the co-op people included. Simon seemed to expect me to follow him if he decided to leave town. I didn't come here to be with him, Mum, but that's what he thinks. Or seems to. I'm not sixteen anymore.'

'Did you tell him how you feel?'

'Yes, and he was upset.'

'Who doesn't he want you to talk to? Everyone?'

'Flynn.'

'He's jealous.'

'Why?'

'Ant, darling ... do you see a lot of Flynn?'

'More or less. He comes into the cafe and he's the agent for the house. It's a small town, people see each other all the time.'

'So do you think Simon has reason to be jealous of Flynn?'

'I'm not...'

'I think maybe you are, darling. And maybe Flynn is too. Your dad thought so.' Mum chuckled. 'Let me know what time your flight comes in and we'll meet you. Love you. Love to the twins.'

***

'How much will it cost to leave my car at the airport? And how do I find the parking station?' Antonia asked Cath the next morning. Flying to Sydney was obviously quickest and she'd be met at the other end, but the logistics of negotiating the airport with two small children and luggage, coupled with never having flown before, were daunting.

'There'll be signs but I've no idea of the cost. Ask Flynn when he comes in.'

She'd have to. Simon wouldn't know anything about it and she really didn't want to talk to him at the moment. Not that she wanted to talk to Flynn either, but she had to ask someone for help or she'd get completely lost and miss their flight.

He didn't come in until well after lunch. Cath had gone to the bank.

Antonia was clearing tables and serving coffee and dessert to the lingerers when he took his regular spot at the counter.

'Hi. The regular?' she asked. She could make coffee to Cath's satisfaction now, which meant Cath could have a breather when the lunch crowd rush died down.

'Hello. Yes, please. How's Sarah?'

'She seems okay. She went to school happily enough and I haven't had a call.'

'That's good.'

She concentrated on making his espresso. When she placed it before him, she said, 'I have to go Sydney on Sunday. Dad has organised the air tickets but I've never flown before. What time should I get to the airport? Cath said you'd know. Apparently I can leave my car there too but I don't know where or how much it costs. The flight is at one forty-five.' Did she sound as anxious as she was?

'Are the twins going too?'

'Yes.'

'You'll need to be there about an hour before the flight time to check in your bags and go through security. Will you have luggage?'

'One bag. We're coming back on Tuesday afternoon.'

'Okay, so you'll need to leave here by nine-thirty or ten at the latest. Two hours drive, say twenty minutes to park and get to the terminal, check-in etc. That would get you there and ready in plenty of time.'

'As long as I don't get lost.'

'There are plenty of signs and you can ask for directions. Or you could leave earlier to make sure.'

'I suppose.'

'Are you worried about it?'

She realised she was biting at her lower lip and stopped. 'A bit. Everything is slower with the twins in tow and there'll be lots of traffic, won't there?'

'Probably on a Sunday it won't be so bad. Tuesday might be worse but you'll know where you're going then.'

She gave a doubtful little snorting laugh and went to take the money from a customer who was leaving. When she returned to take his empty cup he said, 'I could drive you and pick you up when you get back.'

The offer was overwhelmingly tempting but ... 'Thanks Flynn. I think I really need to be able to do this stuff myself. I don't want to be helpless and have to rely on people for things.'

He studied her for a moment. 'Accepting help occasionally isn't being helpless. Sometimes it's just practical. I can drop you at departures and you can take it from there. It just means you won't have to worry about parking and getting to the right terminal.'

'But it means hours of driving for you.'

'I can catch up with friends and come back in the evening. No worries. I've done it before.'

The friend being the woman he went out with before? 'I'll have to think about it. But thanks.'

'Okay. Whatever you decide. See you later.' He slid off the stool and headed for the door.

Antonia wiped the countertop, pondering the concept of Flynn. Was he so insensitive to what Simon might think about his offer, or did he just not care? Why was she thinking about Simon's reaction anyway? She'd made it clear to both of them she was her own boss. Flynn was simply acting on that assertion. Wasn't he? Or was he deliberately trying to upset Simon? She hadn't taken him for a petty man.

Simon would be upset, that was for sure, but she knew for certain he hadn't been anywhere near Brisbane airport or any other airport in his life. He didn't read newspapers, didn't watch TV. He hadn't been farther than Kurrajong since he'd moved here. He'd told her himself. If he had to go to Sydney he'd drive.

She shook her head free of such annoying thoughts. Flynn's offer was kind and would save her a lot of stress, which she didn't need given the reason for the trip. And on the return journey she and the twins would be tired. Driving home in the evening would be downright dangerous.

She'd call in to Flynn's office and accept on the way home.

Chapter 12

Would Antonia tell Simon how she was getting to Brisbane and back? She was fighting hard to be strong and independent but in some areas she was vulnerable and unsure of herself. Endearingly so. When she walked through the door just now his heart did a hop and a skip, and when she said 'yes please' to the ride he had to force himself not to jump out of his chair with delight.

Instead he nodded with a reserved but friendly smile and said, 'Fine. I'll swing by at ten.'

She hadn't said why she was going to Sydney at such short notice. It wasn't a pleasure trip; he could tell by the tension in her body. Something to do with her abusive ex, perhaps? At least she wasn't prepared to leave the twins with their father, which meant Simon was no closer to her than he was. And she hadn't gone to Simon for help either. A small but satisfying victory on the road to gaining her complete trust.

On Sunday he arrived at the Mango House just before ten. Jacob was sitting on the steps. He waved at Flynn and scurried inside. Moments later, Antonia appeared clutching a suitcase. Both twins ran to the car where Flynn waited with the boot open.

'Hello, everyone,' he said.

'Hello, Flynn,' they chorused. No shyness now.

Antonia caught his eye in the midst of the whirlwind, smiled. 'Good morning.'

'We're going on an aeroplane,' said Jacob.

'That's exciting. You'll like it.'

'Will we?' asked Sarah doubtfully.

'I think so.'

Antonia handed him the suitcase and he slung it into the boot. 'Packing light,' he said.

'We don't need much.'

'We're staying with Gran and Frank while Mummy goes to talk to someone,' said Sarah.

'That'll be fun.'

Antonia clicked the children's seatbelts. Would she tell him why she was going or not? He couldn't ask, he'd have to wait for her to speak.

She didn't say anything beyond short replies to questions from the back seat. That she was eaten up by nerves was obvious, but was it the plane ride or the someone she was going to talk to?

'When you go into the terminal, look for the Qantas check-in counters,' he said. 'They have auto check-in stands. All you have to do is follow the onscreen instructions and put in your flight number and name and so on and it will print your boarding passes. Then you take your bag to the Bag Drop counter and that's it.'

'What if something goes wrong?'

'It won't, but if you get confused there'll be staff to help you. Then you go through security. Make sure you don't have anything metal—scissors or nail clippers, knives, guns, a bomb, in your carry-on bag.' He gave her a sidelong glance and caught her looking at him in surprise.

'A gun?' she said.

He laughed and she laughed too, but it was brittle.

'You put your handbag and Sarah's backpack through the X-ray and walk through a scanner. You'll see what to do. Sometimes it'll beep if you have a metal belt buckle or something but don't worry if that happens. They'll check. When you're through that, look at the board for the departure gate for your flight and go there and wait.'

'It sounds very complicated.'

'It's not really. It's more of a nuisance than anything.'

'I'm glad you know what to do,' she said. 'Thank you.'

'No worries.'

But she didn't look any more relaxed.

When they finally reached the departure drop-off zone, he took the suitcase from the boot and placed it on the footpath.

'Just go through there,' he said, indicating the sliding doors.

She nodded and grasped the handle of the bag as though it was a life preserver.

'I'll be waiting outside the arrivals hall on Tuesday afternoon in the pick-up lane. Look for the car,' he said. 'Call me if the flight's delayed.'

Another nod. Why was she so nervous? He should be going with her but couldn't have suggested it. Instead he took the risk and kissed her cheek, lingering as long as he dared. Her body quivered under his hands when he held her lightly.

'Take care,' he said and released her.

'Thanks,' she murmured, but this time her little smile was genuine, shy, and her cheeks turned a rosy pink. He stole another quick kiss.

'See you later, kiddos,' he said to the twins. 'Have fun.'

'We will,' they said.

He waited until they'd disappeared through the glass doors before getting back into the car and heading for home. Spending the day in Brisbane held no appeal whatsoever.

***

Monday dragged. Tuesday morning dragged. Flynn checked the flight arrival time twice, discovering it was scheduled as 'on time' both times. Antonia hadn't called or texted. Not that he expected to hear anything. He'd leave just before two to meet her flight at four-twenty.

At twelve forty-five, when he was contemplating going along to the pub for lunch before hitting the road, Aidan called.

'Better get out here, Flynn. Baldessin is knocking down the house next door and there's a bit of a protest brewing.'

'Oh Christ. Is it a police matter?'

'Not yet but it might turn into one. Some of the protesters aren't locals.'

'Jesus. Okay I'm on my way.'

'What's up?' asked Brandon.

'They're demolishing the house on that block next to the co-op. Some out-of-town protesters are there.'

'Wow. Why?'

'Indeed. See you later.'

Cursing, Flynn flung himself into his car and careered down the main street. What the hell did they think they could do about it? Chain themselves to the wrecking ball? Bloody idiots. And what God-awful timing. With any luck he could deal with it and be on his way on schedule. He couldn't possibly leave Antonia stranded.

The protest group was relatively small—about ten people, some of whom he recognised, others as Aidan had said, he didn't. A photographer he knew from the *Kurrajong News* was there, accompanied by a young female reporter, blonde hair scraped back in a knot, smart in a red blouse and white jeans and talking to Lauren and Rufus who held placards saying 'Save our National Park' and 'Stop the Development'. The strangers stood across the driveway, creating a barrier. Professional protesters he'd guess by their confidently aggressive attitude. The other locals stood to one side watching—Simon, Hugo and another equally unkempt person from the commune, Mary, Helen and Glenda, of course. Aidan had stayed away.

A large dump truck was parked on the road with the driver sitting in the cab smoking while he waited. A bobcat and an excavator were at work dismantling the old wooden-framed house.

Flynn walked across to the group. Simon folded his arms but said nothing.

'This shouldn't be happening, Flynn,' said Mary. She gestured at the wrecking.

'Why not? The land was up for sale and someone bought it. The owner can knock the house down if he wants to.'

'It's what he's building in its place that's the problem,' said Glenda.

'And what is he building there?' asked Flynn.

'You know perfectly well.'

'I don't. Do you?'

'Don't play the innocent,' said Mary. She'd had it in for him ever since he'd turned down her blatant attempt at seduction a few years ago. A woman going through a messy divorce wasn't one to be tangled with and when he'd sold a house near Whiterock to her ex and his new partner a year later, his name was mud—even though she had a new man in her life.

'I'm not. As far as I know, and the council knows, Baldessin hasn't got approval to build anything. I know he has plans for improvements, which would benefit everyone in the town, but as far as I know he hasn't secured any government backing and hasn't made any final decisions. I do know he really likes the area.'

'Are you trying to tell us he might be building himself a house?' Glenda spat venom like a cane toad. She even looked a bit like one.

'He might be. I don't know. It's his land. Would you have a problem with that?' he glanced at Simon but received nothing by way of acknowledgement. Did he know where Antonia was and why? He must.

'No, but how we do know for sure?'

'You could ask him.'

Flynn left them muttering to each other, turned and strode across to Lauren and Rufus. The photographer clicked off a few shots and said, 'G'day, Flynn.'

'G'day, Bob.' Balding, overweight and cynical.

The reporter, eager as a terrier after a rat, stepped forward. 'Mr Flynn,' she said. 'Megan Raynor, *Kurrajong News.* Can you tell us what's planned for this site?'

'No.'

'Surely you have an idea what Baldessin has in mind here. It's no secret a resort development is on the cards.'

'Nothing's been decided yet in that regard. Mr Baldessin bought this property and he can do what he likes with it, including knock down the existing buildings.'

'What stage are the resort plans at?'

'Planning.'

'So it will go ahead, completely ignoring the community concerns.'

'I can't say one way or the other. Speculation is rife as it is.'

'Is Mr Baldessin keeping you informed of progress?'

'Yes, but these things take time.'

'So why is this building being demolished so quickly?'

'Ask Mr Baldessin.'

'I will.'

'That's bullshit, Flynn,' Rufus broke in. 'You know exactly what he's doing and you're helping. He wants to buy out the co-op and he's preparing the ground so he can get cracking as soon as he gets approval. This side of the block is where he wants to build his resort and we're in the way of his expansion. Get rid of us and he's away.'

'Any comment?' Megan's bright blue eyes fixed on Flynn.

'No. Mr Baldessin has assured me he has no intention of forcing anyone off their property. If conditions aren't right he'll take his ideas elsewhere. That, in my opinion, would be a great shame and a terrific opportunity lost to Flynn's Crossing.'

'In what way?'

'Flynn wouldn't get a cut out of whatever deal they're cooking up.'

Flynn didn't give Lauren so much as a glance. Simon came to stand by her side but still said nothing.

'Because small towns like ours lose our young people to the cities and we don't attract enough people to replace them. Unemployment is a big problem, our population is ageing and we don't get the resources we need to support the people who stay here. If our primary school numbers drop below a certain number it will close. We'll lose our post office and our supermarket. We're already down to one bank when ten years ago we had three. Who knows how long that one will stay? Tourism is the obvious answer. We have a fantastic drawcard right on our doorstep. Why not open it up and tell people about it?'

'We don't need a whacking great luxury resort to do that,' said Rufus.

'I agree and so does Sean Baldessin.'

'Sure,' said Lauren. 'You can always believe a billionaire businessman. Those people don't make their money by being restrained by the opinions of locals.'

Flynn checked his watch. Nearly one-thirty. He'd have to leave.

The truck's engine burst into life with a throaty roar. The five or six people blocking the gate linked arms. The driver leant on the horn but they didn't move.

'Who are those people?' asked Flynn.

'Sympathisers,' said Lauren.

'Where from?'

'Sydney mostly, but a couple are from Brisbane.

'What do they have to do with this?'

'They care about the environment.'

'Really? Friends of yours, are they?'

'One of them is. He brought the others.'

'Do they know anything about the town?'

'They know how precious the forest areas are.'

'For God's sake! No one's bulldozing the forest.'

'Yet,' she said.

The truck edged forward. Flynn turned away, pulled out his phone and dialled.

'Pat, Flynn.' He outlined the situation.

'Did you call the cops?' demanded Lauren.

'Yes. This could easily get nasty.'

'Whose fault is that?'

'Not mine if that's what you're implying, Lauren. I didn't invite a bunch of professional protesters here to cause trouble.'

The truck moved forward till the bumper was almost touching the barricading line of bodies. The excavator and bobcat fell silent. The bobcat operator jumped down from his cabin and walked across to the gate, talking on his phone. The excavator driver followed, swigging from a water bottle.

The truck's engine stopped and a ragged cheer went up from the protesters.

'You're a bit late, aren't you?' said Flynn. 'The house has been knocked down already. What's the point of preventing them clearing away the rubble?'

'Bloody idiots,' said the excavator driver to no one in particular.

'Get out of the way,' yelled the truck driver. 'I've got a job to do.'

'So have we,' someone shouted back.

'Bloody good-for-nothing layabouts.'

The three workmen glared at the protesters.

Flynn said, 'The police will be here soon.'

'Who are you?' asked the truckie.

'Flynn, head of the local council. I'm sorry about this. These people aren't locals. Those are.' He indicated with a nod of the head.

'What the hell are they protesting about? That house wasn't worth anything.'

'There's a proposal for a resort to be built on this land and they think it'll damage the National Park.'

'No protected trees here.' The excavator driver spat on the ground.

'No.' Flynn sucked in air and checked the time again. Five to two. He'd be late. 'I have to go.'

He headed for the car but Simon and Lauren cut him off.

'Where are you running off to?'

'Shouldn't you stay and see this through, Flynn?' asked Simon. 'This is your project, after all.'

'For God's sake! It's not my project. I didn't know this was happening here today. Why should I?'

'You take a personal interest in other clients' affairs though, don't you?'

Lauren's head whipped towards Simon. She frowned.

'If you mean Antonia, she's a friend,' Flynn said.

'What are you on about, Simon?' Lauren demanded. 'Why shouldn't Flynn see Antonia and the twins?'

'They're my kids, not his.'

'So? Aren't they allowed to see anyone else? Isn't she?' Lauren's voice rose. All her attention was on Simon now, the protest forgotten. 'She's not interested in you other than as father to her kids. She told me herself. Stop pressuring her and let her make her own decisions. She's been through enough.'

'I have to go,' Flynn said swiftly. This was getting very personal very quickly.

'You have no idea what she's been through,' Simon snapped.

'Do *you?*' Flynn paused. He'd never heard Simon raise his voice as much as in the last few weeks. 'You haven't seen her for years.'

'Yes, because she told me when she first came to see me. If she hasn't told you, and I doubt very much she ever will, it's because she doesn't trust you. And I don't blame her.'

'What happened to her?' asked Lauren.

Simon shook his head. 'Antonia trusts me not to say anything.'

'Do you know why she went to Sydney?' Flynn asked.

'Of course I do.'

Lauren sighed and caught Flynn's eye.

'See you later.' He headed for the car. So that meant Simon knew of his involvement in the trip. Or did he? He hadn't mentioned it and he would have if he'd known. What a mess this was turning into. Secrets were dangerous things. Divisive and corrosive.

***

Antonia scooped her bag off the luggage carousel then, with a child on either side, she headed for the exit and the passenger pick-up lanes across the road. Sarah hadn't slept well in Sydney, too excited by the whole excursion. Now she was grumpy and exhausted. Jacob was too but he tended towards silence while Sarah whinged.

'Where are we going?' She slapped her feet down noisily on the tiled floor and let the backpack fall to be dragged along behind her.

'Carry her bag please, Jacob,' said Antonia.

'No, it's mine.' Sarah jerked the bag out of his reach.

'Then put it on properly, please. We're going outside.'

She herded them over the pedestrian crossings, scanning the slow-moving traffic and waiting cars.

No sign of the black BMW. Flynn promised he'd be here but he wasn't.

He hadn't texted or phoned either. Had he forgotten or was he just late, held up in traffic? She parked the twins on a bench and tried calling him. Straight to voicemail.

The flight had landed a few minutes early but still ... She sat down next to Jacob.

'Where's Flynn?' he asked.

'I don't know. He'll be here. Watch out for his car.'

'How will we get home if he doesn't come?' Jacob leaned his full weight against Antonia.

Good question. 'He'll come.'

'Daddy could come.' Sarah said.

'Maybe, but Daddy's ute won't fit us all in and he doesn't have the key for our car.' It was on the key ring in her handbag.

Half an hour later, Flynn still hadn't arrived. Sarah and Jacob fidgeted, whined, argued and asked every few minutes when he was coming. In desperation, she tried Simon but he didn't answer either. What to do? It was after five. Decision time. At worst they'd spend the night in a Brisbane hotel and get home somehow tomorrow.

Surely there was a bus service. This was not a disaster, they weren't stranded in the middle of nowhere. She had a credit card and a brain.

They couldn't sit here forever. She drew in a deep breath, stood up and said, 'Come on.'

'Where are we going? I'm tired,' said Sarah.

'We're going back into the airport to find out how to get home.'

'I need to do a wee,' said Jacob.

'Okay, we'll do that first. Then we'll get a drink and something to eat and work out what we're going to do.'

With a stride more confident than the hazy plan in her head, she headed for the terminal. Fifteen minutes later, bodily essentials taken care of and the twins marginally happier, she approached the Information desk and stated the situation to a plump-faced woman. She tried hard not to but she may have sounded a tad desperate. The woman cast a glance at the two faces staring up at her over the counter and smiled.

'Aren't you two just the cutest ones?' she said. 'Let's see what we can do.'

After perusing the coach-line timetables, frowning and murmuring to herself, she pointed to a car-hire desk.

'That's your best bet, in my opinion, especially with the little ones. You'd have to stay overnight in the city or go down to the Gold Coast to catch a bus in the morning. The train is across the way, but by the time you'd done that and found a hotel you could be nearly home by car. It'd be cheaper to drive, I think. And much faster.'

'Are we going in our own car?' asked Sarah.

'A rental car,' said the woman.

Antonia did some quick calculations. It was now past five-thirty but wouldn't start getting dark till at least eight. If she didn't get lost on the way out, they'd be home before night fell. She could do this. She'd watched fairly closely when Flynn had driven them in. She needed to get onto the M1 and go south. The roads were well signposted and the car might have a GPS. She'd driven to Flynn's Crossing from Sydney, she could drive home from here.

'Thank you very much.'

'Safe trip.'

On legs gone suddenly weak, she approached the car rental desk.

***

So far so good. The car was a new model silver hatchback, nippy and far more responsive than her own car. Once she'd remembered the indicator lever was on the other side, she settled in and began to enjoy herself. Traffic had been heavy close to Brisbane because it was the evening rush hour and she hadn't factored slow-moving queues and impatient drivers into the time frame. But once they reached the M1, the cars flowed along faster even with the vast numbers leaving the city. She still had at least an hour of driving to go and it was nearly seven-thirty.

Jacob said, 'I'm hungry.'

Antonia threw a quick glance at the back seat. Both of them had gone to sleep quite quickly once the new car excitement wore off and the trip home began in earnest, but now they were awake.

Sarah stretched and yawned. 'I need to do a wee.'

'You're a pair of sleepyheads,' Antonia said. 'You've been asleep for ages. I suppose we should eat dinner then you can go straight to bed when we get home. How about a burger?'

'Yes.'

'Keep your eyes peeled for a place to stop.'

Shortly after, she pulled into a roadside cafe, which proudly boasted the best burgers in Australia.

The place was busy, but fortunately most customers were waiting for takeaway orders. Toilet stop taken care of, Antonia secured a table and scanned the menu. It was like the Bluebird Cafe at home, same basic fare. While they waited, she checked her phone. Still no messages. She tried Flynn again. No answer, which was a little concerning now.

But this time Simon answered his phone.

'It's Antonia.'

'I know. How did it go?' His voice was curiously flat and toneless, with none of the usual warm cheer.

'Okay, I guess. He asked all sorts of things, some of which I'd told them before, other things I hadn't. I'm glad it's over. For now anyway.'

'Yes.'

'What's up? You sound strange.' She lowered her voice and turned away from the twins who were giggling together across the table.

'We had a bit of trouble next door. There was a protest when they started demolishing the house on that block Baldessin bought.'

'Why? What happened?' The Flynn's Crossing protest issues had gone completely out of her head. Was Flynn involved? Was that why he hadn't turned up?

'A couple of Lauren's friends were arrested.'

'Gosh. What about Lauren?'

'She's okay but she's furious with Flynn.'

'With Flynn? What did he have to do with it?'

'He was there talking to a reporter but he cleared out after he called the cops.'

'Why did he call the police?'

'The protesters blocked the gate and wouldn't let the truck go in to clear the site.'

'Did locals do that?' It sounded rather extreme for someone like Mary or hippy Hugh, but then she didn't really know the depth of feeling in town.

'No, Lauren's friends brought people with them.'

'Why would they get involved? It all sounds really stupid to me.'

'Yeah, well it would. It doesn't affect you, does it?'

Antonia closed her eyes, perilously close to yelling, 'Grow up, Simon.' Soothing his wounded ego wasn't her job. 'Simon ... I have nothing to do with any of this. Right now I'm tired and I want to get myself and my children home.'

'I thought you were home. Where are you?' A spark of interest at last, maybe even concern.

'Driving back from Brisbane. We're having dinner in a cafe at the moment. We're about an hour away.'

'Oh, right.'

'Where's Flynn?'

'I've no idea. Why?' Sullen again but that was no surprise.

'I tried to call him but his phone's been off all afternoon.'

'I don't know. He said he had to go somewhere and took off.'

'When was that?'

'About two. Why?'

'He was supposed to meet us at the airport.'

'Didn't you drive?'

'Flynn did and he was supposed to pick us up but he didn't. I hired a car to come home.'

'Why didn't you ask me?'

'I tried but your phone was off.' Hard to keep the annoyance out of her voice. He was so childish sometimes.

'Oh—yes, it was for a while. I was in the bush taking photographs.'

'Simon, do you think Flynn is all right? He might have had an accident.'

'I doubt it.'

'Can you call someone and find out?'

'Who? Flynn lives on his own.'

'The police? The hospital?' Was he being deliberately dense?

'I suppose I could call the Kurrajong Hospital.' Said grudgingly.

'Simon, Flynn's your mate. You introduced me to him and said I should trust him. I do and he's been very helpful. What's your problem?'

The waitress arrived with the food. Three plates of burgers and chips. Two marginally smaller but still more than any of them could eat.

'I have to go. I'll phone when I get home.' She pressed 'Off' before he could reply.

'Why are you cross with Daddy?' asked Sarah.

'I'm not.'

'Is Flynn in hospital?' asked Jacob.

'I hope not, but he might have had an accident when he was coming to collect us.' Which was the only explanation she could think of to explain why he didn't answer his phone or call her. And for that to happen he would have to be injured badly enough to be incapable.

She stared at the plate of food with no appetite whatsoever and a lump of dread expanding rapidly inside her.

Chapter 13

Simon tossed the phone onto the table. Damn Flynn. He should never have introduced him to Antonia, but he'd been so keen to help her he never dreamed she'd fall for that bastard and vice versa. And here she was not telling him Flynn had driven her and the twins to the airport. Why didn't she ask *him?* It was his job to do that sort of thing, not Flynn's.

Somehow he'd bungled the whole thing. Lauren didn't understand what it was like to be a father—the love and the overwhelming need to be there for his kids, to help them and protect them. She was angry with him and so was Antonia. Antonia kept secret the fact she was asking Flynn for help, Lauren took her side and told him to back off. Why?

And Flynn was most to blame. He knew Antonia was off limits but he went there anyway. Damn him to hell and back. He didn't even bother to say he was rushing off to Brisbane to collect Simon's family from the airport. Antonia had let him assume she was driving her own car to Brisbane. Why would he think otherwise?

He ground his teeth and went to the fridge for a beer, then flung himself down on the couch. Rain beat against the window, preventing any more work today. For the first time in his life, getting drunk seemed like a good idea. Only problem was he probably didn't have enough beer on hand.

***

Flynn opened his eyes and closed them almost immediately. Nothing made sense. Why was he lying down? Was he dreaming? No, it was cold. His head hurt, and a stabbing pain shafted through his chest as he attempted to move. The seatbelt was cutting him half, holding him in place like an iron bar across his belly. Something was wrong with his right leg. His right arm was trapped, immobile. He concentrated hard on his left hand and managed to move the fingers.

His eyes flickered open again and focused this time. A mass of leaves and branches obscured the windscreen, falling onto the dashboard. Why were they there? How? Where was he? Leaves glistening with water. Raining? Soft drops pattered on the foliage, landed on his face and slid down to wet his shirt. He blinked.

There was no windscreen. The glittering remains of the glass hung from the frame. He lay crushed against the door. The car must be on its side, angled down a slope wedged against a tree. In a burst of memory, a pair of roos came from nowhere right in front of the car. No time to stop, wrench the wheel, frantic instinctive braking, useless ... a slide ... thunderous crashing ... then what?

Undo the seatbelt.

Fingers groped feebly for the catch, found it and pressed. Nothing happened. He tried again, holding the button down as hard as his weak thumb would allow. It popped free and he lurched forward with a hoarse scream as his head connected with the steering wheel and the stabbing in his chest turned into a chainsaw attack.

Barely drawing breath, he lay still, waiting for the agony to subside. He could move his right hand now but the shoulder must be damaged, because every movement sent shock waves up his arm and neck. The remains of a deflated airbag lay on his lap and another draped over his shoulder. He peered through the broken windscreen trying to assess where the car lay, how precarious its position on the slope. Where exactly was he?

He forced his battered brain to remember. Driving somewhere. Going to Brisbane. Antonia. Late, in a hurry. Drizzling rain. Roos on the road. How far along? Through Whiterock, over the ridge ... then what? Nothing.

Antonia. Beautiful, beautiful Antonia. Had to get there for her.

The short cut wound over the ridges. Not much traffic, quicker if you knew the road. He did. He was late for Antonia. Couldn't let her down.

Phone. He groped at the centre console between the front seats. Not there. Could be anywhere. Wait for help. Better to stay in the car. Too wet outside.

He drew a shuddery painful breath. How long?

***

Antonia kissed the sleepy twins goodnight. Thank goodness they'd stopped to eat when they did, because this pair were asleep most of the way home and could barely stumble from the car to their bedroom.

She phoned Simon but he didn't answer so, annoyed, she left a message. Had he found Flynn? Had he tried? She made herself tea and sat at the kitchen table with the phone in front of her. Who could she ask? Something had happened to him, she knew with a deep certainty. He was hurt somewhere, unable to contact her.

She found the local police number and rang it. She knew the constable, Pat. He'd been into the cafe a few times. A friendly man heading for retirement but happy to finish his career taking care of the local area. His main job seemed to be issuing traffic violations, sorting out the odd punch-up and chasing one or other of the Kurrajong Cardews when they decided to try their luck with a bit of theft or vandalism in Flynn's Crossing and surrounds.

'Flynn's Crossing Police, Constable Symonds.'

'It's Antonia, Pat.'

'Hello, love, how are you? Something wrong?'

'Yes, well, no I hope not. I was wondering if you know where Flynn is.'

'At home or at the pub, I'd say. Why?'

The words poured out in a torrent. 'I've been away for a couple of days and Flynn was supposed to pick me and the twins up at the Brisbane airport today at about twenty past four but he didn't turn up and I can't contact him. His phone isn't on. I'm worried he might have had an accident and be hurt somewhere.'

'Mmm. Have you checked his house? He could have been taken sick.'

'No, I've only just got home. I hired a car and drove. The twins are asleep. I can't go out.'

'All right, love. I'll drop over to his place and call in at the pub on my way. Don't worry.'

'Thank you. He wouldn't just forget to come and he'd call if he couldn't get there. I know he would. Simon saw him at two at that protest and said he was in a hurry to go somewhere. That would have been to collect us.'

'I agree. Do you know which road he was taking?'

'Not for sure. He took the main road out when he drove us on Sunday. Through Kurrajong and then across to the M1. I came back the same way.'

'No sign of a breakdown or an accident?'

'No.' But would she have seen anything?

'I haven't been notified of any accidents in the area but I'll put out an alert just in case. If the police were involved they'd have his car registration information, and if they couldn't contact next of kin, they'd contact me.'

'Thank you.'

'I'll get onto it. Goodnight, love. Try not to worry. Flynn's tough as an old boot.'

'Okay, yes. Thanks.' He was being kind but he was wrong. Flynn was flesh and blood. He could be hurt and he could die. No one was immune to pain and suffering. She was about to disconnect when a question popped into her head. 'Did Simon phone you earlier?'

'No. I'll keep in touch. Sit tight.'

The phone went dead in her ear. Why hadn't Simon called Pat? That was ages ago, about seven-thirty, now it was after nine. He said he'd phone the police and the hospital and she'd bet he'd done neither. Flynn could be lying somewhere injured and in shock. It was raining too. He could be out there all night. If Simon had called earlier Pat would have had several hours of daylight to search in, now it was dark and wet.

Who were his next of kin? Did he have anyone besides parents in Perth or Fremantle or wherever they were? She knew nothing about his personal life. Who would be listed on his phone? The councillors. Margie was very much in favour of the resort development. They'd hatched the plan together. Apparently she knew Baldessin personally and it was her idea to ask him. So said the grapevine.

A flip through the phone book and Antonia dialled. Margie knew nothing but she was immediately concerned.

'That's not like Flynn,' she said decisively. 'He must be in trouble. I'll send Bernie over to his house.'

'No, don't. Constable Pat's going,' said Antonia. 'I called him when I got home a little while ago.'

'Good thinking. We'll stop by anyway, and if he's not there at least we can take a drive along the Whiterock road and see if we see anything. He might have taken that route as quickest.'

'Now?' Rain lashed against the kitchen window and pounded on the tin roof.

'Yes. If he's had an accident he could be stranded out there. There's no reception when you're on that road and not much traffic. Hell of a night to be stuck.'

'Gosh. Be careful in the rain.'

'I'll call you. Bye.'

Hell of a night all right. Margie had refrained from saying what she knew they both feared. Flynn was injured, too badly to seek help, and unless he was found he'd be spending the night outdoors in the rain and a rapidly dropping temperature. Winter was mild in this area compared to Sydney, but the mountain areas were becoming chilly at night now. Please let him be in the car and have some shelter. Exposure could be lethal to someone seriously hurt.

Antonia picked up her mug of tea with a shaky hand and put it down. Cold. She got up to make more, then wandered into the living room clutching the warm mug between her hands, trying to ward off the sudden chill enveloping her. Don't think the worst. There were other reasons. Maybe he was at the pub. Maybe the BMW had broken down. Maybe he'd become involved in the protest and forgotten about her.

But she knew that last bit was wrong. He'd left the protest and Margie would know if he'd been involved in urgent council business. It had to have been for the airport pick up.

He hadn't stayed in Brisbane with his friends, or friend, longer than planned either because he was here on Tuesday.

'Where are you?' she whispered. If Flynn wasn't here in Flynn's Crossing, her life would suddenly have a huge gap in it. A Flynn-shaped hole she hadn't realised he'd been filling. Slowly but surely he'd insinuated himself into her life before she realised he was doing it. He'd ignored all her protests in that breezy way he had—not ignored exactly, kind of sidestepped with nifty footwork so that she found herself agreeing with him after all.

But it wasn't just her, everyone would miss him. Even those people he annoyed. They'd realise he was a driving force in this town and without his energy and enthusiasm the place would slowly wither away. The same way she would.

Flynn had brought her alive, dragged her into the light, forced her to make decisions and respected her choices. More than that, he'd expected and allowed her to make those decisions where Simon tried to stifle her, unintentionally of course, but the effect was the same. He wanted to bend her will to his using love as the lever.

Flynn didn't. He cared for her and was very fond of the twins. But was it love? There was physical attraction, she knew, but after their frank conversation and her declaration of her life as a no-man's-land he was very careful not to make her feel uncomfortable in his presence. A few light kisses on the cheek was it. The way her Dad and Frank did when they greeted her or said goodbye.

But kisses from Flynn had a hugely different effect. His lips sizzled on her cheek, sending hot blood racing in her veins. And when he stole a second kiss at the airport she could barely breathe. Did he realise? Did he care? Maybe he was more than happy to relegate her to the friends basket with the likes of Margie and Cath, and Donna at the pub.

She didn't want to be relegated.

'I want to be special,' she said aloud. 'I want to be special to Flynn.' Tears leaked out and fell as fast as the rain outside.

***

A car engine. Flynn roused himself from the stupor of pain and listened. Definitely a car, changing gears as it climbed the ridge. Thank God. Water bounced off leaves to drip relentlessly through the broken windscreen and onto the dashboard, where it flowed in a constant chilly stream onto his legs and down to pool on the floor. Branches scraped desiccated fingers along the roof.

The engine grew louder, carrying clearly over the patter of rain. High above him. How high? How far down the slope was he? Panic burst in his chest. Would they see the BMW? Was there a trail where he'd crashed off the road? Would it be visible in this sodden blackness? If they weren't looking for him they could drive straight on, oblivious.

He stretched out a hand and felt for the dashboard to turn on the lights. Couldn't reach the switch with his right hand, the pain was too intense in the shoulder and his left was just as useless because leaning across felt as though a sword was driving through his chest. Broken ribs, for sure. He didn't want to puncture a lung. He collapsed back, straining his ears for telltale sounds that the car had stopped. The engine ground on, louder then fading as it turned and headed away round the next bend.

Gone.

With the despair came uncontrollable shivering. He had nothing to cover himself. No jacket, no rug. He closed his eyes and sank into the darkness. Images and thoughts wheeled in slow motion through his head, dancing on the pain racking his body.

Was this how it ended? Was this his punishment for the other life lost in a car crash all those years ago? To die alone and in pain, suffering? Years ago. Yesterday. A life for a life. Two lives. His life wasn't worth two lives.

Antonia's was. Antonia was pure gold. Diamonds and pearls. She was worth all the treasure in the world. She came towards him smiling. Her fingers caressed his cheek, her soft lips pressed on his. He kissed her and drew strength and warmth from her body. She murmured words he couldn't hear, spoke softer still and drew away. 'Stay,' he cried but his voice was silent. No sound came from his throat. She turned and the smile turned into a grimace. Disgust.

'Murderer,' she said.

He called her name but she was gone.

He had nothing. He was nothing. A broken and useless carcass. Good for nothing. Nothing.

A heavy thud on the roof jerked him to consciousness. Scuffling in the branches outside made every hair on his head stand on end.

'Help,' he croaked.

The scuffling stopped.

'Help.'

Silence.

Had he slept? Antonia had kissed him, so soft and lovely ... He was alone. The pain had backed off. A silvery sliver slanted across the bonnet of the car. Moonlight. Eyes staring wide in the blackness, he could make out lighter patches of night sky through the windscreen. The rain had stopped.

Antonia ... beautiful wondrous girl, Antonia. Strolling into his life and blinding him, Blindsiding him. Innocent and lovely. Adored her instantly.

If he survived this he'd tell her... And if they were still on speaking terms after she knew, he'd ask her, beg her if necessary, to give him a chance.

A chance is a fine thing. Fine. Fine line. Fine line between pleasure and pain and this was pain. No pleasure here. Not for Flynn of Flynn's Crossing.

If she said no, he might well die. Right here. Die. But he couldn't—not without asking her. Not without finding out. He had to stay alive.

He had things to do.

Questions to ask.

Flynn forced himself to straighten, ignoring the sudden pain in his shoulder and leg as he levered himself into a different angle. Using the broken steering wheel as a prop, he dragged his left leg back and pushed up, propelling his body agonisingly slowly towards the passenger seat on the higher side of the car. If he could reach the door ... but the centre console was in the way, wide and bulky. Difficult even for an able-bodied person, impossible for him.

He fell back panting, lying awkwardly across the seats, teeth gritted against the agony, eyes clamped shut.

Darkness overwhelmed him.

***

Pat didn't phone but Margie called at eleven-thirty.

'Nothing,' she said. 'But it's impossible to see anything properly at night, and with the rain. Pat's sending people out first thing in the morning. He said Flynn hasn't been admitted to any hospitals.'

'Thanks for calling, Margie, I'm ... I've been...' A sniff betrayed her.

'I know, Antonia,' she said gently. 'Go to bed. There's nothing you can do at the moment. And it's thanks to you we even know he's missing.'

Antonia went to bed but worry gnawed relentlessly, snatching her from the brink of sleep countless times. Now she knew how her parents felt when she disappeared from their lives. Devastating, crippling anxiety, robbing her of breath, swamping her brain, leaving her a brittle shell of herself. If she transferred this feeling of loss to one of the twins, she'd be incapable of coherent thought, go mad with worry. Now she understood when people said it was the not knowing that was worst. The imagining and the helplessness, the frustration, the incapacity to do anything but wait.

But her dad had never given up on her, neither had the police. She wouldn't give up on Flynn. On that thought, she drifted into a restless sleep to jerk awake with the screeching of parrots flying overhead. Pale dawn light crept through the blind.

Flynn! Was he found? Antonia sprang out of bed then stood swaying for a moment, gathering herself as her body reacted to the sudden vertical activity after insufficient sleep. A quarter to five. The twins would sleep until at least seven.

Showered and dressed, she sat in the kitchen and spooned in cereal and banana, tasting nothing. When could she call Pat? The search should be well underway by now. Who would go? Locals. The volunteer firefighters probably, from the areas along both routes. They knew the terrain, knew the danger spots, had the equipment to handle emergencies.

She dumped the bowl in the sink then walked out to stand on the front verandah. The silver rental car sparkled in the sunlight. That had to be returned to an agency in Kurrajong by this evening. She'd have to ask Simon to help this afternoon after work. He could follow in her car with the twins. There wasn't anyone else she could comfortably call on to help out. Only Flynn and he was ... where?

Movement next door caught her eye. Her elusive neighbour was out snipping at the sunburst of flowers along his front fence.

Antonia sprinted down the steps, across her front yard and along the footpath. He looked up, startled.

'Good morning, Josef,' she said. 'I'm Antonia, I've been wanting to say hello but I keep missing you.'

'G'day.' He returned his attention to the flowers.

'Your flowers are lovely.'

'They're all right.'

She searched her brain for something to say and came up blank.

He wasn't helping. He edged away slowly, trimming dead leaves and flowers, ignoring her. Antonia gave up. She didn't have the energy to persist this morning. She turned slowly and went home with the urge to sob welling in her throat.

The twins were still fast asleep, exhausted after yesterday's adventure. All in all they'd coped well. She scooped up dirty clothes and loaded the washing machine. Still only six am. Her early burst of energy was wearing off. She yawned and began making more tea.

Someone tapped on the door. Constable Pat with news? Heart in mouth, she ran to open it.

But it was Josef, holding a large bunch of the flowers she'd admired. She only recognised pink carnations and white stocks along with some big bright daisy-looking things.

'These are for you,' he said and thrust them towards her. 'For the shortbread.'

'Thank you, thank you very much.' She smiled but a tear escaped and she dashed it away.

He peered at her, frowning. 'Something wrong?'

'No ... well, yes. Flynn's missing.' Another couple of tears trickled after the first. 'I'm worried.'

'What do you mean missing?'

Antonia gave a brief summary then said, 'Would you like to come in? I was making a cup of tea.'

'All right.'

He tottered after her, pausing to inspect the changes she'd made to the furniture arrangement in the living room.

'Still got Jean's couch,' he said.

'Yes, I don't have much of my own so I was pleased some of her things were left here.'

He grunted. 'Thought you'd get rid of the old stuff. Want new.'

'No. I like some of her things to be here. Sort of a link to the past, you know? She lived here for so long I can feel she loved this house. I think that was why I loved it too. Right away.'

'I reckon you and Jean would have got on real well,' he said.

'You and she did?'

'Yeah, we were mates. After my Greta died ... Jean made the best scones I've ever eaten.'

'I like cooking. I'll have to have a go at scones.'

'Your shortbread was pretty good.' He chuckled and she smiled.

'Thanks. Come into the kitchen and I'll find a vase. There was some glassware and crockery left here too. I found a box in one of the rooms.'

She opened a cupboard and reached for a big cut glass vase.

'Jean used that plate to serve her scones,' he said.

'This one?' Antonia removed a pretty, floral-patterned cake plate, which she'd propped up so the picture was visible through the glass-panelled door. She handed it to him and he held it carefully, remembering.

'She was a great mate,' he murmured.

'Would you like to keep the plate as a memento?' Antonia asked softly.

'I would, yes. I don't have anything. Thanks. That's very kind.' Was she imagining the moisture in the grey eyes?

'Sit down and I'll make the tea.' She set the jug to boil and arranged the flowers in the vase, placing it on the table. The scent of carnations perfumed the air. 'They're lovely. Thank you very much.'

'Flynn will be okay,' he said. 'He's a survivor.'

'Pat said they'd start searching at first light.' She opened the tea caddy.

'They'll find him. Unless the aliens have taken him.'

Antonia's hand remained suspended over the teapot, tea scoop in hand. Was he serious?

'Do you think that's likely?' she asked carefully, without turning to face him.

'What do you think?'

'I'd say it's very unlikely.'

She finished the tea and brought it and two mugs to the table. He sat there with a massive grin on his lined old face. She laughed.

'Aliens.'

'You thought I had a few screws loose, didn't you?' He cackled with delight.

'I did for a moment. Mind you, the aliens would have their work cut out with Flynn.' She poured the tea, glad of the company; glad he was making her laugh and taking her mind off the agony of waiting.

'Mummy?' Sarah in the doorway, pyjama-clad, hair tousled, rubbing the sleep from her eyes.

'Good morning, sweetheart. This is Josef from next door.'

'I know. Hello, Josef.'

'Good morning, Sarah.'

Antonia stared from one to the other. 'When did you two meet each other?'

Sarah shrugged. 'Jacob knows Josef too. Josef has a cat called Smokey.'

'The grey one?' She'd seen it stalking through the garden on occasion.

Sarah nodded.

'We've had a chat over the back fence,' said Josef.

'Can we have a cat?'

'Maybe. Is Jacob awake?'

'No.'

'Go and wash your face and get dressed, sweetheart.'

'Is Flynn all right?'

'I haven't heard yet but everyone's looking for him.'

'He'll be all right, don't you worry about Flynn,' said Josef.

'Okay.'

When she'd gone to the bathroom, Antonia said, 'I'm glad you came in, Josef. I can't stand not knowing where he is. If he's all right.'

The phone rang, shrill and demanding.

Antonia dived for it and pressed the button with a trembling finger.

'Antonia? Constable Pat. We've found Flynn.'

Chapter 14

Simon woke with a foul taste in his mouth, a pounding head and the certain knowledge that finishing the four beers in the fridge and moving on to the half-bottle of whisky last night had not been the smartest decision of his life. He sat up and groaned as the pounding increased in strength. His stomach roiled and twisted. Bile rose in his throat and he launched himself towards the bathroom, making it just in time to throw up in the toilet.

The phone started ringing in the other room, a hideous clanging beating at his head. Bloody hell. He threw up again, sprawled on the floor clutching the porcelain rim as though his life depended on it. Never again would he drown his sorrows in booze.

Fifteen minutes later, his stomach seemed to have emptied itself and he was able to stand on feeble legs under the shower. He closed his eyes and let the hot water cleanse the foul stink from his skin. Eventually enough energy filtered back into his body for him to dry himself, drag on shorts and a T-shirt and head into the kitchen for a few litres of water and coffee.

The phone lay on the table but he ignored it. One thing at a time. He moved slowly and deliberately to avoid any sudden shocks to his fragile system. The water helped a bit and the coffee sent a caffeine boost to his engine. He reached for the phone and checked the missed call. Antonia. Twice. The first time last night. He dimly remembered the phone ringing.

Did he want to speak to her? Not really, not yet.

Why was she calling so early? At ... He blinked and focused on the time. Twenty past eight? Was that right? He hadn't slept so late in years. Not since high school.

Last night's conversation filtered back into his brain. Flynn had stood her up. Left her stranded at the Brisbane airport, the bastard, but she hadn't called him for help. No. She'd hired a car and driven. And she'd wanted him to phone the cops and the Kurrajong Hospital. He hadn't. A little of spasm of guilt made him squirm.

He drained the mug and poured himself more coffee. Maybe he should eat something. A piece of toast was all he could visualise without the urge to throw up.

As he waited for the toast to pop, someone tapped at the door.

'Come in,' he said and winced. Too loud.

Georgia pushed the door open. 'So you're up,' she said. 'Are you okay?'

'More or less.' He might be able to pretend he had a twenty-four-hour bug.

'Ade said to let you sleep it off.'

'What?' He must have looked moronic, staring open-mouthed at her.

'The binge you went on last night.'

'I...'

She held up her hand, unsmiling. 'I don't want to know.'

How...'

'Did he know? He came over before dawn to wake you but he said you were dead to the world and smelled like the inside of a whisky vat. They all went out searching for Flynn. He went missing yesterday on his way to Brisbane to collect Antonia and the twins. She was worried and when she got home she got onto Pat. It's lucky she did.'

My God. He was totally in the poo with her now. And Flynn...

'Did they find him?'

'This morning.'

'Is he all right?' Barely audible.

'Just.'

***

Going to work that morning was torture. All Antonia wanted to do was rush over to the Kurrajong Hospital and see Flynn, but she couldn't leave Cath in the lurch having already taken Tuesday off. The day plodded by.

Pat came in with an update on Flynn's condition: two cracked ribs, badly sprained right ankle, badly bruised right shoulder and knee, dehydration and the usual after-effects of being injured and outside overnight.

'Came out of it pretty well,' he said. 'Good thing you called when you did, Antonia. The car was right down in the gully, invisible from the road, which is why Margie and Bernie missed it last night. Went right past it they did, twice. On the way out and on the way back.

Could have been there for days. He couldn't get out on his own. It took the SES guys two hours to get down there and cut the door open. Then they had to winch him back up on a stretcher.'

'He was lucky,' said Len, who had come out from the kitchen to hear the news. 'Remember that other crash? About six years back, when that young girl drove off the road up on Sawyer's Ridge and same thing happened—car was out of sight down near the creek. She wasn't found for three days.'

'How long will Flynn be in hospital?' asked Cath.

'Another day or so I reckon. He needs somewhere to go after they let him out. They won't discharge him on his own.'

'He could stay at the pub,' said Len. 'Plenty of people there to look after him.'

'Rubbish,' said Cath. 'He'll need proper care.' She looked at Antonia. 'He could stay with you, couldn't he?'

'Me?' The idea filled her equally with excitement and dread. Could she have a man living in her house, sharing the bathroom, sleeping under the same roof, sitting in the lounge room, eating meals at the table? Even Flynn? Her house was her sanctuary. She forced her breathing to slow.

Flynn was different and he was in need of help. He was injured. What harm could he do injured?

'Why not? You've got a spare room. It would only be a few days—until he's able to go home.'

'I don't know. He might not want to stay with me.' A weak response and everyone knew it but they'd assume she was being coy about her feelings for him. That part of her wanted him to stay, wanted to care for him, nurture him, heal him. The other part was terrified.

'Of course he will.' Cath laughed.

Luckily a customer walked in and saved her from replying.

Snatching a few minutes before the lunchtime rush, Antonia tried calling Simon again. If she didn't need help returning the rental car she wouldn't bother talking to him at all, but she had no choice. This time he answered, sounding very subdued. She stated her request, expecting some sort of objection but instead he said, 'Sure. I'll come at three.'

'Thanks. I'll see you then.'

She disconnected. He could take her to the hospital as well and mind the twins while she visited Flynn.

***

The four-bed ward was a bloody noisy place. They'd wheeled him in from the Emergency Department that afternoon and he was looking forward to a decent sleep, aided by the painkillers they'd given him. One bed was empty but the two occupied ones more than covered the gap in noise production. The old bloke in the next bed, recovering from an operation, swore and complained nonstop until he went to sleep, and then he snored for Australia. The fellow opposite had both legs in plaster and must be related to half of Kurrajong, judging by the visitors who crowded round the bed and all talked at once.

Flynn closed his eyes and tried his best to ignore them. He was alive, he was safe and relatively intact. The ribs hurt like hell if he moved the wrong way or tried to take a deep breath, but it was the shoulder that was most painful. The doctor told him he could leave the day after next if he had someone to look after him at home.

'I'll be all right,' he said.

'Quite possibly, but I'm not going to take the risk. If I discharge you and something goes wrong, you'll be back here with your lawyer.'

He looked at Flynn over his black-rimmed glasses, daring him to disagree. Covering his arse. Fair enough, but where could he go? The pub? Would Donna take responsibility for him? She had her own family. Margie and Bernie? Maybe. They weren't that close. Same with Phil, not that he could stand staying at Phil's place. His wife doted on dogs and had about half a dozen yappy, smelly little fur balls running around underfoot.

Once he would have asked Simon and the co-op crew but not now. Antonia? Why would she say yes? She had enough to do with her job and the twins and she wasn't likely to offer. He couldn't ask.

Being single had a few problems. No man is an island, indeed. He didn't even have a change of clothes to go home in and was wearing a hospital-issue gown along with a crop of stubble.

Shooed off by a nurse, the current crowd of visitors left like a flock of chirping birds and he dozed for a while. When he opened his eyes, the curtain was drawn, shielding him from his snoring neighbour, but he had his own visitor sitting by the bed.

A dark-haired vision. He tried to raise a hand to touch her but grimaced. Wrong arm. Was she real? She'd been in his dreams, he wasn't sure she still wasn't.

She smiled that sweet tentative smile he loved so much and leaned forward, touching his hand gently with hers. 'How are you feeling?'

'Bit rough.' His voice wasn't working properly, his mouth couldn't form the words.

'Constable Pat said you're as tough as an old boot.'

He concentrated hard. Had to tell her something, something important. 'Sorry I didn't meet you. Didn't forget.'

'I know you didn't. We were fine. I hired a car and drove.'

'Did you? Well done.'

Her smile widened. 'I thought so.'

'So you managed? Okay?' Better now but his thoughts came in stuttery slow-motion bursts.

'Yes.'

'Pat said you raised the alarm. Thank you.'

'I knew you wouldn't forget. Simon said you left that protest because you had somewhere to go. I knew then that something had happened.'

'I don't remember exactly...' His eyelids felt like lead.

'Don't try. It doesn't matter.'

'They've got me pretty doped up.'

'You need sleep.' She stood up. 'I'll go.'

'Thanks for coming,' he murmured.

Soft lips brushed his cheek but it may have been a dream. A sweet dream suffused with a fragrance belonging only to her.

When he woke next, Antonia had gone—if she'd ever been there at all—and a short plump woman was placing a tray of food on the wheeled table. He was starving. A nurse came in and helped him spoon in pumpkin soup and roast chicken followed by canned fruit salad and custard.

'Did I have a visitor earlier?' he asked between mouthfuls.

'I don't know, I've only just come on duty.'

She wiped his mouth and moved the table away from the bed. She checked the levels on his drip, lowered the back of the bed and straightened the bedclothes with deft movements. 'Try to get some more sleep.'

This time, aided by drugs and exhaustion he did sleep, deeply and well.

The following day brought a physiotherapist to check his mobility and the range of movement in his shoulder and ankle. He was put through a barrage of tests, some of which he did easily and some he couldn't do at all.

'Basically you've torn the muscles and ligaments,' she said. 'It needs rest to heal, then later, exercises to build up the strength again. You can go to your own physio for that.'

'I don't have one.'

'I'll give you a list. In the meantime we'll keep that arm in a sling to prevent you trying to use it for a few days and we can fit a moon boot to keep your ankle stable. You'll be able to remove it for showering and sleeping but the more you wear it the better.'

'Okay. When can I go home?'

'As far as I'm concerned you can go now, but it's up to your doctor.'

'He said tomorrow.'

'Then it's tomorrow,' she said.

And he still had no one to collect him and nowhere to go.

Margie strode in after lunch carrying an unfamiliar overnight bag. After the exchange of greetings and asking how he was she said, 'I brought you some things. Pat let me into your house and I raided your closet. He had your keys by the way. They're in the bag. And your phone but it's broken.'

Keys hadn't entered his muddled head. His car was a write-off, he knew that. He'd been there when they cut it apart to get him out.

She produced some bathroom gear, underwear, a T-shirt and a pair of trackpants he hadn't worn for years. His shoes and socks had survived the ordeal and were in the drawer by his bed.

'Thanks, Margie. That's very kind. I was wondering how I'd go leaving hospital in this gown.'

'I didn't know what you wear to bed,' she said. Nothing was the answer to that. 'I couldn't find any pyjamas so I brought some of Bernie's.' She held up a red and blue striped outfit.

'Thank you.'

'When are they throwing you out?'

'Tomorrow with any luck.'

'Okay, I'll come and collect you. I'll get them to call me.'

'They don't want me to go home alone,' he said. 'But I reckon that's bullshit. I'll be all right.' If he didn't move around too much he'd manage. No need for a shower if he didn't have to go out for a day or two, or three ...

He could telephone. Someone would bring groceries in.

'You won't be going home alone so you can forget that,' she said.

'But I don't want to impose on anyone.'

'You won't be. That's what friends are for,' she said.

Margie was so matter-of-fact there was no point trying to argue with her. When she made a statement like that, the subject was over.

'I won't need to stay with you for very long,' he said.

'You won't be staying with us at all. Not that we'd mind, of course, but no, Antonia insisted you go there. She feels responsible for what happened.'

'She's not responsible! How could she be?' She insisted? Did Antonia insist on anything? This sounded like Margie-speak for Cath and sundry others having exerted pressure on her to agree.

'Of course she isn't, but you were going to pick her up so...' She smiled. 'Anyway. She'd come to get you herself but she has the twins to collect from school and she's at the cafe most of the day so I said I'd take you to her place.' He opened his mouth and drew breath but she held up her hand. 'No point, Flynn. It's all arranged. See you tomorrow. Take care.'

She gave him a brisk kiss on the cheek and left.

With the help of a nurse, Flynn took a shower and shaved then, clad in Bernie's roomy pyjamas, lay in bed contemplating the next few days with Antonia. And the twins. Mustn't forget those two. What day was it? He'd been driving to meet them on Tuesday, he'd been rescued on Wednesday so this must be Thursday. He'd be captive at Antonia's over the weekend.

How would they all cope? How would he endure the torture of living in the same house, seeing her every day, up close and very personal? And a new thought struck him. How would he shower? He needed assistance but it wouldn't be from Antonia and he couldn't go three days without washing. What a nightmare.

***

Flynn was sitting glumly on his bed with an overnight bag on the floor at his feet when Margie arrived. When Cath and Margie joined forces, backed up by Len, Bernie and heaven only knows who else, the deal was done. He was being looked after whether he liked it or not.

'Hello. How are you?'

'Not bad. I don't know why they're insisting I stay with someone. I'm perfectly capable of going home.' And they'd insisted he take the damn crutch with him too, even though he didn't need it.

'They don't want you to end up back in here five minutes after you get home. Anyway, you need a lift back to Flynn's Crossing regardless of where you end up.'

'Right. Sorry, I'm being rude. Thanks for coming.' He stood up but rested his hand on the bed for a moment, steadying himself before bending for the overnight bag. Maybe she hadn't noticed ... No such luck. Margie stepped forward and scooped it up.

'I can take it,' he said.

'No, I will,' she said. 'You just keep quiet and sit in the wheelchair.'

'Wheelchair?' Was there no end to this indignity?

'The orderly will be along in a minute. They're not taking any chances, Flynn. They want to see you safely off the premises so you can't sue them for negligence if you fall over in the corridor.'

Even though he grumbled and would never have admitted it, the walk would have been slow and awkward with one leg unwieldy in the moon boot, one arm strapped in place, that damn crutch under the other and a couple of busted ribs.

In the car, he sat beside her quietly as she drove. Apart from a grimace or two as he lowered himself onto the seat, he figured he'd got away with how painful and exhausting any movement was. He did allow her to fasten his seatbelt.

'I'm really very grateful to you for coming to get me, Margie. Thanks.'

'No worries, Flynn.'

'What's happened with the protest at the site?'

'Nothing. Pat turned up and they finished clearing the rubble away and that was it.'

'Waste of time protesting about it. Who were those ring-ins?'

'We don't know. They didn't stick around but they'll probably be back.'

'Great. Any word from Sean?'

'No.'

To his surprise, she swung down his road and into his driveway when they reached Flynn's Crossing. Had Antonia changed her mind about having him stay? Had she asserted herself and said no? He didn't dare ask. A small part of him was disappointed.

'Don't get your hopes up,' Margie said. 'We're just stopping in here to collect your mail and let you pick up a few more clothes.'

'Are you sure Antonia is happy to have me there?'

Margie opened her door before she answered.

'Yes, she is. Why wouldn't she be?'

'I thought you and Cath might have talked her into it. It's not like I know her as well as I know the rest of you.'

'We would have had you, of course, but Bernie's got some sort of stomach bug and you don't want that along with all this...' She waved her arm vaguely at his strapped-up arm. 'Tell me what you want me to get.'

So she wasn't even letting him out of the car. He gave up. 'A couple more T-shirts, long-sleeved ones should be in the drawer too, and the blue sweatshirt on the chair in the bedroom. More underwear and a pair of shorts from the shelf in the cupboard, thanks.'

'Back in a minute.'

***

Antonia opened the front door with a wildly beating heart. Margie had reported in at the cafe after she dropped Flynn off so he was here, safely ensconced in her house.

'Grumpy as all get out but he's in a fair bit of pain though he won't admit it, the stubborn idiot,' Margie said. 'What is it with these men? They're either completely helpless with the slightest thing—Bernie thinks he's at death's door at the moment—or they pretend everything's fine when it's clearly not.'

Antonia didn't know what to say to that. She hadn't had enough experience with men. Murdoch had never been sick and Dad rarely. Even if he was, first her mum and now Jax would care for him.

The door swung wide. Jacob and Sarah pushed in ahead of her, dumping their school bags on the floor and running into the living room in search of their guest.

'We're home, Flynn,' they yelled.

'Pick those bags up, please,' Antonia called. 'And be quiet, Flynn might be asleep.' Fat chance of that after their entrance.

Contrary to her own misgivings, the twins had none. At some stage Flynn had been received into their inner circle, which was good because it meant they were losing their fear of men but not so good because it meant she would be forced to pretend she was equally accepting of his proximity. Which she was on one level but on another, a deep-seated primal one, she was terrified. Not of him so much as herself—how she would cope sharing the same space, helping with personal things. How she would breathe and how she would stop the fantasy of Flynn touching her, kissing her.

'I'm lying down,' he called.

By the time Antonia reached the spare room, Jacob and Sarah were already there, leaning on the bed and asking about the support on his foot, the sling and the crutch propped against the bedside table.

'I don't need that thing,' Flynn said. 'I've got this moon boot.' He looked up at Antonia and smiled, sending her pulse into overdrive.

'A moon boot,' Jacob said. 'You're a spaceman.'

'Go and put your bags in your room, please,' she said.

'Can Flynn watch our afternoon TV program with us?'

'If he wants to. Bags. Now. And wash your hands and change your clothes too.'

The pair trailed out of the room.

She turned to Flynn. 'Sorry. They're very excited. How are you?' Amazingly, somehow, her voice sounded normal.

He sat up slowly, using his good arm as leverage but grimacing with pain. Should she offer assistance? She stepped forward hesitantly, arm outstretched, but he managed and swung his legs to the floor, the moon boot clunking on the mat.

'I've been better.' Those blue eyes had lost none of their laser power, holding her effortlessly. 'What about you? Are you okay with having me here? Don't let Margie and co railroad you. They're good at that.'

'I know they are. But it's fine. Really. You can see how keen the twins are.'

'What about you?'

'It's fine.' She turned away, took the crutch and handed it to him. 'Use this.'

'Thanks. I just need it to stand up. I reckon I could manage at home but no one else seems to think so.'

She shook her head. Margie was right. 'Don't be mad, of course you can't, you can barely move. I'm making afternoon tea for the twins. Would you like something?'

'I'll come to the kitchen. Would you just give me a hand with my shoe, please?'

A sandal lay on the floor. She knelt quickly and slipped it onto his good foot.

He ditched the crutch and hobbled after her to the kitchen where she set about making tea and pouring glasses of milk while he settled himself at the table. The twins came in all giggles and questions, which Flynn answered as best he could, smiling at their excited chatter. She placed a plate of oatmeal biscuits in front of them.

'Is your car all smashed?' asked Jacob.

'Yes.' Flynn caught Antonia's eye and grimaced.

'I'm so sorry,' she said.

'The accident wasn't your fault.'

'But you were coming to pick us up. I should have driven myself in the first place. I could have managed. I was...'

'Why did you crash?' Sarah asked through a mouthful of biscuit.

Flynn looked at Jacob and Sarah. 'A couple of roos came from nowhere. It happens all the time in the bush and sometimes they're impossible to miss, no matter how careful you are. Some of them are really big and fast. It was in a mountainous stretch with thick trees and lots of corners.'

'What happened to them?'

'I don't know but they weren't on the road later. Constable Pat said.'

'So the roos weren't hurt,' Sarah said. 'That's good.'

'Yes it is.'

'Will you get a new car?' asked Jacob.

'Yes. When I'm better.' And when the insurance company had paid up. He'd have to go down-market with his next car, given the state of his finances at the moment. No more brand new BMWs.

'Can we go in your new car?'

'You can be the first passengers.'

'What colour will it be?'

'Eat,' said Antonia. 'And give Flynn a chance to have some tea.' She picked up her own cup. 'Sorry. They won't stop unless you tell them to.'

Flynn smiled. 'I don't mind.' He winked at Sarah, who tried unsuccessfully to wink back.

'If you get tired you can go back to bed,' Antonia said.

'I will.' He speared her with a look, which sent hot blood to her face. 'Don't worry.'

'Can we watch our program now?' asked Sarah.

'All right.'

'Come with us, Flynn.'

'I will in a little while.'

'Okay.'

The silence was almost oppressive when they'd gone. Did he feel it too, or was it just her? Antonia poured more tea into her half-full cup. Flynn had barely touched his but he took a second biscuit.

'Did you make these?'

'Yes. I love cooking.'

'They're very good.'

'Len said I should take some to the cafe and see how they go.'

'You should.'

'One day I'd like to study cooking properly, but first I have to...' She'd been going to say finish high school. That would have to wait until next year the way things were shaping up at the moment. She'd had such plans when she arrived but time had slipped out of her grasp. Earning money, being a mother, running the house...

'Have to what?'

'Oh, you know, get settled, earn some more money.'

Why couldn't she simply tell him? He wouldn't think any the less of her. Why was she so nervous while he sat there relaxed and looking as comfortable as anyone could with broken bones and bruises? It was ridiculous. She was ridiculous. He was a man she knew, a man she trusted, a man who posed no threat to her at all. He needed her help and she was providing it. He'd been helping her when he crashed—she owed him.

So why couldn't she look him in the eye and why was it suddenly much hotter and where was the air in the room? She swigged down her tea.

He shifted in his chair and hissed through his teeth at a stab of pain. 'I must remember not to do that.' The action instantly refocused her.

'I feel so guilty,' she said. 'If you hadn't been coming to get us this would never have happened.' She clenched her fist and banged it lightly on the table. 'I was so stupid. There was no reason I couldn't drive myself.'

His warm hand closed over hers, sending a jolt of electricity up her arm. 'Hindsight is a wonderful thing,' he said. 'But we do what we think is right at the time. That's all we can ever do.'

'Sometimes it's completely wrong.'

She relaxed her clammy fingers but he didn't release his hold and she didn't pull away. She didn't dare look into his eyes; instead she studied the tanned skin on the back of his hand.

How different Flynn's situation would be if she'd gritted her teeth and refused his offer of a lift. How different her life would be if she'd walked away from Murdoch instead of with him. Or had walked into the clinic. Or had left Simon alone at school and not become a teenage pregnancy statistic in the first place.

'Are we talking about the same thing?' he asked softly.

She flung him a weak smile. 'I think so.' The past was gone, unchangeable. Focus on now. 'Chance plays a big part too. If you'd driven a fraction faster or slower, or left five minutes earlier or later, or taken the other route this wouldn't have happened.'

Flynn laughed. 'That's right. I might have been hit by a semi-trailer and killed.'

'No! That's not what I meant.'

'I know but as you say, it's chance, isn't it, what happens to us and how we make choices based on those things?'

Antonia sighed. 'Seems to be. Although sometimes good things come out of the bad.'

'Like?'

'If I hadn't become pregnant at seventeen I wouldn't have my beautiful children.'

'That's true, but if your parents hadn't been supportive you would have been bundled off to have a termination.'

She pressed her finger on a biscuit crumb and dropped it on her saucer.

He said in a voice tinged with doubt, 'They *were* supportive, weren't they? You said...'

'Yes, of course. It took a while but ... yes.' She stood abruptly and began clearing the table.

'I always have the feeling you're not telling me everything.' He was probing without actually asking outright. He just couldn't let it be.

'Of course I'm not. Why should I tell you everything about myself?'

'Because I'd like to know everything there is to know about you.'

She faced him then, anger rising. 'Why? Have you told me everything there is to know about you?'

'Would you like to know everything about me?' he countered.

'Not particularly.' She turned back to the sink and began washing the cups and plates. Liar. She wanted to know about Flynn, about the woman in Brisbane, what she meant to him.

'I'll tell you one thing if you tell me one thing.'

She bent her head and tried not to laugh. He was as bad as the twins. 'You've been mixing with five-year-olds too much.'

'Five-year-olds are very open.'

Antonia hesitated but maybe Flynn did deserve something. He'd probably find out soon enough, when the trial started. 'Now mine are,' she said. 'They weren't before. We lived with a man who wouldn't let them speak unless spoken to. He was very strict. They had to be quiet all the time. They were frightened of him and that's why they were afraid of you at first. They thought all men were like that.'

'He didn't hurt them did he?' Anger darkened his face.

'No, not physically.'

'Why did you stay? Did you love him?'

She pulled the plug and the water drained away with a gurgle and slurp. 'That's my one piece of information. Your turn.'

'Fair enough. I wish I could stand up.'

She swung around, indignant. 'That's it? That's not fair.'

Flynn laughed. 'No, that's not it. Come here so I can tell you.' He held out his hand and she took a step closer. 'Come on, I won't bite. I can barely do anything, let alone something classed as dangerous.'

She smiled. 'Makes a change, doesn't it?' But she came to stand next to him.

He grasped her hand and gently pulled her closer and down so she had to lean over.

'So what are you going to tell me?'

'I've wanted to kiss you since the first moment I saw you.' He paused, giving her time to react, to pull away but she didn't. Slowly the pressure on her fingers increased and she found herself bending towards his face, hypnotised by the thought of his lips on hers, incapable of resisting, stunned by his words. He stretched up to meet her, slipped his hand around her neck and planted his mouth firmly on hers.

Antonia froze.

Chapter 15

Flynn released her instantly.

'I'm sorry,' he murmured. 'I couldn't resist any longer.'

Her mouth was still inches from his. She didn't move, eyes locked on his, wide with surprise.

'Antonia?' he whispered.

She straightened abruptly and turned away, but not before he saw the rush of hot blood to her cheeks. At least she hadn't screamed or whacked him with the teapot.

'Actually, I'm not sorry at all,' he said, encouraged. 'Not about kissing you. I'll never be sorry about that. I'm only sorry I surprised you.'

Still she didn't turn but the hands clenched by her sides relaxed and she raised her palms to press against her cheeks. 'It's okay,' she said softly. 'I didn't mind. Not really.'

'I can do better than that,' he said. 'I will next time.'

'Next time?' As he'd hoped, her voice gained strength at the teasing tone.

'Oh yes, there'll definitely be a next time, but not until you say I can.'

She faced him then, a tentative smile on her lips. 'Okay. Deal.'

'Flynn,' yelled Jacob from the other room. 'Come and watch with us.'

'Coming,' he called. He hauled himself to his feet, wincing as his cracked rib sent a stabbing pain through his chest.

'Are you all right?' Instantly she was by his side, grasping his arm, steadying him.

'Yes, fine.'

'You are not,' she said. 'Don't be so macho.'

'I'm not macho, I'm a sensitive new age guy.'

That brought a laugh. 'Sure you are.' She guided him towards the door; hopping out of the way when, losing balance, he clumped his foot down. 'Watch where you put your moon boot, rocket man.'

Flynn grinned. 'Hear that, kids? I'm a rocket man, your mum said so.'

'Sit there.' Sarah pointed to the couch. She and Jacob were sprawled on big cushions on the floor.

He hobbled across and eased himself down. 'What are we watching?'

'Cartoons with Daffy Duck.'

'Looney Tunes. Great!' Better than expected, much better.

'Don't overdo it,' murmured Antonia.

'What? I love Looney Tunes, don't you? I haven't watched cartoons for years.'

'Watch with us, Mummy.'

'Yes, watch with us, Mummy,' said Flynn. He patted the couch next to him.

'Okay, just for a little while, then I have things to do.'

'They can wait,' said Flynn.

The twins beamed at him then turned their attention to Porky Pig. Antonia sat next to him, leaving a sizeable gap, but that was fine. She wasn't upset by the kiss and she hadn't vetoed more in the future. Not a bad state of affairs.

After dinner Flynn was co-opted into reading stories, which turned out to be surprisingly enjoyable, especially as his audience encouraged his attempts at character voices.

'I haven't read *Winnie the Pooh* since I was a kid,' he said when he rejoined Antonia in the kitchen, having discovered his fans were asleep. She wiped the sponge over the bench and dried her hands.

'We're working our way through the classics,' she said. 'They've missed out on so much. *Winnie The Pooh* is a favourite at the moment.'

'You're a good mother,' he said.

'I'm trying to be.'

'You're succeeding. Those kids are terrific.'

She smiled. 'Thanks. I told you they'd be okay after they got to know you.'

'Yes, you did.'

'School's making a big difference to them. They love it.'

'They're very bright. Sarah loves wordplay, doesn't she?'

'Yes, she always has. Some words made her laugh like crazy when she was tiny.' She firmed her mouth. 'But she didn't have much of a chance to ... never mind. Would you like coffee?'

'No thanks. I think I'll sit out on the verandah for a bit.'

'All right.'

She made no move to join him, instead heading for the doorway to the bedrooms.

'Will you come out too?' he asked.

She paused, half turned towards him. 'Maybe, in a bit.'

'Okay.' He pushed the screen door open to the backyard. Cool evening air washed over him. This would be much easier than he expected, this sharing a house with Antonia and the twins. Almost like being part of a family. A proper functioning family where love was the driving force, rather than a reluctant sense of obligation.

But he mustn't get used to it because this family wasn't his, they were Simon's and Antonia wasn't in the market for any sort of expanded family unit, she'd made that very clear. He'd have to make do with that. It didn't mean the occasional kiss was out of line, if she was willing.

***

Antonia closed the bathroom door and sank onto the edge of the bath. Flynn's kiss teased and tormented her. She'd wanted him to, but now he'd done it she wasn't sure what happened next. He'd left her in control of any follow up, confident she would give him the okay in the near future. She couldn't possibly summon the courage to suggest it. A kiss was one thing, but he could get entirely the wrong idea and assume she was willing to go further. To go to bed with him.

A shiver of apprehension made her gasp. The thought of fingers on her skin made her shudder. She couldn't.

She sprang to her feet and splashed cold water on her face.

If she sat on the verandah with him in the balmy evening air, would he expect the follow up? She couldn't hide away from him in her bedroom. It was way too early to go to bed and she usually sat outside after the twins were asleep, enjoying the few moments of peace and the quiet of the beautiful natural bushland over the back fence.

She stared at herself in the bathroom mirror, breathing slowly and deeply, willing her mind to calm, the tense muscles to relax. This fear was something she had to conquer or that monster would succeed in ruining her life.

She picked up her toothbrush and added toothpaste. The mindless routine soothed her as she scrubbed. Then she brushed her hair. By the time she'd finished, she was ready to face Flynn again.

He looked up as she joined him, his face shadowy in the dim light coming through the kitchen window. Insects banged incessantly against the glass but she'd placed the old cane outdoor chairs farther along, away from the light-seeking hordes.

'Lovely night,' he said.

'Yes. I often sit out here in the evening. I love the sounds of the bush at night.'

'Thank you for dinner.'

'You're welcome.'

'I'm sorry I'm no use as an assistant in the kitchen.'

'That's okay.'

'When I'm better I'll cook for you.'

'You don't need to do that, you've done enough for me already.'

'I'd like to,' he said. 'I'm good with a barbecue.'

She smiled. 'So is Dad.'

His voice coming at her through the half-light changed subtly. 'I never asked ... never had the chance ... but did everything go okay in Sydney?"

'Sydney? Oh! Yes, it did. Funny, I'd almost forgotten we'd been there. It seems ages ago.'

'It was only last Sunday. Will you need to go again?'

'Not for a while. Maybe at the end of the year or the beginning of next.'

Flynn fell silent. Was he about to ask the direct question? She couldn't blame him for being curious. Should she tell him? Was her secret safe with him? It wasn't a very good secret, considering how many people knew about the case and how many would have read about it at the time. Was she being unnecessarily close-lipped?

'I went to Sydney to speak to a lawyer,' she said.

'You don't have to tell me.'

'I know, but I think you'll find out anyway sooner or later; everyone will. As long as you won't spread it around ... if I tell you.'

His hand closed over hers and squeezed gently. 'Of course not. Was it to do with a divorce? The man who abused you?'

'Not a divorce. I'm not married. I was giving evidence to the prosecuting lawyer who is preparing a case against a man who...' She stopped, breathing hard, the words jammed in her throat. Flynn stayed quiet. She swallowed and began again. 'When I was seventeen I discovered I was pregnant. I told Simon and I told my best friend Bryony. Simon's parents were super religious and they would have ... I don't know what ... Dad was pretty strict with me back then and I was too scared to tell him. We three figured we could deal with it ourselves and no one would ever know. I was going to have an abortion after school and stay overnight at Bryony's. I went by myself but when I got there I had second thoughts. It was such a big thing to do and I was scared. There were people outside the clinic doing a prayer vigil and a man and a woman spoke to me. They were nice and they asked me to come home with them and think about it.'

She sucked in a deep breath. Flynn's hand was still warm on hers, comforting and strong.

'I thought they lived close by, but they drove for over an hour south out of Sydney, to a house in the bush. At first he was nice to me but when I said I wanted to go home he ... wouldn't let me. He locked me in along with Hannah, the other woman. He made her go with him to Sydney and locked her two daughters in the house so she'd do what he wanted while she was out.'

'My God,' hissed Flynn. 'Did anyone look for you? How long were you there?'

'Five years. I was listed as missing, of course, but the police thought I was a runaway and my friends never told anyone ... they didn't know.' She cleared her throat and continued. 'The twins were born there. Hannah is a midwife and she saved my life.'

'And he was violent?'

She nodded.

'The man's an unspeakable bloody monster. He's locked up, I hope?'

'Yes, they had enough evidence to hold him in custody until the trial. Flynn, I don't want to keep thinking about that part of my life. I came here to start fresh and so the twins could meet their real father and learn that men aren't all like that man.'

Flynn exhaled long and deep beside her. 'So Simon didn't know any of it until you arrived that day.'

'No. He thought I was dead. Most people did, except my dad. He never gave up.' She pulled her fingers gently from his and wiped her hand quickly across her eyes, blotting the tears that threatened to spill. 'I told Simon what happened, of course. He promised not to tell anyone and he hasn't.' She licked her lips. 'We made up the bit about Dad and Mum taking me away to have the babies and not telling Simon.'

'My God, it must have been an incredible shock when you appeared. He's been very supportive, hasn't he?' he said slowly. 'No wonder you were scared when you turned up here and no wonder those two beautiful little kids were petrified of me. I'm so sorry, Antonia.'

'It's not your fault, Flynn. You've been very kind.'

'But I didn't ... I...'

'It's okay,' she said. 'I don't want sympathy or special anything. I just want to live my life and raise my children the best way I can.'

'I understand.' He paused then added, 'And you want to do that alone.'

'I think I have to.' She rose and stood in front of him. 'I'm sorry. At the moment I can't...'

'It's okay. I understand, really I do. I just wish I was the man who could make it right for you.'

She leaned forward quickly and brushed her lips over his. 'So do I,' she whispered, before she straightened.

After she'd gone inside, Flynn sat a while longer, digesting the hideous information she'd imparted. How did she survive that experience and emerge the stronger for it? She was an amazing person and he was honoured to know she'd trusted him with such a deeply personal revelation. Honoured and humbled.

He understood, now, Simon's protectiveness of her and the children and why he exhibited such strong emotions towards her. He must feel unbelievably guilty for letting her go to that abortion clinic alone. Guilt similar to his own.

Flynn hauled himself to his feet and hobbled inside. Antonia appeared from the living room.

'Do you need help going to bed?'

'Only taking this boot off. I can't reach it or do it one-handed.'

'Okay. Let me know when you're ready.'

'Thanks. And thanks for telling me ... what you did.'

She ducked her head. 'Like I said, it'll be in the news soon enough.'

***

Antonia answered her phone the next morning. Saturday meant everyone was at home. Flynn, sitting on the back verandah watching the twins playing with a ball, heard it ring inside. He'd have to buy a new phone but it was strangely relaxing not having to answer it or talk to people.

Antonia appeared, phone in hand.

'It's Sean Baldessin,' she said.

Flynn raised his eyebrows. How did he know where he was? The answer came immediately. Margie, of course.

She'd have filled him in on all the details.

'How are you? I've only just heard the news or I would have rung earlier.'

Flynn gave him a brief summary, emphasising that he'd be back in business very soon.

'That's good to hear. Listen, I wanted to touch base with you about the development proposal. We've had a rethink, and after discussions with the National Parks people we've come to an agreement about that block I bought recently. There'll be a visitors' centre run by the government on land leased from us and we'll build a small lodge and bistro style restaurant for hikers and campers. Low-cost shared and dormitory-style accommodation and a camping ground. All environmentally friendly, of course. No one should object to that.'

'No, that sounds very reasonable.' Flynn hid his disappointment. Any development was good but a smallish low-key place wouldn't bring much in the way of employment and money for the area.

'It should take the heat off you. That protest can't have been pleasant.'

'It wasn't, but the main troublemakers weren't locals.'

'I see. Now, there is one other matter I wanted to run by you. I'm still very interested in opening a boutique-style resort. Not on a massive scale and not on the same block, but in the Flynn's Crossing area with reasonably close access to the new visitors' facility. When I was in town I had a look around, as you know, and I was very taken with an area of bushland on the eastern side of the town. It runs along the back of Randall's Road. Is that town land?'

'No, it's not.' Flynn stood up carefully and leaned on the verandah railing, excitement beginning to swamp the disappointment. Privately owned but a perfect site for a secluded bush retreat-style resort. Close enough to the National Park for it to be a drawcard. Even closer to the town centre than the other site.

'Who owns it, do you know?'

'It's a part of a large block owned by a local family who have been here for generations. They run a mix of cattle and crops but that section bordering the town has never been farmed. It's rocky and steep in places with a ridgeline right at the back of their property. Their entrance is on the highway, about twenty kilometres out of Walen.'

As he spoke, he envisaged the view from that ridge. Spectacular in all directions but particularly towards the mountains.

'So it's not part of Flynn's Crossing?'

'No, Walen is east of here. The town border is a fence line about five metres in and parallel to Randall's Road.' As he spoke, he looked across the yard at the land in question. Unused, not protected by any government legislation. Open for development.

'So who would I speak to about acquiring some of it?'

'Bruce Curtin is the owner but I can certainly approach him for you.'

'Do you think he'd be amenable?'

'Possibly. But what about access? It's an awkward area to get to, quite a distance from the highway. You'd have to build a road in for at least ten or fifteen kilometres.'

'Not if I could gain access from Randall's Road. It's a dead end, a cul-de-sac, isn't it? What if I could get hold of one of the properties, both would be better because of the narrow frontage, at the end of the street? Do you know who owns them?'

'Yes. I do.'

Baldessin laughed. 'Yes you know or yes you own them.'

'I own one of them.' He glanced towards the kitchen door hoping Antonia wasn't within earshot.

'Is the other owner-occupied?'

'Yes.'

'How do you feel about selling? You can name your price. Within reason.' The laughter had left his voice, this was business. 'How would the other owner feel, do you think?'

'You'd demolish them?' His breathing almost stalled as the realisation of what Baldessin had in mind sank in.

'Have to.'

'I have a tenant.' How much was he willing to pay? He squashed the thought immediately. He couldn't sell, wouldn't, no matter how much he might need the money.

'Move them.'

As simple as that. Was this how he himself came across to the townspeople in regard to the resort plans? To the co-op? Ruthless and calculating, profit at any cost?

He looked at the twins running and laughing on the grass as they tried to kick the ball. Antonia loved this house, they all loved their new home and it meant far more to them than a rented house usually did. For Antonia it was a symbol of her freedom and independence, the start of a new life. And over the fence were Kev and Bron, who'd told him they felt secure here as they worked to get back on a safer financial footing. He'd sold their house to them for less than what he paid for the place so they could own their first house. Not that anyone knew that detail.

'It's not so easy, Sean.'

'It can be. Money works wonders, Flynn, when administered in the right amounts. Think about it. Give me a call when you've decided.'

Antonia reappeared with a tea tray loaded with cold drinks and biscuits and set it down on the table.

'Bad news?'

He handed her the phone and manoeuvred himself onto a chair while he regrouped. 'No, not really. Baldessin is going to build a visitors' centre and a lodge on that block next to the co-op. Smaller than he originally planned so it won't generate as much employment as we'd hoped.'

'But it's a good result in the end, isn't it? He might have pulled out all together and no one would get anything.'

'That's true. And Simon and Aidan and co should be happy. It won't interfere with them at all. The road will be fixed up too, I imagine.'

'That would be good. It's an awful road, especially when it rains. Some of those potholes turn into lakes.' She sat down, smiling. He returned the smile, wishing the moment would last, that he could sit here in the shade with the woman he loved, her children happy and playing in the garden, basking in her care and attention. That he could ensure her happiness would last ... But he couldn't.'

How would she feel if she knew the offer Baldessin had made? He couldn't tell her, not yet. He was duty-bound to pass on the information to the council and the news was sure to leak out. He sighed and drank some of the fresh mango and orange juice she'd given him.

The twins ran across, red-faced and panting. 'Did you see us, Flynn?' They flopped down on the steps to slurp their drinks.

'I sure did. You were doing really well. When my ankle is better I'll play with you.'

'Why don't you have your sling on today?' asked Jacob.

'I didn't like wearing it. It's a nuisance,' he said.

'Aren't you supposed to?' asked Antonia.

'Probably.'

Sarah frowned. 'That's naughty. You should do what you're told.'

'The doctor said I didn't have to wear it for very long and my shoulder feels okay without it.'

She seemed happy with that explanation and he caught Antonia's eye and grimaced. She hid a laugh but her eyes sparkled. Flynn relaxed back in the chair. He could get very used to this, being part of a family, but he mustn't, he must remember that.

'Will you tell the co-op people about the revised plans?' Her voice broke into his reverie. 'Simon will be pleased.'

'Yes, of course. I'll have to tell the council first, so Aidan will know. In fact, can I use your phone, please? I need to make some calls. I'll make them short.'

'That's fine.'

Antonia stayed outside with the twins while Flynn hobbled inside to make his phone calls. Thank goodness all that nastiness about the resort had been resolved. It was a good solution; the best compromise because it meant no one lost out. Now life would settle down into the peaceful routine she'd so enjoyed. Simon would calm down and forget the harsh exchange of words with Flynn and they'd resume their friendship.

She had no regrets about telling Flynn about her past. It was time he knew. And the knowledge would make him all the more wary of trying to break down her resistance to starting a relationship, with all the tension that would produce. Now he might back right off.

She ran her tongue over her lower lip. Was that a good thing?

The more she saw of him the more attracted she was, despite all her reservations and intentions. Helping him meant touching him and touching him meant rapid changes in pulse and heart rate, not to mention body temperature. All uncomfortable and uncontrollable reactions and all, she was positive, clearly evident to such an experienced man as Flynn. The trouble was she had no experience with normal adult feelings of love and attraction. How could she tell which was which? As a teenager she'd had crushes on various people and had been wildly attracted to Simon, but was it love? Not the enduring kind, that was for sure, because now that compulsive, red-hot desire to be with him had faded to grey.

What did she feel for this man she'd so dreaded having in her house? Physical attraction, definitely. Love? The idea of losing herself so completely in a man was frightening.

The screen door banged open and she looked up, startled, cheeks immediately hot.

He grinned. 'What are you thinking about?'

'Uh ... I...' How did he do that to her? Those clear blue eyes penetrated her layers of defence and struck her heart as easily as blinking.

'About our next kiss?'

'No!'

'That's a pity.' He sighed and the grin faded. 'Margie's coming to pick me up in half an hour. I'll be at the pub for most of the day.'

'Is that a good idea?'

An expression that could have been annoyance flashed across his face. 'I'm fine. Don't worry about me.'

'Sorry.' She turned away to where the twins were examining something in the vegetable plot.

'Oh, Antonia.' His voice was soft. 'I love that you're concerned for me. I'm just not used to being looked after.'

She couldn't bring herself to face him. Light fingers stroked her hair, moved to caress her cheek.

'I promise I'll take it easy and if I get tired I'll ask someone to run me home. Here, I mean,' he amended swiftly. 'Not to my home.'

'You probably could manage on your own,' she said, risking a glance at his face. 'If you don't need the sling.'

'Would you rather I went home?' Was that disappointment?

'No, not at all. I don't think you should go but if you'd rather ... I mean, if you don't want to be looked after, if it's a nuisance, or annoying...'

'It's not. Please, can I stay?'

She nodded. 'As long as you need to.'

When he'd gone to get ready, Antonia started work in the vegetable garden. Weeds grew faster than anything else but she had a good crop of lettuces and more carrots, silverbeet and leeks than they could possibly eat. Maybe Josef would like some.

'Jakey,' she called. 'Would you run inside and get me a plastic bag, please? We'll pick some veggies for Josef.'

Sarah came across to help. 'I love our Mango House, Mummy. Can we stay here forever and ever?'

'I hope so, sweet pea. I don't see why not.'

'Goody. And can Flynn stay here with us?'

Antonia nearly dropped the weeding fork. They'd been here nearly six months and already he'd wormed his way into all their hearts. But were they as strongly lodged in his or was he enjoying the novelty of living with a family after so long alone?

'He has his own house,' she said weakly. 'And he's just our friend.'

But why was he so adamant about not deserving or wanting a family when it was clear how much he liked the children?

Perhaps it was time to ring Anita for another appointment.

Chapter 16

Five of the seven councillors were able to come to the short-notice meeting in the rarely used upstairs lounge at the pub. Judy and Phil were unavailable, unfortunately, but Flynn had given them the basic information and both were pleased with the outcome.

The councillors arranged the armchairs around a coffee table set with a platter of sandwiches and drinks for lunch. Flynn sat on the two-seater couch, his leg stretched uncomfortably before him. The climb up the stairs had been laborious and painful but he wasn't admitting that to anyone and assured all enquirers that he was fine.

'I hope the co-op is happy, Aidan, it's a good result, I think,' said Margie. She took a healthy bite from her sandwich.

'Seems so on the face of it. The thing is, can we trust Baldessin to do what he says he will?'

'I think we can,' Flynn said. 'He has another plan in mind. I didn't mention it on the phone because it's better if I tell you all together.' He looked around at the expectant faces. Aidan's had taken on a resigned expression but he shouldn't be upset by this new idea; it had nothing to do with his side of town. 'He asked me about Bruce Curtin's land. Not all of it, he's interested in the bit that backs onto Randall's Road.'

He outlined the new proposal and as he'd predicted it was met with surprised but overwhelmingly positive comments.

'Access is a problem, isn't it?' asked Bill. 'How much land will Bruce sell? I know he's in a bit of financial strife like everyone on the land, but he won't want to walk away completely. Curtin's have been there for five generations.'

'No question of that. Baldessin is only talking about the bushland along the ridge.'

'He'd get a wonderful view,' said Margie. 'But Bill's right. It's hard to get at.'

Flynn swallowed. Here was the cruncher. 'He asked about buying the two houses at the end of Randall's Road and cutting through from there.'

Silence greeted his remark. A few frowns appeared.

'You mean he wants to bulldoze Kev and Bron's place? And Antonia's?' asked Aidan.

'She's only renting,' said Margie. 'It'd be the owner's decision. What's Sean offering?'

'Whatever they want, within reason.' Flynn sat back and drew in his leg. His ankle and shoulder were both aching. The shoulder in particular was sending a throbbing pain through his arm. The painkiller he'd taken this morning was wearing off and he'd forgotten to bring more with him.

'He's keen.' Bill, munching steadily, took another sandwich.

'Kev would probably go for it,' said Aidan. 'He'd make a nice profit and could buy somewhere bigger. Those boys of theirs aren't getting any smaller.'

Margie nodded. 'I agree. He'd be mad not to take it.'

'Jean Tracey's heir would jump at it, I imagine,' said Walter. 'She's never going to sell it otherwise.'

'She has sold it.' All eyes focused on Flynn. 'I bought it a while back.'

'Well, in that case,' declared Margie with a broad smile, 'there's no problem. Sean has himself a deal.'

'Will Bruce sell?' asked Aidan. He raised an eyebrow at Flynn.

'I haven't approached him yet. I wanted to run it by you first. Keep you all up to date.'

'It's nothing to do with us whether Bruce sells his land or not, though, is it?'

'No, but Sean needs our permission to extend Randall's Road,' said Margie.

'And the owners of the land need to agree to sell,' said Walter. 'Will this resort benefit us much?'

'I think together with the other development we'll gain quite a bit,' said Flynn. 'There'll be jobs, of course, and more visitors in town. Everyone benefits from that.'

'Sounds good to me,' said Bill. 'When will you talk to Bruce?'

'Monday morning. I'll do it from the office. We need to keep this quiet until we've spoken to everyone who's involved.' Flynn made sure the councillors nodded their agreement. 'The last thing we want is gossip starting up about houses being knocked down before the residents know anything about it.'

'Absolutely,' said Margie. 'No one else knows so if word gets out we'll know where it came from.'

'How will Antonia feel about losing that house?' asked Aidan.

'She won't like it,' said Flynn. 'But I can find her somewhere else.' The words were ash in his mouth. He couldn't do it to her.

'Good luck with that, mate,' murmured Aidan. 'She loves that place.'

'It's just a house,' said Margie briskly. 'And she's only been there a few months.'

Flynn remained silent. It wasn't just a house to Antonia but how could he say this situation was different when he'd wanted the co-op to accept a development right next door? If he refused to sell, no one would let him forget the double standard and his reputation for straight dealing would be mud. If he sold, Antonia would be heartbroken and would never forgive him or trust him again. He couldn't bear that.

Aidan shook his head and said it for him. 'It's not just a house, it's her home.' Then he added, fixing his attention on Flynn. 'But I guess you find that hard to understand. And as you're the owner, she has no say.'

***

Antonia was surprised when Margie dropped Flynn off barely two hours after he'd left. She opened the screen door for him as he clambered up the steps, one hand clutching the railing, his face pale and drawn beneath the tan and dark shadows underlining his eyes.

'You're going straight to bed.' She took his arm and supported him inside to his bedroom. The fact that he didn't resist demonstrated how exhausted he was.

He sank onto the bed and lay back with a sigh of relief as Antonia removed the moon boot.

'Are you in pain?'

'A bit,' he murmured, eyes closed. 'I forgot to take the pills with me.'

She went to the kitchen for a glass of water. When she returned he hadn't moved but he opened his eyes when she picked up the tablets from the bedside table.

'Here, take these.'

He sat up slowly and did as he was told. 'Thanks. You were right. I should have listened to you and stayed here. I didn't realise how little energy I have.'

'You had a pretty bad experience and you're injured,' she said. 'Give yourself a chance to recover.'

He lay back. 'I need an afternoon nap like an old man.'

She smiled. 'Are you hungry?'

'No, I had something at the pub. Antonia?' She paused, about to leave.

'What?'

'I ... I'm ... there's something...' He exhaled fiercely. 'Sorry ... I can't...'

'Tell me later. Sleep.'

She lowered the blind and pulled the door closed behind her. Poor Flynn. She'd never seen him so vulnerable, so lacking in that confidence he wore like a second skin. Whatever it was he'd wanted to say to her would have to wait until his brain was working properly. He wasn't used to being dependent; that was his problem. She smiled. Who'd have thought she'd be the one in control where Flynn was concerned? Usually she was so out of control in his presence she didn't know what to do or say. This evened the odds quite a lot.

'Is Flynn home?' Jacob and Sarah crashed in through the back door to the kitchen.

'Yes, but he's very tired and his ankle and shoulder are hurting so he's having a sleep. You need to be quiet.'

'Okay. Can we take the vegetables to Josef?'

'By yourselves?'

They shared a look then nodded. 'Yes. We like Josef. And Smokey,' said Sarah.

'Can we have a cat?' asked Jacob. This had become a recurring theme since Josef's visit.

'Would you feed it?'

'Yes. Every day.'

'I suppose we could have a cat. I'll ask Cath if she knows anyone with kittens for sale.'

'We know someone,' Sarah announced. 'Annabel in first class has a cat and it had five kitties on Wednesday in the night.'

'Black and white ones,' said Jake. 'But she's not allowed to keep them so we can have one of those.'

'Did you tell her that?'

'No,' he said doubtfully.

'We said we might be allowed,' said Sarah and Jacob nodded vigorously.

'Is Annabel's sister Ellie in fifth class—in the recorder group? They both have red hair?'

'Yes.'

'Can we pleeeaaaase, Mummy?'

'All right. I'll ask Ellie on Monday. Now, take the vegetables to Josef but don't stay long.'

When they'd gone amid a barrage of excited chatter, Antonia leaned on the bench, tears pricking her eyelids. Her darlings were discovering the joys of childhood and growing brave and adventurous faster than she'd dared hope. Flynn's Crossing was a life saver, not only for them but for herself as well. This house was a home, their first home and just as it had been a haven for Jean Tracey and her family for many, many years, so it would be for her.

The mango tree had stopped producing fruit for the time being, but next year they'd be the first to taste the fresh crop. The garden was already showing the results of care and attention and every week brought a new surprise when a plant flowered or appeared from among the weeds. Her dad had said don't make big changes for a year so you can see what grows each season and he was right. One day she might be able to make an offer to the new owner...

A gust of wind rattled the screen door. Antonia shivered. She hadn't expected the temperature to drop as much so far north in the state but Cath had told her some years they had single-digit overnight temperatures and they were in a mountainous region. No frost though. Today had begun with mild sun, but since Flynn had returned clouds had accumulated and turned the sky a dull grey.

She'd become used to the sultry heat of summer, which had lingered on past its usual date, and enjoyed the balmy evenings after the years of cold, damp autumns and winters in the other house. Now, however, she went to don a sweatshirt and jeans.

By the time she'd changed, the wind had picked up. The trees over the back fence were whipping their top branches about in a frenzy. Antonia ran outside to collect the gardening implements and shut them away in the shed. She stacked the outdoor chairs in the laundry. Her car was safely in the carport away from the threat of a falling branch from the mango tree, but when she looked up uneasily at the giant in the front yard, several limbs looked like they might reach the house, or at least the verandah, if they decided to part company with the trunk.

'Knock knock. Anyone home?' Bron's voice at the back door.

'Hi, come in.'

'Hello. I just popped in to see how Flynn is. If you need any help don't hesitate to ask.'

'I won't, thanks Bron. Cuppa?'

'No thanks, love. I won't stay. How is he?'

'He's asleep at the moment. He's in more pain than he'll admit, I think, but generally he seems pretty good, considering.'

'Yeah it must have been a rough night stuck out there in the cold and the wet.'

'He went in to town to a council meeting this morning and said he'd be out all day, but Margie dropped him home just after lunch. It wore him out.'

'Silly bugger.'

Antonia grinned. 'He snapped at me when I told him to take it easy.'

Bron laughed. 'Men! What was the meeting about?'

'Baldessin is going ahead with the visitors' centre and a scaled back low-cost lodge and restaurant on that block. It sounds like a good compromise to me but Flynn was disappointed because it won't bring much in the way of jobs.'

'It'll bring some work, and that's a good thing.'

'That's what I said. And more hikers and people will visit so everyone benefits from that.'

'I'm surprised Baldessin's satisfied with just a hikers' lodge. It sounded to me like he wanted to go upmarket like his other places. Five-star resorts, they are.'

'Well, that's what Flynn told me after he got off the phone with him.'

'Okay, I'd better go, I've got something in the oven.' She opened the screen door. 'Storm coming. That wind's really picked up. I hope your mango tree doesn't drop any branches.'

'Does it do that often?'

'Sometimes. Took out the front fence once. That was a while back.'

Big fat drops of rain began soon after Bron had departed. Antonia ran next door to bring the twins home but they were already running along the path, with Josef watching from the front gate. She waved and he waved back then retreated inside.

'Josef said thank you,' said Sarah when they were safely inside.

'I'm glad he liked them. How about we do some cooking this afternoon?'

'Can we make chocolate cake? Flynn likes chocolate cake.'

'How do you know?'

'He liked it on our picnic.'

'Can we go on another picnic?'

'Yes, but hand washing first. Quietly,' she said before they rushed out the door.

* * *

When Flynn woke, a delicious smell permeated the house. Baking. Cake, at a guess. And it was raining. Hard. Wind howled around the eaves and the room was dim and shadowy. He sat up and pushed the quilt off his legs. Where had that come from? He smiled. Antonia, taking care of him.

He stretched cautiously, mindful of his ribs and shoulder, but his ankle wasn't as sore and he felt better overall. His watch said it was after four-thirty—he'd slept for nearly three hours.

After a slow visit to the bathroom and an awkward donning of warmer clothes, he ventured into the kitchen where three faces turned his way with big smiles. Two of the faces had chocolate icing smeared around their mouths and all were gathered round a partially iced cake.

'We're making chocolate cake,' announced Sarah.

'With icing,' added Jacob. 'It's very, very, very yummy.'

'That looks terrific. Did you help make it?'

'Yes, and now we're doing the icing.'

'Looks more like you're eating the icing.' He caught Antonia's eye and grinned.

Her cheeks reddened and she focused on the cake but she did laugh. 'It's very hands-on. How are you feeling?'

'Much better. Can I help?'

'You can use my spoon.' Sarah held it out.

'I'll get Flynn his own clean one.' Her fingers grazed his as she handed it over but she avoided eye contact. Skittish as a wild horse.

Flynn said, 'What do I do?'

'Spoon some icing on and Mummy will smooth it on the cake, but you have to put it where she tells you,' said Jacob.

'Okay. My right arm is sore and I'm not very good left-handed so I might make a mess.' He scooped up a big dollop of icing and dumped it more or less where Antonia pointed. 'When can we eat it?'

'After dinner. It's for dessert,' said Sarah.

He pulled a face. 'That's a long time to wait.'

The twins laughed. Antonia frowned and shook her head as she smoothed the icing over the cake. 'You're a bad influence.'

'I try,' he said and gave the twins a big stagey wink, which produced more giggles.

'We're getting a kitten,' said Sarah.

'Are you?'

'Josef has a cat and they've decided they'd really like one. Pets are good for kids,' Antonia said. 'We couldn't have one before, but now we're settled we can.'

'We had a dog when I was a kid,' said Flynn. 'He was a bitser.'

'What's a bitser?' asked Jacob.

'Bitser this and bitser that. No special breed.' Antonia smoothed the last of the icing and collected the dirty utensils.

'What was his name?' Sarah asked.

'Freddie.' A black and white scruffy little dog that his mother adored more than her kids, it seemed to him. 'He was old. My mother had him before she got married so by the time I was born he was already about six or seven. I remember him being a bit deaf and very snappy. He died when I was twelve.'

'Do you like cats better?'

'I don't know, I've never had a cat.'

'You can have one of the kittens from Annabel's cat too.'

'I don't think I want a kitten.'

'But you'd like it,' Sarah insisted.

'We haven't even asked Annabel ourselves,' said Antonia. 'They might have given the kittens away already.'

'They can't leave their mummy until they're six weeks old,' said Jacob. 'Annabel said.'

'Into the bathroom, you two, and wash your face and hands,' said Antonia. 'Then your cartoons will be on.'

Flynn sat down while she bustled about tidying up. Rain and wind pelted against the roof, the old timbers creaked and groaned under the onslaught, but the house was solid and had weathered many similar storms.

'It's getting wild out there,' she said.

'It won't last too long. These things blow over in a few hours usually.'

'I'm a bit worried about the mango tree. Some of those branches could hit the house.'

'We'd better get them trimmed.'

She nodded. 'I think so. It'd be terrible if one crashed into the verandah.'

'I'll see to it this coming week.' If he sold from under her the whole house would come crashing down. And the tree would be the first to go. That might cause a bit of public resistance.

'It's not urgent. You shouldn't go back to work until you're stronger.'

'I do need to replace my phone. I'll have to go to Kurrajong.'

'We could go on Monday morning when the twins are at school. I don't have to be back until after lunch for the recorder group.'

'It's a date. Thank you.'

'Is spaghetti all right for dinner?'

'Sounds good to me. Give me something to do, please.'

'No need.' She flashed him a smile and bent to pull a saucepan from the cupboard.

Flynn relaxed and watched her move purposefully about, collecting the ingredients for the sauce. She began chopping onion and garlic with deft strokes of the knife then dumped the onion into the pan to brown.

She turned to face him, wooden stirring spoon in hand. 'Why do you feel you're not worthy of having a family? You'd be a great father.'

The suddenness of the question took him by surprise.

'I told you my secret...' she said.

'Yes, and I'm honoured you felt you could.'

'So?'

She'd been brave, so could he.

'I was a pretty out-of-control kid from about eleven or twelve on. Don't ask why, I'm sure there are plenty of reasons to do with my parents, but basically I was a little ratbag. When I was thirteen I got in with a group of older boys who were really bad—burglary, muggings, drugs, you name it. I know two of them have been in prison for most of their adult lives and one of them died of a drug overdose at eighteen.'

'But you came good,' she said softly.

'Only after...' He stopped, the memories flooding in. The exhilaration that turned to fear, then shock and outright panic. The screech of brakes, the frantic swearing from the driver, the scream and the terrible thud...

'Flynn?'

He swallowed, continued. 'We stole a car. At least they did, I went along for the ride, thinking I was something else—a big tough gangster instead of an unhappy, ultimately stupid fourteen-year-old. I was in the back seat. There were four of us. Jacko was driving. He had a licence but he was crazy reckless and the others kept egging him on to go faster. There was booze too, but weirdly enough I didn't drink because I didn't like the taste. Anyway, at first it was fun, a lark, a bit of excitement on a boring Thursday night but we were roaring down a suburban street and suddenly a woman came from nowhere, crossing the road.'

Antonia gasped but didn't interrupt.

'The car hit her going full speed. Jacko braked but it was way too late. She died instantly, they said, and so did her baby. She was six months pregnant and she'd just gone across to visit a neighbour—to return a book.'

'Oh my God.' It came as a whisper.

'Jacko died later in hospital. No seatbelt and he was crushed against the steering wheel and cracked his head open on the windscreen. The rest of us weren't badly hurt.'

The onions sizzled vigorously, the mouth-watering smell permeating the kitchen. Antonia turned abruptly to stir them.

'I vowed there and then that I would never have my own family because I didn't deserve to have what that poor woman's husband had lost in one stupid, senseless act.'

'What happened to you?'

'I was a minor, we all were. I wasn't deemed accountable for the death but I was involved in the car theft. I was given counselling and community service and a good-behaviour bond. Which I kept. As far as the law is concerned I've paid my debt, but as far as my conscience is concerned I never will.'

Antonia dumped mincemeat into the frying onion and garlic. She stirred without saying a word. What was she thinking?

'Do you know what happened to the woman's husband?'

'Actually, yes I do. I did a search and found him through Facebook a few years ago but I didn't contact him. I'd never do that.'

'And?'

'He's married with two children. He lives in Grafton now.'

'So he's happy. That's good to know, isn't it?'

He nodded. He had been pleased when he saw the man's page, glad he'd managed to overcome the tragedy and find happiness again.

She turned the heat down and faced him. 'Nothing you do or say will bring her back, Flynn, you know that. Why deny yourself something that would make you happy? You were a kid; no one holds you responsible for the accident, because that's what it was. Jacko died and he paid the ultimate price for what essentially was his fault. The others have learned nothing, apparently, but you have. You turned your life around and I imagine if that woman's husband knew, he'd be pleased she didn't lose her life in vain. I can't think he'd want you to pay for the rest of your life.'

'I don't know.' He shook his head, lips clamped together. What she said made sense and others had told him that at the time; and afterwards, police and counsellors who urged him to learn, to change his life for the better, take a new path. He had, but the black hole of remorse remained.

'Neither do I but that's what I think.'

'Do you want your abductor to pay for the rest of his life?'

Her expression changed instantly, blank but at the same time a fierceness blazed from her eyes as she spoke.

'Yes, but he set out deliberately to do what he did and he was an adult. He'd been doing it for a long time and he allowed at least three girls and their babies to die in order to protect himself from discovery. It's not the same thing at all. None of you went out that night looking for someone to run down and kill. You were all brainless, mad kids acting in a criminally reckless manner but you weren't psychopaths.'

'I suppose not.'

'No suppose about it,' she said viciously. 'Believe me, I know. Murdoch will never feel the remorse you feel. He's incapable of empathy in any way, shape or form.' She snatched up a tin of tomatoes and ripped the ring-pull top off before dumping the contents in the saucepan.

'Are you saying I should get over myself? That I'm being self-indulgent?' he said stiffly. How could she be so callous? He'd thought she'd be sympathetic, understanding.

Antonia stopped stirring, hesitated. She added a couple of dollops of tomato paste, water and a sprinkle of herbs to the mix. When she spoke, she was calmer. 'I think you should live your life and be happy. You can't allow events in the past to ruin your whole life. All you can do is try to live a better life for yourself and other people. Flynn, you're already doing part of that here in town. It's the part for yourself...' Her burst of candour fizzled. She turned back to the stove and began poking and stirring at the fragrant sauce. 'Sorry,' she muttered. 'I don't know anything about it, really.'

Flynn pushed himself to his feet. 'No, and I don't know how to stop feeling the way I do.'

'Maybe you need to let yourself...'

'What?'

'Get close to someone...'

A loud crash and thud came from outside and a moment later the power went off.

'Mummy, the TV stopped,' yelled Sarah.

'It's okay, it's just the storm,' she called back. 'Press the off button.'

Flynn was already out the back door, peering into the gloom towards the street. Antonia followed him to the corner of the verandah, her hair whipping about in the wind.

'Was it the mango tree?'

'I don't think so. It looks okay to me and it's not near the powerlines. I think it was at the back but there aren't any wires there either.'

She ran back to the steps into the yard.

'It's the shed. A branch from one of those gums landed on it,' she called. Leaves and smaller branches almost covered the shed but it was still standing. 'It's too wet and nasty to check now.'

'The powerlines must have come down somewhere else.' Flynn walked carefully around to the front of the house, mindful of the slick boards underfoot and the wind tugging at his clothes. No lights came from across the road or next door, although it wasn't really dark enough to need them.

'Oh well, at least we can eat chocolate cake for dinner,' Antonia said behind him. 'It'll be back on soon, probably.' She opened the front door and slipped inside, shivering, then closed it firmly behind them both.

Flynn wiped drops of water from his face and hair. 'It could take a while for them to find the fault. One of the benefits of living in the country. Do you have candles? A torch?'

'No, I don't think so.'

'Okay, well, we could go to my house. I have solar power with battery storage and a backup generator for emergencies. I also have a stack of candles and a gas stove so we can finish cooking dinner. And I wouldn't mind collecting some warmer clothes.'

'All right. I'll get organised.' She was already heading for the kitchen, calling the twins as she went.

'Make sure you turn the stove off in case the power comes back on.'

***

Antonia had never been to Flynn's house. It was on the far side of town in a more recently developed area. The houses were newer and more expensively designed and built, but surprisingly his house was an old-style wooden-framed bungalow similar in design to her own. The difference was Flynn's sat on a rise with a view flowing away to the far hills and much more money had been spent on the upkeep and interior.

The contrast with the Mango House was even sharper inside. Polished wood floors, white painted walls with a few landscapes and presumably his own photos hung in strategic places, an open living area which led onto a lovely garden space. At the moment, in the wind and rain, it was grey and sodden, but when the sun was shining it would be beautiful—a little corner of rainforest with ferns and flowering vines.

Antonia insisted on taking her and the children's shoes off and leaving them in the entrance foyer in spite of Flynn telling them not to worry.

'It's so clean,' she said. 'We don't want to a make a mess in your house.' So clean and uncluttered it was like a showroom.

'Here's the kitchen,' said Flynn. 'I hope everything's there that you'll need. I'm not much of a cook but over the years I've collected some bits and pieces.'

Granite benchtops, polished wood cupboards, all clean and tidy and functional. Antonia put the two bags containing the spaghetti sauce and chocolate cake on the bench, then set the saucepan of sauce on the stove to continue cooking. Flynn flicked on a few lights and pulled the curtains while the twins stood awkwardly together, looking around at the unfamiliar house.

'Are you warm enough?' asked Flynn.

They nodded and edged closer together.

'Will we see if your cartoons are still on?'

'Yes, please.' All their bravado had disappeared in the face of this new situation. Despite their liking for Flynn, being in his house was disturbing.

'You can sit down,' Antonia said and they walked across and perched on the edge of the black leather couch facing the large-screen TV. All the houses they'd lived in had been messy, family homes, crammed with the junk of daily life. Even their captor's house had the feel of family, an atmosphere the women had struggled to maintain for the sake of the children despite the lack of freedom.

This house was like a display home. Beautifully furnished but with an unlived-in feel to it.

'Have some cushions.' Flynn took a couple of red cushions from another chair and tossed them over. Jacob grabbed one while Sarah scrambled for the other. 'Have some more,' he said, and threw another two, which elicited giggles from the recipients and a failed attempt at retaliation from Jacob.

'No pillow fighting,' Antonia said sternly. She knew exactly where this would end up.

'Flynn started it,' said Sarah.

'And I'm stopping it,' she said, hands on hips. They settled back to watch the remainder of the program surrounded by red cushions.

Flynn joined her at the bench, which divided the kitchen from the living area. 'There should be some wine in that cupboard.' He pointed. 'And glasses up there.'

Antonia poured two glasses. 'This is a lovely house. It's a similar floor plan to my place.'

'I like it. It's the original old weatherboard structure but I pretty much had the whole of the inside redesigned and modernised. It's solar passive too. I got most of those ideas from Margie. It's very cost efficient.'

'It's beautiful.'

'It needs more living in. I'm not home much.'

'You won't be going far without a car,' Antonia said.

Flynn groaned. 'I'd almost forgotten about that. I haven't even called the insurance company.'

'You don't have a phone and you're injured. Give yourself a break.' She smiled.

'I know, but I need to get onto both things quickly so I can get back to work. My insurance will cover a rental car for a while. In fact, I should call them now.' He slid off the stool. 'I have all the details here in my study. Make yourselves at home.'

'Okay.'

While Flynn was busy doing that Antonia explored the kitchen. His stove was brilliant. She could do wonders in a kitchen like this but it was clear he rarely cooked because the utensils were so neatly stacked in the cupboards. There was a dinner setting for eight, which she would swear hadn't been used, and a matching set of blue-patterned mugs, plates and bowls, which would be for daily use. Six all-purpose tumblers had never been bought for their contents of jam or vegemite. Nothing was chipped and everything was part of a set.

He must think her mishmash of crockery and cutlery completely hopeless and wonder why on earth she was so passionate about the run-down old house. She pulled out a large saucepan and filled it with water for the pasta. The sauce was simmering nicely but would need at least half an hour.

Flynn's voice came from another room, too far to hear what he was saying.

'I need to do a wee,' said Sarah from the couch.

'Let's find the toilet. It should be down this hallway.'

Flynn was in the first room they passed, sitting at an office desk with a computer and papers spread before him. The door was open and he smiled and rolled his eyes. 'I'm on hold,' he said.

'Where's the loo?'

'Second on the right.'

The bathroom and toilet were in separate rooms just like at home, but his bathroom was ultra-modern with a walk-in shower and a spa bath and looked like an extension to the original building or an adaptation of a smaller bedroom. Why not, if you had the money and the space? He probably had an ensuite in the main bedroom too. Antonia sighed as she waited for Sarah.

The more she saw of the house, the more she realised just how far he'd lowered his standards to stay in the Mango House. He'd jumped at the chance to return to this comfort and warmth. She'd hardly been aware of the storm since they'd arrived, whereas at home every gust of wind and slash of rain rocked the house and threatened to tear it apart.

He'd probably want to stay here now he was back and she couldn't blame him at all. Staying with her was slumming for him. They'd have dinner, she'd borrow some candles and she'd take the twins home.

Chapter 17

Flynn concluded his conversation about the insurance but he didn't immediately rejoin Antonia; instead he checked email and dashed off a few replies before his ribs and shoulder began to ache and he realised he'd been sitting in the office for half an hour.

'Sorry,' he said as he went back through the living room. The twins had turned off the television and were reading the books they'd brought with them, still snuggled amid the red cushions. 'I caught up with some emails.'

'Did you get the insurance sorted?'

'Yes, but it'll take a while for the money to come through. I can rent a car in the interim.'

'That's good except you can't drive it.'

'Hmm. Maybe I...'

'You can't,' she said firmly. 'You'll have another smash.'

'I can't keep asking people to drive me all over the place.'

'No one would mind.'

'I would.'

Antonia lifted a strand of pasta from the pot and tested it. 'This is ready. Go and sit down. Twins, dinner's ready.'

His rarely used dining table was set with a bowl of salad, bread, cutlery and plates. The wine bottle and glasses of water for the children were already in place. Flynn took his half-full glass from the bench and sat down, amazed at the difference a woman made in his house. This woman. She'd only been here about an hour and already the place felt like a home. The fragrance of food cooking, the chatter of children's voices, the pile of shoes in the foyer, four places at the table.

Was she right about accepting the past as over? That he was as entitled to have his own family as anyone else? If he accepted that, and right now it was a very appealing argument, the problem remained that the family he wanted was this one. Antonia and Sarah and Jacob, living in his house, bringing warmth and colour and love to his world. But Antonia didn't love him the way he was beginning to love her, hopelessly and forever.

The twins climbed onto the high-backed wooden chairs opposite and slurped down water. Antonia placed a bowl of steaming sauce and another of pasta on the table. She served the twins, Flynn and herself and fussed about with salad and parmesan before settling to eat.

Flynn raised his glass. 'To the blackout.'

She snorted with laughter and clinked her glass against his and the twins.

'And chocolate cake,' added Sarah.

'Absolutely. Here's to chocolate cake.'

Silence descended, broken only by munching and the clink of cutlery.

'This is very good!' said Flynn.

'Thanks.'

'I'd like to go to Italy one day.'

'It'd be lovely but I can't see myself going anywhere for a while.'

'There are lots of places to visit in Australia,' he said. 'Plenty the twins would enjoy.'

'I know. I suppose one day I could drive us somewhere for a holiday.' She meant herself and the twins. He meant with him included. Family holidays.

Was he mad? Just because she said he deserved to be happy didn't mean she wanted to be involved in providing the happiness. After what she'd endured, she deserved to live by her own rules. Just like the promise of another kiss, the first move would have to come from her.

After dinner and cake, Antonia began packing up her carry bags and stacking the dishwasher.

'We should go soon.'

'It's still nasty out there. Why don't we stay here tonight?' Flynn asked as casually as possible. 'I have a couple of spare rooms.'

Antonia looked up from her packing. 'All of us?'

'Yes, of course. Why not?' He couldn't hide the surprise.

'I thought you might want to stay here alone.'

'You've already pointed out I can't manage by myself yet. And the power might not be back on. If we stay here we can check it out tomorrow after breakfast. We can cook here.' He smiled. 'And have hot tea and coffee.'

A shadow swept over her face. 'I should take the twins home.'

'Why?'

'It's getting late.'

'Okay, if you insist. I'll get the candles and a torch.' He turned for the laundry but her voice stopped him.

'Do you want to come with us?' She sounded doubtful, but was it more that she would rather he stayed here? Had he outworn his welcome? 'If you don't mind. I'm sorry, I thought...' He grimaced. She'd said he could stay till Sunday. He wanted to be with her, where didn't matter.

'No, it's fine. It's just ... I thought ... nothing.' She made no move to pick up the carry bags but looked at the twins who were half asleep, ensconced on the couch again with the red cushions. 'Do you have room for us?'

'I have two spare rooms. There's a queen-sized bed in one and a double in the other. Take your pick.'

She hesitated, pondering her decision. Made up her mind. 'They'd be happier if we share the queen. Thank you.'

Fortunately, he always had the bed made up so it was easy to provide towels and another pillow. After being washed and the outer layer of clothing removed, the twins happily climbed into the big bed. He left Antonia tucking them in and went back to the living room with a small glow of happiness in the region of his heart. This is what being part of a family would feel like. He began making tea, slowly and carefully with his limited strength and movement.

But why would she think he wanted to stay here on his own and send her back to a dark, cold house? Was it a residual lack of self-esteem, a result of being treated as an object by that monster of a man? When she reappeared, he said, 'Antonia, I'm really happy to be staying with you and I want to thank you again for taking me in. I only suggested we stay here tonight because of the power situation, nothing else.'

She joined him in the kitchen and took over the tea making, standing beside him intent on the task, her hair a curtain obscuring her cheek until she tucked the strands behind her ear. 'Are you sure? This house...' She waved an arm vaguely, '...it's so much more comfortable than mine. The furniture, the kitchen, the bathroom, the fittings, everything is so much better...'

He plunged. 'Not everything.'

She laughed softly. 'Oh, yeah? Like what?'

'You. This house doesn't have you in it.' His voice caught on the truth of the words.

The exposed cheek turned a deep pink. The tea was ready but she stayed facing the bench, head bowed. He risked moving closer, stroking the silky length of hair from her shoulder, gently turning her face to his, knowing at any moment she might shy away.

'You are the most extraordinary woman I've ever met. Every time I see you I'm amazed at how beautiful you are, how strong you are and how brilliantly you look after the twins. I want to be near you, Antonia. Always. Forever.'

'Flynn,' she whispered. He placed gentle fingers against her soft lips. Her eyes were soft, moist with unshed tears as she gazed at him, but she was trembling. Was it fear?

'I know,' he said. 'I know you don't want a man in your life messing it up, getting in your way. I know that but I can't help the way I feel about you and I just had to tell you.'

Antonia closed her eyes against the passion in Flynn's voice and the way those blue eyes penetrated to her soul. She'd longed to hear him say those words, longed to feel him close beside her, be in his arms ... When he was missing she'd been distraught with worry, wanted to be special to him. But it was all in theory, a kind of fantasy. Now, in the searing moment of reality, she had no idea what to do with the overwhelming declaration he gave her and the emotions powering through her body. Her breath came in jerky spasms and she teetered on the edge of an abyss so vast and terrifying one small movement might topple her over the edge. If she succumbed to her desire, could she follow through with what he would understandably expect? No, not yet...

She leaned against the solid bulk of the bench, gripping with fingers tense as claws, legs weak and shaking.

Flynn moved away. 'Antonia, it's okay. You don't need to say anything.'

He poured tea. She heard the liquid gurgling into the mugs and the clink of china, and slowly opened her eyes. Flynn was two paces away holding his mug, leaning on the bench and staring into the living room, his expression incomprehensible.

Her hand shook as she picked up her tea but the hot drink soothed her. Was he angry?

'Wind's dying down,' he said after a while. He walked across and opened the curtains onto the back garden and peered out. 'Rain's still coming down pretty hard.'

'I'm sorry,' she said. 'I'm ... you surprised me. I'm not ready...'

'I know. Don't worry about it. It's my problem, not yours.'

What was he thinking? In her present jangled state she couldn't tell, but a man like Flynn wouldn't be used to the reaction she'd given him to his declaration. No man would be happy if the woman he'd opened his heart to couldn't hide her fear at his words. And she'd told him he should try to get close to someone. What kind of heartless creature did that make her?

***

The Mango House and tree had escaped the storm unscathed and the morning sun shone, making diamonds sparkle from the newly washed leaves and blades of grass. Josef's riotous display of flowers was slightly bent and some had fallen flat but otherwise nothing was damaged. The power was back on when the twins ran inside to check. 'The lights are working,' yelled Jacob.

'Good.' Antonia lugged the carry bags through to the kitchen and began unpacking while Flynn took his bag of extra clothes to his room.

The embarrassing exchange may as well not have happened for all the signs he showed this morning. He was his usual self with her and the twins but she couldn't help the nagging feeling that something had shifted in their basic relationship. What had been an easy friendship now had the undercurrent of unfinished emotions, of words still to be spoken and feelings not fully explored. Or was this all on her side alone?

He'd be going home soon so she need only survive the next few days. They'd go to Kurrajong for a new phone in the morning and afterwards she could drop him at his office. There were plenty of people who would drive him home if necessary.

On Tuesday she'd be at work and so would he. After that ... life would return to normal. If she could forget what he'd said and the way he'd looked at her as he said it.

After lunch, Kev and two of his boys came over from next door to remove the fallen branch from the garden shed. Antonia didn't even realise they were there until a chainsaw burst into life. The twins came rushing out to see but sat out of harm's way on the verandah steps to watch, as she instructed.

'G'day, love.' Kev cut the saw as she approached. 'Storm made a bit of a mess, thought we'd get rid of it for you.'

'Thanks very much. I hadn't even begun to think how I'd do that.'

'You're lucky, it's only dented the roof a bit. The main part didn't reach the fence.'

Antonia looked up at the tall gums along the back of the properties. 'They're beautiful trees.'

'Yeah, but treacherous in a storm. And there's always the fire danger in summer. If they put that road through it'll make a bit of a break.'

'What road?'

'They reckon Baldessin is putting his fancy resort over the back there on Bruce Curtin's land. Along the ridge. The only decent access is from this side so they'd have to come in from the outskirts of town out past the motel somewhere. It's long way though.'

'I hadn't heard about that.'

'Better ask Flynn,' he said with a little smile. He started the chainsaw and Antonia retreated to the house.

Was that what his meeting had been about? Why hadn't he mentioned the second part of his news when Baldessin had phoned? Bron was right, that man wasn't satisfied with a low-budget hostel at all. But it was a much better site because it didn't physically affect anyone in town but was still close enough for the local businesses to reap the benefits of the extra cashed-up visitors. Flynn must be pleased.

He was in the kitchen watching through the screen door. 'Nice of Kev,' he said.

'Yes, they're terrific neighbours. Why didn't you tell me about Baldessin's new plans for the land over the back?'

His face darkened with annoyance. 'Who told you that?'

'Kev.' She couldn't resist a smirk. 'Is it a secret? You told me yourself everyone knows everything about everything in Flynn's Crossing.'

He exhaled fiercely. 'Nothing's been decided. I haven't even talked to Bruce yet. He owns the land. What else did Kev say?' He fired the last question at her with surprising vehemence.

'Nothing much. Just that access is only available on this side of the ridge and they'd have to cut in from the road. Near the motel he thought, but that's a long way, isn't it?'

'Nothing's been decided. Sorry, can I make some calls?'

'Of course.'

Antonia went to sit with the twins and watch the workers. Her query had upset Flynn no end. The council must have tried to keep the news quiet but surely they all knew how hopeless that was in this place. She chuckled softly. Heads would roll.

***

Flynn didn't come back to the house until after five on Monday. He'd bought a new phone in Kurrajong and Antonia had dropped him at his office just after eleven. He hadn't mentioned the resort but he'd been preoccupied and a bit snappy since he'd made those calls the previous day. Clearly something had gone awry with the council machinations. Why it should be such a big secret she didn't know. Flynn's Crossing wouldn't be involved much at all as far as she and Kev could tell. They'd had another discussion about it when she helped load the sawn-up branches into his trailer.

'I suppose if no one's asked Bruce yet they don't want rumours going round,' he said.

'Yes, it's a bit rude if everyone knows except him.'

'He'd find out pretty quick, his daughter lives here. Mary. She runs that craft shop.' He caught her eye and she laughed.

Flynn knocked as he opened the front door. 'Hello, anyone home?'

'We are,' shouted Jacob from the living room. 'And we're getting a kitten.'

'In the kitchen,' called Antonia.

Flynn spent a few minutes listening to the excited chatter about the kitten then went to the kitchen and slumped onto a chair at the table. His ribs ached and his ankle was throbbing, although his shoulder was much better.

'I should be able to manage at home tomorrow,' he said. 'My arm is feeling pretty good.'

'How will you get around?'

'Brandon will pick me up.'

'Are you sure? You can stay longer if you want.'

'No, no. I've been in your way long enough.'

'Okay.' She nodded and turned back to whatever she was doing at the sink.

Her calm acceptance of his proposal was disappointing but the longer he stayed here the more uncomfortable it would be for both of them. Him with his unrequited love and his searing passion, her with her friendship and desire for a life unencumbered with male complications and demands.

'Did you talk to Bruce Curtin?' she asked, still with her back turned.

Had she heard? She'd been at the cafe today with plenty of wagging tongues coming in and out all day. He may as well tell her the truth.

'Yes and he's interested in negotiating.'

'That's good then.' She turned. 'Isn't it?'

'So far.'

'There shouldn't be anyone protesting about that site.'

'Hope not but you never know.' He stood up. 'I'll go and lie down for a bit.'

'Dinner will be a while yet.'

Coward. He'd spoken to Sean, and after discussing Bruce's terms he'd immediately got onto the subject of access. Sean had done his homework and discovered what Flynn already knew, that cutting in from anywhere along the road into Flynn's Crossing would mean building a bridge over a ravine. The only feasible way in was from either Randall's Road, which was shortest, or farther north on the Kurrajong side. That land belonged to the commune and there was no way in the world they would allow it.

The amount offered for Kev's and Antonia's properties was generous but much less than the other option of building a twenty-five kilometre road through thick bush and rough terrain, with a bridge. Flynn sounded out the possibility of only buying one block—Kev's.

'The frontage is wider than the other one,' he said.

'Yes, but I wanted a proper entrance with gates.'

'Couldn't you do that on the one block? It's a good size.'

'I'd rather not have a house sitting right next door to the entrance. It's not really in keeping with the exclusive image.'

Flynn almost growled at the slur on the Mango House. 'This is a residential street in the town you're talking about,' he said. 'It's full of houses.'

'Sorry, mate. I know it's your property and the residents might not want to move but I can offer a bit more if it will help convince you to sell.'

And he had offered quite a bit more. Flynn said he'd get back to him about it and hung up. With that money he could slice a massive chunk off his mortgage, which had expanded frighteningly due to the Mango House. And cover the gap the insurance would leave when replacing his car. He'd be able to buy something close to new.

If anyone else was his tenant he wouldn't hesitate. But if anyone else was living there he wouldn't be involved other than applying pressure for the owner to sell. He was only the owner because of Antonia and his problem now was entirely of his own making because he'd fallen in love. Becoming emotionally involved was disastrous for business. He'd known that for years and until now it hadn't been an issue, hence his reputation in the area.

If he refused to sell and Antonia continued to resist his advances, where would that leave him? If there was no chance of being with her in the future, he would have to love her and let her go, join the ranks of the unrequited lovers and continue with his life of emotional detachment. She knew how much this project meant to him and his plans for the town. It wasn't just him involved; it was the community.

He had to sell.

***

'He's offered us a fair whack of cash,' said Kev.

Bron sat beside him at Antonia's kitchen table, fiddling with the handle of her cup. 'It's hard to turn down, especially as the house isn't really big enough now the boys are teenagers,' she said.

'We've been stuck a bit because we don't have the money to extend or move but now this offer makes it viable. Flynn's found us a beaut house up his way. We could buy it outright.'

Antonia sat dumbfounded, trying to absorb what they were saying. They were moving, selling the house to Baldessin for a vast sum of money so he could knock it down and build a road through to his resort.

'What about my house?' she whispered.

Bron and Kev shared a frowning glance. 'He's made the same offer to Flynn.'

'But the new owner doesn't want to sell,' she said. 'Flynn told me they were happy to rent it.'

'Flynn *is* the owner, love,' said Kev.

'Flynn?'

He nodded. 'Baldessin made the same offer to him.'

'Why does he want two blocks?'

'He wants a wider frontage because he wants to put in a security-access gate. Fancy-shmancy for the rich customers.'

'But Flynn won't sell.' As she said it, she wondered. Would he? Baldessin could offer a lot of money and that was Flynn's business. Property investment.

How much would his feelings for her and the twins count when it came to the crunch? He hadn't mentioned a thing to her when he'd told her about Baldessin's revised plans and he must have known.

And another question raised an ugly doubt. How much part would her refusal of his advances play in his decision to sell or not?

'If he doesn't,' said Bron, '... we're stuffed because Baldessin wants both or neither. He'll take his idea somewhere else.'

'That's blackmail!'

Kev shrugged. 'It's the way these blokes operate. It's business to them.'

***

Simon didn't want to discuss the new resort plans with Lauren. She was all for mounting another protest against Flynn, whereas he was torn. He knew Antonia loved the Mango House and it represented much more to her than just a house, but she hadn't lived there very long and she could put down roots somewhere else just as easily. He could help with that, he wanted to help. Flynn had proven to be a false friend, and many people, including Lauren, thought he was interested only in his own wellbeing. Now he might have a chance with Antonia.

Despite the falling-out over Flynn's accident, Simon was bound to Antonia for life through their children. Flynn wasn't and was about to prove where his priorities lay. It would be in Simon's interests if he sold. He was ready to step in with comfort and advice. If she wanted to pack up and leave town, he'd go with her. He was smart enough not to say as much to her or anyone else.

Lauren, along with other like-minded townspeople, had organised a public meeting to discuss the project. Flynn and surprisingly, Aidan, maintained that it was a private matter between the property owners and the developer and had council approval in a general sense. The protesters maintained pressure was being applied to people who had no real choice in the matter and their homes were under threat, that it was a dangerous precedent in that large wealthy companies could buy up property and exert undue influence as a consequence.

'He could buy up the whole town,' snarled Lauren. 'And turn it into a theme park if he wanted to.'

***

Flynn tried phoning Antonia several times but she'd switched her phone to voicemail, which he took as an indication she was blocking his attempts to talk to her because she never returned his calls. The furore that had erupted over the present situation had staggered him and the council. As Aidan said, 'I thought this would be the end of the protests.'

No one had anticipated the depth of support for Antonia and Flynn hadn't anticipated the rise of feeling surrounding him. He had supporters and detractors in equal number but the only opinion he cared about was Antonia's and she refused to speak to him. He couldn't walk across the street and confront her in the cafe, it was way too public, and he couldn't visit her at home because he couldn't walk that far and wasn't going to ask someone to take him to the Mango House and wait and watch while the door was slammed in his face.

***

'I don't know what's going to happen,' Antonia said miserably to Cath as they cleaned up after closing time on the day of the meeting.

'Have you talked to Flynn?'

'No, I don't want to. I think I might say something I'll regret, I'm so angry with him. Why didn't he tell me he owned my house?'

'I don't know but I'm sure he had no idea this would happen. He probably just wanted you to feel secure.'

'Well, I don't.'

'But that's not Flynn's fault.'

Antonia wiped the counter with vicious swipes of her sponge. 'I trusted him ... he's the first man apart from my family and Simon that I trusted.' She looked at Cath, conscious of the tears pushing at her eyelids. Trusted him and loved him. Missed him in her life, desperately.

'You can still trust him. He's a good man.'

Cath was guaranteed to be on his side. She knew that. 'He lied to me.'

'Yes he did—sort of—if you can count not saying something as a lie ... but I think you're the first woman he's...'

'What?'

'Become more involved with than usual ... he looks to me like a man who's fallen in love but isn't sure what to do about it.'

Antonia snorted. 'Flynn has plenty of women.'

'Have you seen him with any of them? Where have they all been lately when he needed help?'

There was no answer to that. Did he really love her? He said so but that could mean nothing coming from him. How could she tell? She was back on quicksand again.

'Has he said anything to you?'

A flush crept up Antonia's neck, prickling at her cheeks. 'Yes,' she muttered. She sprayed disinfectant on the nearest stool and ran the sponge over it. 'I told him I wasn't ready for anything like that.'

'What did he say?'

'Nothing much but this is probably his way of letting me know he's pissed off. Selling my home.' But that was wrong and she knew it. Wrong and unfair.

'Flynn isn't like that,' said Cath firmly, echoing her thoughts. 'He's not vindictive. This is a very difficult decision for him. Don't you see that?'

Antonia didn't reply. She moved on to the next stool. Cath was beginning to sound annoyed.

'If Flynn sells he upsets you, the woman he loves. If he doesn't sell, he messes up Kev and Bron's chance to buy a bigger house and he also puts the resort plan in jeopardy, which won't help the town. He's been working on trying to boost the town's fortunes for years and years. This is the best thing to happen in the area that I can remember. What's he supposed to do?' Cath dropped her wiping cloth into the sink and stomped into the back room.

Antonia cleaned in silence with Cath's tirade revolving in her head. Put like that, Flynn *was* in an awful position. She had no rights over him and no right to claim precedence in the town over long-term residents and their futures. She was being selfish and mean while Flynn ... She sniffed. Cath thought he loved her. If Cath thought so maybe she was right. Flynn loved her and tried to protect her future by buying the house. If that wasn't a gesture of love what was? And all she'd done was push him away.

She'd go across the road and tell him to sell as soon as she finished in the cafe. And while she was there she might just suggest she was ready for that second kiss.

But Flynn wasn't in the office. Brandon said he was at Margie's preparing for the meeting this evening in the pub.

Antonia went to collect the twins. They'd begged to be allowed to go home with Annabel and Ellie after school to see the kittens and check on the one they'd chosen. Visiting someone else's house wasn't terrifying anymore, and was one more thing she had to thank Flynn's Crossing for. Could she give up the Mango House and start somewhere else? See it bulldozed? And they'd cut down the mango tree. The thought sent a knife to her heart. All those memories lost, hers and Josef's. He'd be upset too.

On the way home, she broke the news to the twins that they might have to move.

'That's what Annabel said,' said Jacob.

'Did she say why?' The grapevine no longer surprised her.

'Because our house is going to be turned into a road. But that's not true, is it?'

'I don't know. Someone wants to buy our house and Bron's house. They want to build a hotel in the bush and our houses are in the way of the driveway.'

'But we love our house,' wailed Sarah.

'I know. But if it happens we'll have to move. We can do that.'

'Where to?' asked Jacob.

'Can we go to Flynn's house?' Sarah said through a few sobs.

'No, not Flynn's house.'

'Why not? He lived in our house.' Jacob, with almost unanswerable logic.

'He wouldn't want us living there.'

'Yes he would,' said Jacob. 'He likes us.'

'And we like him,' said Sarah

'I know, darling, but ... I don't know what's going to happen. I'll find out this evening.'

'At the meeting?'

'Yes.' She had no choice but to take the twins with her because everyone who they might have agreed to stay with would be going as well.

Streams of people headed into the pub when Antonia arrived with a twin clutching each hand. People greeted her with smiles and allowed her through the crush to the front of the room, where Bron and Kev waved her to their table. Simon was already there, which surprised her but at the same time having his support was comforting. The twins were delighted.

'What do you think will happen?' he asked.

'I've no idea. But if he sells I can understand why he'd do it.'

Simon nodded. 'Money,' he murmured.

Not what she was thinking, but Antonia firmed her mouth and stared around the room. Simon would never miss an opportunity to have a go at Flynn. There were others in the room who thought the same way as Simon but they were all wrong about him because they didn't know what she knew. They didn't know about his past and his guilt-fuelled attempts to redress a terrible wrong even though he'd paid his debt and wasn't at fault. Flynn had a conscience, so much so that he was prepared to deny himself happiness because of it. As Cath said, he was a good man.

On impulse she pulled out her phone and sent him a text.

Whatever you decide, it's okay.

She'd be okay. If she lost the Mango House she'd survive, because it was just a stepping-stone and she wasn't dependent on it for her wellbeing. She had Flynn to thank for letting her live there. She had him to thank for many things; not least was showing her she was a competent, strong woman who could manage her life and those of her children. She'd survived far worse than this.

A small group pushed through the crowd. Lauren led the way, followed by Flynn, Margie and two men Antonia didn't recognise. Flynn looked pale and tired. He still wore the moon boot and by the way he sat down she guessed his ribs were sore. He scanned the crowd and when he spied her, paused for a moment but didn't smile. Had he got her text? There'd been no reply.

Lauren took the microphone and began by welcoming everyone to the meeting, then launched into the main topic.

'We've called this meeting because of the concerns many of us have about the recent spate of development proposals put forward by the council on behalf of the Baldessin Resort Group. While we appreciate the need for some sort of outside economic stimulation to keep our town viable, we can't allow unlimited access to wealthy companies such as Baldessin's who have no interest in maintaining the community standards we enjoy and every interest in maximising profits.'

A round of applause greeted her remarks.

'The council seems hell-bent on letting this man come in here and railroad our residents into selling their land or houses. I want to know where this will end? Is there no limit?'

Beside her Kev grunted. 'All very well for her to complain. She hasn't got four kids to support,' he growled.

Margie stood up. 'If I may say something, Lauren?'

Lauren handed her the microphone and Margie calmly pointed out the economic benefits of the already agreed-upon lodge and visitors' centre. 'In conclusion,' she said, 'we're not offering unlimited access to Baldessin or anyone else. That's a complete exaggeration.' She paused and her gaze swept over the silent assembly. 'There's no downside to this agreement. Ten new jobs will be created, maybe more, with training for young people in the National Parks Service as local rangers.'

One of the unknown men took the microphone. 'I agree that outcome is a good one, but it wouldn't have been if we hadn't mounted a protest and had it scaled back. Baldessin wanted to take over that whole area, including the co-op.'

Flynn said loudly, 'No one can do anything if the landowners won't sell. The co-op proved that. Bruce wants to sell his land and you have no right to stop him.'

'So do I,' called Kev. 'I can't see there's a problem and it's none of your business what I do.'

'Can't you see how he's blackmailing us into agreeing with his plans?' Lauren yelled. 'He offers you lots of money and then says if you don't take it he'll go somewhere else.'

'That's business,' said Kev. 'If I charge more than a bloke down the road you'll take your car there to be fixed instead. Fair enough, I reckon. It's your choice.'

'Sean doesn't want to take over the town,' said Margie. 'You're overreacting.'

'Are we?' Lauren glared at Flynn. 'You're one of the landowners. Will you take his money and turf Antonia and her children out of their home?'

Flynn stood up slowly, steadying himself before he moved forward. Antonia held her breath. The room went completely silent. He took the microphone from Lauren, and when he spoke his voice was low with a raspy edge and to Antonia's ear, exhausted.

'I know a lot of you think I'm a complete bastard when it comes to business dealings. I admit I'm in the property business to make money, and why not? Any business owner or employee is working to make money. But I also want to do the right thing by Flynn's Crossing and I think everyone would agree that the council has done a pretty good job so far. You keep voting us in so we must be getting something right.' A few claps and laughter. 'But this decision Lauren has highlighted is the hardest one I've ever had to make. It's never been personal for me before, the buying and selling of property. Now it is.

'Many of you know Antonia. She hasn't been in town long but she's made it her home and she's made many friends. I know for a fact she's had a tough time of it in the last six years; she's told me things ... things I could hardly believe, they were so terrible. Coming here to our town was, for her, a fresh start in life and she's done it very well.'

Antonia bent her head as eyes bored into her. Simon took her hand and squeezed. She glanced up and caught Flynn's eyes upon her but couldn't smile. He went on. This time his voice was stronger and he spoke faster as though he wanted to get it over with, spit out his decision and be done with it. Her throat was so tight she could barely breathe.

'Kev and Bron have already decided to take advantage of the offer and sell their house, but for me selling the Mango House would be a betrayal of the woman I have grown to love with all my heart, so I've decided I can't do it. Regardless of how she feels about me, Baldessin will have to find another way in. I'm sorry Kev, Bron, but I can't sell.' He sat down abruptly.

Antonia gasped. The room erupted in a roar of voices. Kev and Bron stared at each in shock. Simon swore. Lauren laughed in delighted astonishment.

Flynn sat with the wash of noise breaking over his head. Margie was yelling on one side, asking what the hell he was thinking, Lauren was shouting into the mic asking for quiet but the only voice he wanted to hear was Antonia's. He couldn't see her through the crowd, let alone hear her if she spoke. Simon was there sitting next to her, holding her hand, being where Flynn wanted to be—with her. But that didn't matter if she was happy, and he'd done his best to make it so.

Then she was there in front of him, asking Lauren for the microphone.

'I'm Antonia and I need to say something, please.' The roar subsided instantly. She was nervous, her voice trembled and the hand holding the microphone shook. 'Since I arrived here I've come to realise many things, but the main one is about Flynn. He's a good man and he's always tried to do the right thing by the town and his friends, but I think in this case, my case, he's got it wrong. I think...' She licked her lips and took a couple of deep breaths. 'He knows how much my house means to me, but it's just a house in the end. I have had some ... hard times and when I came here I was scared most of the time as a result.

But now I know I can make a home for myself and the twins ... anywhere, really. I've learned that since coming here, and I want to thank everyone for helping me and accepting me.'

She was leaving. Flynn couldn't look at her, at anyone. He stared unseeing at the floor. He'd declared his love for her in front of the whole town and she was turning him down again, in public this time. She'd go away with Simon and set up a new home in some other town and forget all this. Forget him.

She said very slowly and clearly, 'I want Flynn to sell but I want to make one proviso, if he can. Don't let Baldessin cut down the mango tree.'

He knew she was looking at him, as was everyone else, but he couldn't meet her eyes. If he did, he'd break down. She was cutting her ties and giving up the Mango House. She was doing it for him, and for the town. A few people clapped and he wanted to get up and run for his life, for his sanity and his dignity slowing being shredded here in front of everyone.

Kev shouted, 'Good on ya, love. Thank you.'

She went on, but she turned her back on the crowd and faced him; he knew because as she came closer he could see her pink-painted toenails in the red sandals she wore. She spoke to him, still with the microphone in her hand. Telling the town. 'Flynn, I told the twins we might have to move and they asked where we would go. I said I didn't know and Jacob said, "We could live with Flynn. He likes us."'

A ripple of laughter ran round the room. Flynn looked at her then. She paused, waiting for the laughter to die down. 'I said we couldn't do that. But we want to stay here in Flynn's Crossing and we want Flynn to find us a new house to make our home ... and who knows ... what might happen ... later.'

What was she saying? Her lovely brown eyes swam with tears but there was also something else there. Hope mixed with fear. Fear he might say that wasn't enough, that he'd want what she wasn't ready to give, that he wouldn't wait. And above all, love was there, in her face, her eyes and her voice.

Suddenly he was on his feet, arms extended, incapable of speech. She dropped the microphone and walked into his embrace.

'Can I have that second kiss?' he whispered but he knew the answer even before she pressed her lips on his.

Margie's voice came through the haze of emotion, saying they'd have a break before the meeting continued. 'You two should go somewhere private.' She was grinning. 'I can handle this.'

Flynn took Antonia's hand and pulled her through the throng to his office, ignoring the slaps on the back and congratulations as he went. She stumbled after him, conscious only of the warmth of his hand in hers while a delirious swirl of excitement turned her body to mush.

'What about the twins?' she asked when he closed the door on the racket and faced her. The colour had returned to his face and the blue of his eyes seemed deeper, drawing her in, enthralling her.

'Simon's with them. Did you really mean what you said? About staying?'

She nodded. 'This is our home now. We don't want to leave. Can you find us somewhere to live?'

'You could do what Jacob said,' he suggested, but he sounded more hopeful than demanding.

'No, I'm not ready for ... that. Are you? Really? It's too much.'

'Probably not.' He stole a quick kiss. 'I understand. It was worth a shot. But one day?'

She touched her fingers gently to his face, tracing the line of his cheek. 'I love you, Flynn. I only just realised how much, this afternoon. I think I've loved you for a while but ... I'm sorry I'm so ... I don't know how long...' She stopped, brow creased, searching for the right words but he kissed her and she forgot what she was trying to say and it didn't seem to matter.

Holding her tight in his arms, he whispered, 'You don't need to apologise for anything. Not to me. I'm happy just hearing you say you love me and letting me hold you like this. When you're ready for the next step, we'll work it out together. I don't care when that is.'

'You're an extraordinary man.'

'You're an extraordinary woman. Remember, too, that a family is something I never thought I'd have so this is a massive change for me. I love those two but being a second father to them ... wow.' He shook his head. 'That'll take a bit of getting used to.'

'They're used to you already. I told you they'd accept you after they got to know you.'

'You did. I just wasn't sure *you'd* be as easy to win over. A few "knock, knock" jokes wouldn't do it.'

She laughed. 'You'll regret teaching Sarah those jokes.'

'Maybe we should go back or God knows what they'll think we're up to.' Flynn reluctantly released his hold even though hugging her increased the pain in his ribs, but kept her hand in his as he opened the door. 'What do you think Simon will do now?'

'No idea, but he should realise that nothing much will change for the co-op. Not sure about Lauren.'

'I meant about you and the twins. Us.' Facing more insults from Simon wasn't the best way to finish off such a momentous occasion.

'He knows how I feel so he'll have to accept that this is how it is,' Antonia said with a firmness he couldn't have imagined she possessed when he first set eyes on her that hot summer's day.

He smiled and squeezed her fingers. 'I like that.'

The meeting had collapsed into a babble of talk and the bar was going full bore as groups settled down to discuss the events and the likely ramifications. As he led Antonia to the table where Simon and the twins waited, hands slapped him on the back and a ragged cheer went up amid the applause and good-natured laughter and wisecracks. He turned to see Antonia blushing crimson but with her head high, her hand still firmly in his.

His ankle hurt like hell and he sagged onto one of the chairs recently vacated by Bron and Kev who were now celebrating a few tables away. Antonia took the other chair, next to Sarah. Lauren was sitting next to Simon but her expression was difficult to interpret and Flynn had neither the energy nor the interest to try.

'Mummy said we can't live in your house when ours gets knocked down, Flynn,' said Sarah. She and Jacob had half-finished glasses of orange juice in front of them and seemed to be enjoying themselves immensely.

Flynn winced at the bald word choice but he smiled at the resilience. 'I'll find you a new house to live in,' he said.

'With a mango tree?' asked Jacob.

'Maybe.'

'We could plant your own new one if there isn't,' said Simon from across the table. He avoided Flynn's eye but his tone was mild.

Sarah clapped her hands and immediately started nattering to Jacob about what else they could plant in their new garden.

'So, are you staying on at the co-op?' asked Antonia.

'For a while.' Simon glanced at Lauren, still with her inscrutable face. 'I'll see how things turn out. Nothing much will happen for months, I reckon. Anyway, I want to be near my kids.'

'Good. I'm glad.'

'Are you? I didn't think you'd care much one way or the other.'

'Simon.' Lauren suddenly came to life. 'Don't.' She turned to Antonia with a grin. 'I'm glad you two got it together. You have a very good effect on Flynn. He's much more human now.'

Antonia returned the smile in a sisterhood secret knowledge sort of way.

'Thanks, I think,' Flynn said. With any luck, she'd have a good effect on Simon. Some sort of effect anyway. Maybe a strong woman was what he needed, and Lauren was nothing if not strong.

'Simon, of course, you want to be near the twins and they want to be near you, that won't change whatever happens between me and Flynn,' Antonia said, losing the smile.

'They're your kids, mate,' said Flynn. 'But we all have our own lives to lead and we're all finding our way in the dark. It hasn't been easy for any of us, believe me.'

Simon toyed with his empty beer glass. 'I know. It's been a pretty weird time lately. Lot of changes coming out of nowhere. It's hard to adjust.'

'Sometimes there's no choice,' said Antonia softly. 'It's either sink or swim.'

Simon suddenly extended his hand and grasped hers. 'I'm sorry. I don't mean to be ... I'm sorry. You deserve to be happy.'

'Time for another round, this is getting maudlin,' said Lauren, rising to her feet.

'Ask Donna for a bottle of champagne,' Flynn said. 'The good stuff. I think we've all got something to celebrate.'

'You shouldn't be drinking, you're an invalid,' said Antonia.

'I'll risk a sip. I'd risk anything for you,' he said and the smile he received in return washed away the aches in his ankle and ribs and filled his heart with warmth.

***

Simon shovelled the last of the compost into the new garden plot and straightened, rubbing his back. Sweat ran into his eyes and trickled down his back. Bloody hot today, and still hot even though the sun was just about to disappear behind Mount Taylor.

'Haven't you finished yet? Slacker.' Lauren down at the bottom of the slope, shading her eyes as she looked up at him. The golden sunlight bounced off her hair, making it shimmer like copper. The shorts showed off those long tanned legs, shapely from working. He hadn't noticed how good she looked before, not really. A sudden flash popped into his head of her in her flimsy pyjamas that night he'd wanted to talk and she'd chucked him out. Maybe he had noticed...

'Just done the last of it.' He slung the shovel into the wheelbarrow and headed down hill to where she waited by the shed.

'Interesting meeting last night,' she said.

'Yeah. Surprising. I didn't think Flynn would give up a cash bonus and all the rest of it.' He studiously kept his eyes away from her boobs in the tank top.

'I guess he found out that some things are worth more than money.'

'Yeah.'

Lauren opened the shed door and he stowed the shovel and barrow away.

'Did you know?' he asked her.

'What?'

'About Flynn and Antonia?'

'I had an idea. So did a lot of other people. He'll be good for her. And vice versa.'

'I thought you hated Flynn.' A lot of other people? Was he really so clueless as to miss what everyone else could see?

'No, I don't. I don't like some of his principles but as a man he's a pretty good bloke. She's lucky. He'll treat her well. He's kind.'

'How come I didn't know?'

'You didn't want to. You expected Antonia to be like she was at sixteen, with her teenage crush on you.'

'I didn't!'

'Well, as near as. I don't know what she's been through, I suppose she'll tell me one day, but whatever it was made her grow up fast.'

Simon paused, his hand on the shed door, ready to slide the catch across.

'You may as well know. She was abducted and held captive for five years. The trial will come up soon and everyone will see it on the news and in the papers anyway.'

'My God!'

He'd never seen Lauren lost for words but it happened now. She stared at him, completely stunned.

'I suppose you're right,' he said into the silence. 'I wanted to go back to before, even though we'd actually broken up. I thought she'd need me and I could help her and the twins but...' He shrugged. 'I can't. She's outgrown me.'

Lauren shook her head. 'You helped her brilliantly, Simon. You accepted her and the twins instantly, without a moment's thought, and you've proven to her that their father is there for them regardless. What more can you give them than that? A loving, kind father.'

Tears pricked his lids and he swallowed and turned away to walk to his house in the gathering gloom of evening. Lauren walked beside him, a comforting presence, familiar and not familiar at the same time.

'Are you leaving the co-op?' he asked.

'I'm not sure.'

'Don't,' he blurted.

She walked a few paces.

'Why?'

'I'd miss you.'

'Oh. Got a better reason?'

He stopped and she stopped too. He smiled.

'You'd miss me.'

'Would I?'

'Yes. And I need someone to help weed the carrots, and shovel manure.'

'Fool.' Smiling she stepped close and held his face between her palms. 'I'll stay, Simon, on one condition.'

'What?' His breathing hitched and jerked in his throat. Her face was close, lips inviting. Was she about to kiss him? The thought sent hot blood coursing through his body and he leaned in, ready to meet her.

'God, you stink of manure.' She dropped her hands and strode away, grimacing, but laughing at the same time.

'What condition?' Simon followed her and she increased her pace till he was almost running to keep up.

'Have a shower,' she said.

'Is that it? The condition?'

'Right at the moment, yes.' She slowed enough for him to draw level but kept her distance, wrinkling her nose.

'Okay. If I cook dinner for us, will you tell me the other one?'

'I'll help cook. What time?'

'Give me twenty minutes to clean up.'

'You'll need longer.'

'I won't.'

'Righto. See you in twenty.' She waved a hand and walked away towards her own house.

Simon continued on to his A-frame, pondering the condition she might come up with, but by the time he'd pushed the door open he'd decided he didn't much care what it was. He wanted her to stay.

Thanks for reading *The House at Flynn's Crossing.* I hope you enjoyed it.

Reviews can help readers find books, and I am grateful for all honest reviews. Thank you for taking the time to let others know what you've read, and what you thought.

If you liked this book, here are my other books: **Find Her, Empty Heart, Evidence of Love, Mango Kisses, E for England** and **The Ripple Effect.**

Sign up to our newsletter romance. com.au/newsletter/ and find out about new releases, must-read series and **ebook deals** at romance.com.au.

Share your reading experience on:

Facebook

Instagram

romance.com.au

Bestselling Titles by Escape Publishing...

Discover another great read from Escape Publishing...
Find Her

Elisabeth Rose

A chance sighting leads to second chances – for hope, for family, and for love.

Five years ago, teenager Antonia disappeared. With no compelling evidence, the police eventually called her a runaway, and dropped the case. Her teacher, Jax, has always regretted not speaking up about the rumours she heard circling the school that day, but a random sighting at a train station raises the possibility that Antonia is still alive – and not too far away.

Antonia's father, Connor has never given up hope that his daughter will be found and returned to her family. When her old teacher, Jax, calls him with a small spark of a lead, he seizes it with both hands, determined to chase it down.

But there's more at play than simple teenage rebellion and the path Jax and Connor travel rapidly becomes more dangerous than either could have imagined, and opens up new possibilities that neither could have expected.

Empty Heart
Elisabeth Rose

One honeymoon, one vanished husband, one desperate wife – and the cop who is tasked to help her, but can't seem to keep his thoughts on the job.

Honeymooner Nikki Spenser emerges from the surf at Surfers Paradise and can't find her husband, her towel, or her clothes on the beach. Carlos has disappeared from her life as suddenly as he entered it.

In despair, Nikki returns to Sydney where she is contacted by Detective Luke Emerson, a reminder from her past she thought never to see again. Luke informs her that the man she married so recklessly in Las Vegas three weeks prior doesn't exist. Everything she knew about Carlos is a lie, and Nikki realises she knows nothing about her husband—not where he is, not even who he is.

As Nikki and Luke chase down tenuous leads, they soon find themselves plunged into an ever-widening sea of international crime and violence, and Nikki is faced with the hard questions—how much of her love is based on lies, and how much is true?

Evidence of Love
Elisabeth Rose

She survived years as a gangland wife, sacrificing everything to the family. But now they're threatening the one thing that she will never, ever give up – her child.

When Maja's abusive gang boss husband Tony is murdered, she takes the opportunity to flee, change her name, and leave her criminal family and her past behind. As Lara Moore, she and her toddler son Petey live quietly in suburban Sydney. Then, one act of kindness threatens to reveal her secrets and unravel the threads of her new life. But Detective Nick is dedicated and determined, the antithesis of everything she was brought up to believe about the police. Slowly, Maja finds herself drawn out of her shell and into his protective embrace.

Investigating Detective Nick Lawson doesn't know what it is about the prickly, reclusive young mother that attracts and intrigues him, but as the facts about her crime-steeped family emerge, Nick doubts whether his career would survive this relationship, even if she were interested.

Then, to Lara's horror, her past meets her present, and thoughts of love and a future are lost as the fight for her child begins.

Mango Kisses
Elisabeth Rose

A sweet, summery, beachside romance from the author of E for England *and* The Ripple Effect.

Sent to assess a deceased estate in a small coastal town, ambitious city girl Tiffany Holland is initially annoyed by the out-of-the-way assignment. But she soon discovers sleepy Birrigai hides a wealth of surprises: a cross-dressing motel manager, a Kissing College and her client Miles Frobisher, the laid back, surf-shop owning, real life sex fantasy.

Tiffany's ambition is to become a junior partner in her financial firm, but small town life and the proximity of Miles gradually seduce her. But a shocking discovery in the estate papers leads to a dramatic change in Miles's circumstances. Emotionally inept, Tiffany is unable to help Miles through the transition, and drives him away. With misunderstandings and secrets creating frost between them, it seems that their summer romance is destined to go cold. Can they overcome their differences and learn to accept their feelings?